The Lady's Command

Edwina decided that the deck of a ship like *The Cormorant* was an exhilarating place to be.

She remained beside Declan, gripping the rail to one side of where he stood before the heavy spoked wheel; she looked down the length of the ship, then looked up at the masts soaring high above and at the huge kitelike sails. Finally gazing out and around, she felt engulfed by nature's power, by the sheer immensity of the sky and the sea, the force of the wind and the waves. In that moment, she understood why Declan would never give up sailing—would never give up the chance to experience elemental moments like this.

His eyes narrowed against the whip of the wind, Declan glanced, somewhat searchingly, at her. "I forgot to ask—is this your first time at sea?"

She shook her head, glorying in the tug of the wind on her curls. "When we were younger we sailed on the Irish Sea." She lifted her face to the wind. "I used to think that was thrilling, but this... this is nature's power made manifest."

Declan heard the sincerity in her tone, saw the wonder in her face; if he hadn't already fallen in love with her, he would have fallen then.

Other titles from Stephanie Laurens

Cynster Series

Devil's Bride
A Rake's Vow
Scandal's Bride
A Rogue's Proposal
A Secret Love
All About Love
All About Passion
On a Wild Night
On a Wicked Dawn
The Perfect Lover
The Ideal Bride
The Truth About Love
What Price Love?
The Taste of Innocence
Temptation and Surrender

Cynster Sisters Trilogy

Viscount Breckenridge to the Rescue
In Pursuit of Eliza Cynster
The Capture of the Earl of Glencrae

Cynster Sisters Duo

And Then She Fell
The Taming of Ryder Cavanaugh

Cynster Special

The Promise in a Kiss
By Winter's Light

Cynster Next Generation

The Tempting of Thomas Carrick
A Match for Marcus Cynster

Medieval

Desire's Prize

Novellas

"Melting Ice"—from *Scandalous Brides*
"Rose in Bloom"—from *Scottish Brides*
"Scandalous Lord Dere"—
   from *Secrets of a Perfect Night*
"Lost and Found"—from *Hero,*
   Come Back
"The Fall of Rogue Gerrard"—
   from *It Happened One Night*
"The Seduction of Sebastian Trantor"—
   from *It Happened One Season*

Bastion Club Series

Captain Jack's Woman (Prequel)
The Lady Chosen
A Gentleman's Honor
A Lady of His Own
A Fine Passion
To Distraction
Beyond Seduction
The Edge of Desire
Mastered by Love

Black Cobra Quartet Series

The Untamed Bride
The Elusive Bride
The Brazen Bride
The Reckless Bride

Other Novels

The Lady Risks All

The Casebook of Barnaby Adair Novels

Where the Heart Leads
The Peculiar Case of
   Lord Finsbury's Diamonds
The Masterful Mr. Montague
The Curious Case of
   Lady Latimer's Shoes
Loving Rose: The Redemption of
   Malcolm Sinclair

Regency Romances

Tangled Reins
Four in Hand
Impetuous Innocent
Fair Juno
The Reasons for Marriage
A Lady of Expectations
An Unwilling Conquest
A Comfortable Wife

Short Stories

"The Wedding Planner"—
   from *Royal Weddings*
"A Return Engagement"—
   from *Royal Bridesmaids*

STEPHANIE LAURENS

The Lady's Command

MIRA

MIRA

ISBN-13: 978-0-7783-1938-2

The Lady's Command

The Lady's Command

CAST OF CHARACTERS

Principal Characters:

Frobisher, Declan	Hero
Frobisher, Lady Edwina	Heroine

In London:

Staff:

Humphrey	butler
King, Mrs.	housekeeper
Cook	cook
Wilmot	lady's maid

Family:

Delbraith, Lucasta, Dowager Duchess of Ridgware	Edwina's mother
Delbraith, Lord Julian, aka Neville Roscoe	Edwina's older brother and London's gambling king
Delbraith, Lady Miranda	Julian's wife
Catervale, Lady Millicent	Edwina's oldest sister
Catervale, Lord	Millicent's husband
Elsbury, Lady Cassandra	Edwina's sister
Elsbury, Lord	Cassandra's husband
Crawford, Anthea	Lucasta's companion, a distant cousin

Society:

Montgomery, Lady	ton hostess
Mitchell, Lady Cerise	ton lady
Fitzwilliam, Mr.	gentleman of the ton
Holland, Lady	major ton hostess
Marchmain, Lady	ton grande dame
Minchingham, Lady	ton hostess
Forsythe, Lady	ton hostess
Comerford, Lady	ton hostess

Government:

Wolverstone, Duke of, aka Dalziel	ex-commander of British secret operatives outside England
Wolverstone, Duchess of, Minerva	Wolverstone's wife
Melville, Viscount	First Lord of the Admiralty

In Aberdeen:

Frobisher, Fergus	Declan's father
Frobisher, Elaine	Declan's mother
Frobisher, Royd (Murgatroyd)	eldest Frobisher brother

At sea:

Frobisher, Robert	second oldest Frobisher brother
Frobisher, Caleb	youngest of four Frobisher brothers
Frobisher, Catherine (Kit)	female cousin
Frobisher, Lachlan	male cousin

In Freetown:

Dixon, Captain	army engineer, missing
Hopkins, Lieutenant	navy, West Africa Squadron, missing
Fanshawe, Lieutenant	navy, West Africa Squadron, missing
Hillsythe	ex-Wolverstone agent, governor's aide, missing
Holbrook, Governor	Governor-in-Chief of British West Africa
Holbrook, Lady Letitia	Governor's wife
Satterly, Mr.	Governor's principal aide
Eldridge, Major	Commander, Fort Thornton
Decker, Vice-Admiral	Commander, West Africa Squadron, currently at sea
Richards, Captain	army, Fort Thornton
Wallace	house agent in Freetown
Hardwicke, Mrs. Mona	minister's wife
Hardwicke, Mr.	Anglican minister
Sherbrook, Mrs.	local lady
Quinn, Mrs.	local lady
Robey, Mrs.	local lady
Hitchcock, Mrs.	local lady
Winton, Major	Commissar of Fort Thornton
Winton, Mrs.	wife of Major Winton
Babington, Charles	partner, Macauley & Babington Trading Company
Macauley, Mr.	senior partner, Macauley & Babington Trading Company
Macauley, Mrs. Genevieve	wife of Macauley
Undoto, Obo	local priest
Sampson	old sailor
Lashoria	vodun priestess

On board The Cormorant:

Caldwell, Mr. Joshua	First Mate
Johnson, Mr.	Master
Grimsby	Bosun
Elliot	Quartermaster
Henry, Mr.	Steward
Dench	experienced sailor
Carruthers	experienced sailor
Billings	experienced sailor
Higgins	sailor
Upshaw	sailor
Martin	sailor
Ginger	cabin boy
Cam	cabin boy

One

Marrying the lady of his dreams had proved surprisingly easy. Forging the marriage of his dreams… That, apparently, was an entirely different challenge.

Declan Fergus Frobisher stood alongside Lady Edwina Frobisher née Delbraith—his new wife—and let the cacophony generated by the tonnish crowd gathered in Lady Montgomery's drawing room wash over him. The chattering was incessant, like a flock of seagulls squawking, yet such exchanges were the sole purpose of a soirée. In a many-hued kaleidoscope of fine silks and satins, of darker-hued superfines and black evening coats, the crème de la crème of the haut ton drifted and shifted from one circle to the next in a constantly rearranging tapestry. The large room was illuminated by several chandeliers; light glinted on artfully twisted curls and pomaded locks and in the facets of myriad jewels adorning the throats, earlobes, and wrists of the many ladies attending.

One heavily burdened lady swept up in a dazzle of diamonds. "Edwina, my dear!" The lady pressed fingers and touched cheeks with Declan's beloved, who greeted the newcomer with her customary sunny charm, yet the lady's gaze had already shifted to him, traveling down and then up his long length. Then she directed a smile—a distinctly predatory smile—at him. "You must—simply *must*—introduce me to your husband." The lady's tone had lowered to a feminine purr.

Declan glanced at Edwina; he wondered how she would react to the lady's transparent intent.

His wife didn't disappoint; she smiled delightedly—the very picture of a cat who had savored an entire bowlful of cream and expected to indulge further shortly. Her expression radiated supreme confidence; the sight made him inwardly grin. As if sensing his amusement, she cast him a glance from her fine blue eyes and with an airy wave stated, "Lady Cerise Mitchell, my husband, Declan Frobisher."

Hearing the subtle yet distinctly possessive emphasis she had placed on the words "my husband," with his lips curving in a polite smile, he took the hand Lady Cerise extended and bowed. She murmured a seductive "Enchanté," but he'd already lost interest in her. Although he devoted a small part of his mind and his awareness to the parade of people who came up to converse, to answering their questions and deflecting any he considered too prying, interacting with them wasn't why he was there.

On Edwina's other side stood her mother, Lucasta, Dowager Duchess of Ridgware, a handsome, haughty lady of arrogantly noble mien. Beyond the dowager stood Edwina's sister, Lady Cassandra Elsbury, a pleasant young matron a few years older than Edwina. The rest of their circle was comprised of several bright-eyed ladies and intrigued gentlemen, all eager to claim acquaintance with the ducal ladies and, even more importantly, to learn more of the unknown-to-them gentleman who had captured the hand of one of the haut ton's prizes. Declan did his best to meet their expectations by cultivating a mysterious air.

In reality, there was little mystery as to who he was. His family was ancient—the Frobishers had fought alongside Raleigh in Elizabeth's time. They were well-born, with an unassailable entrée to the highest echelons based on their venerable lineage alone, yet from centuries past, the Frobishers had elected to follow their own esoteric, not to say eccentric, path, habitually eschewing even the fringes of the ton. While Raleigh had fought for personal glory first, Crown second, the Frobishers entered battles reluctantly and only at the Crown's command. They were a seafaring dynasty, and battles cost lives and ships; they fought only when they needed to, which was only when they were needed.

They'd been at Trafalgar, but not under Nelson's command. Instead, the Frobisher fleet had ensured none of the French fled north to regroup. Declan's father and his uncles had used their swift ships to good effect, crippling and capturing many French frigates.

Consequently, among the ton, the Frobisher name was well known, easily placed. The mystery, such as it was, had always lain in who the current family members were and in what the family actually did. The manner in which they derived their fortune and the size of that fortune. The Frobishers had never had much interest in land, and what acres they held lay far to the north, close by Aberdeen—a very long way from London. The family's assets were largely floating, which, for the ton, raised the conundrum of whether the otherwise acceptable family had descended into trade. The ton lauded those who lived off their acres, but had difficulty equating acres with ships.

In addition, many of those present had heard whispers, if not outright rumors, about the family's more recent exploits. Most of those rumors—of explorations into the wilds and hugely profitable deals concerned with shipping—had their genesis in truth. If anything, the truth was even more outlandish than any tonnish speculation.

Of course, in society, unsubstantiated rumors only generated more interest. That interest—that barely veiled curiosity—shone brightly in the eyes of many of Lady Montgomery's guests.

"I say, Frobisher," a Mr. Fitzwilliam drawled. "I heard that one of your family recently talked the American colonists into accepting some new trade treaty. What was that about, heh? Was that you?"

That had been Robert, one of Declan's two older brothers and the most diplomatically inclined. The treaty Robert had sailed from Georgia with would make the family even more wealthy and also contribute significantly to the Crown's coffers.

But Declan only smiled and said, "That wasn't me." When Fitzwilliam showed signs of persevering, he added, "I haven't heard that rumor."

Why would he listen to rumors when he knew the facts?

He had no intention of gratifying anyone by explaining his family's business. His entire interest in the evening—the sole reason he was there—was encompassed by the lady standing, scintillating and effervescent, by his side.

She affected his senses like a lodestone, gleaming like a diamond, sparkling and alluring—intrinsically fascinating. From the topmost golden curl to the tips of her dainty feet, she commanded and captivated his awareness. In part, that was a physical response—what red-blooded man could resist the appeal inherent in a tumble of pale blond ringlets framing a heart-shaped face, in bright blue eyes, large and well set beneath finely arched brown brows and lushly fringed by long brown lashes, in a peaches-and-cream complexion unmarred by any blemish beyond a row of freckles dusted across the bridge of her small nose, and in lips full and rosy that just begged to be kissed? Yet on top of that, those lips were mobile, usually upturned in a smile, her expression fluid, reflecting her moods, her thoughts, her interest, while her brilliantly alive, vibrantly blue eyes were a gateway to a keenly intelligent mind.

Add to that a petite figure that was the epitome of the notion of a pocket Venus, and it was hardly surprising that no other being could so easily fix his attention. She was a prize worth coveting; from his very first sight of her, she'd called to him— to the acquisitive adventurer at the core of his soul.

They'd been married for just over three weeks. A year before, having sailed from New York into London and having a month to wait before his next voyage, he'd surrendered to ennui and the entreaty of old friends and had accompanied the latter to a ton ball. Throughout the round-trip to New York, he'd been conscious of a needling, pricking restlessness of a sort he hadn't previously experienced; entirely unexpectedly, his thoughts had turned to the comfort of home and hearth, to family.

To marriage.

To a wife.

The instant he'd laid eyes on Edwina at that very first ball last year, he'd known who his wife would be. With typical single-mindedness, he'd set about securing her, the sometimes-haughty daughter of a ducal house; at twenty-two, having been out for three years, she'd already gained a reputation for being no man's easy mark.

They'd struck sparks from the first touch of their fingers, from the first moment their gazes collided. Wooing Edwina had been blessedly easy. Several months later, he'd applied for her hand and been accepted.

In his mind, all had been progressing smoothly toward the comfortable, conventional marriage he had—in those few minutes he'd spent thinking of it—assumed their union would be.

Then, three months before the wedding, Lucasta and Edwina had braved the winter snows to visit his family at their manor house outside Banchory-Devenick. When he'd learned the purpose of that visit, he'd initially assumed it had been Lucasta's idea. Later, he'd discovered it was Edwina who had insisted that the Frobishers needed to be informed *before* the wedding, rather than after, of the secret her family had been hiding for more than a decade.

Utterly intrigued, he, his parents, and his three brothers had sat in the comfort of the large family parlor and listened as Lucasta had explained. Learning that her elder son, the eighth duke, had taken his own life because of mountainous debts, and that her second son, Lord Julian Delbraith, wasn't missing, presumed dead, as all of society assumed, but instead was masquerading in plain sight as Neville Roscoe, London's gambling king, had definitely been a surprise.

Not, as Edwina had clearly anticipated, a shocking surprise, but an infinitely intriguing and attractive one.

The possibilities every one of the Frobishers had immediately seen in the prospect of being connected with a man of Roscoe's caliber—his power, authority, and assets—had elevated their estimation of Declan's marriage from very good to unbelievably excellent.

Later, in private, his father, Fergus, had clapped him on the shoulder and exclaimed, "Gads, boy—you couldn't have done better! A personal link to Neville Roscoe... Well, no one knew such a thing was there to be had! Such a connection will only make this family all the stronger."

Fergus, Declan's mother, Elaine, and his brothers had welcomed the match from the first, but that wholly unanticipated ramification had been the crowning glory.

In the days following the wedding, a large event held at the local church on the ducal estate in Staffordshire—days he, Edwina, and his family had spent at Ridgware with her immediate family—he, his father, and his brothers had had a chance to meet with the elusive Lord Julian Delbraith, known to the world as Neville Roscoe. Apparently, Roscoe's recent marriage to Miranda, now Lady Delbraith, had forced him to overturn his long-held intention never to reappear under his true name. Julian and Miranda had attended the wedding, although they'd remained carefully screened and out of sight of all the other guests.

Edwina had been thrilled over her brother's presence, and Declan had been pleased on that account alone. The subsequent private meeting between the Frobishers, Roscoe, and his right-hand man, Jordan Draper, had all but literally been the icing on the wedding cake. As a group, they'd explored all manner of potential interactions; it had quickly become clear that Roscoe viewed the match every bit as favorably as the Frobishers. All in all, that meeting had been a coming together of like minds.

That had been the immediate outcome of learning the truth about the Delbraiths, but like a stone dropped into a pool, subsequent ripples continued to appear.

Later, Declan and Edwina had followed his family north to spend a few weeks in Banchory-Devenick; several days after their arrival, Fergus had asked Declan to accompany him on one of his walks.

Once they were away from the house, his eyes on the ground before him, Fergus had stated, "It occurs to me, boy-o, that there's a great deal we could learn from your Edwina's family. I'm not talking about Roscoe, but the others—especially the ladies."

Unsure just what his father meant, Declan had remained silent.

After several paces, Fergus had continued, "It's been a long time since any Frobisher moved among the ton. It was never our battlefield, so to speak. But I look at the old duchess—the dowager—and her daughters, and the daughter-in-law, too, and I think about what they've managed to achieve over the last decade. Given what they had to hide, being capable of...not exactly *hoodwinking* the ton, but veiling the truth, and all so subtly and elegantly done... That takes talent of a sort we, as a family, lack."

Fergus's sharp, agate-y gaze had shifted to pin Declan. "You said you intend taking Edwina to town—that you've hired a house there and that Edwina and the dowager think the pair of you need to appear in society to establish yourselves, whatever that means. I'm thinking that might provide a useful opportunity for you to watch and see what you can learn of how they manage things."

"Manage things." After a moment, he'd said, "You want me to learn how they manipulate the ton into seeing what they want the ton to see."

"Exactly!" Fergus had faced forward. "The Delbraiths might be a family led by women, the duke being so young, but none of those females are fools. They all know how to operate in the ton, how to bend ton perceptions to their advantage. They have skills we could use, m'boy. We might eschew the ton, deeming it irrelevant to us, but you can't duck the weight of a birthright, and who knows what the future will bring?"

That conversation rang in Declan's mind as he smiled and complimented a young lady on her beautifully carved oriental fan. He'd long ago learned to trust his father's insights; Fergus Frobisher was widely respected as a canny old Scot. So as they had planned, he and Edwina had come to London and taken up residence in a rented town house in Stanhope Street. Lucasta had joined them in town, but she was staying with her eldest daughter, Lady Millicent Catervale, in Mount Street. Declan appreciated his mother-in-law's sensitivity in giving him and Edwina their privacy.

Subsequently, Edwina and Lucasta, aided by Millie and Cassie, had put their heads together and come up with a list of events Edwina had declared she had to attend. She'd excused him from all the daytime entertainments, but had requested his presence at the evening events, a request to which he'd readily agreed.

They'd attended several balls, dinners, soirées, and routs over the past week. And tonight, as at those previous events, he was there to observe, to watch and learn how his wife and the females of her family "managed" the ton.

He'd initially studied Lucasta, reasoning that she had to have been the principal instigator in promulgating the non-shocking, acceptable-to-the-ton versions of her older son's demise and of her younger son's disappearance; only because he'd been watching closely had he noticed the difference between Lucasta in private and Lucasta in society. It was like a screen, a veil of sorts, but not something anyone observing her could pierce; even knowing it was there, he couldn't see past it, not while she had it deployed. Lucasta's screen made her appear more rigid, definitely colder, and more arrogantly aloof. It was an emotional screen that held others at a distance and allowed only the reactions Lucasta wished to display to show through.

Edwina's veil was even harder to discern. Only because he'd known it had to be there had he managed to even glimpse it. Because her true nature was so very bright and glittery, her shield was almost like a mirror—something that reflected what others assumed they would see, not necessarily what truly lay behind the screen.

He'd studied Millie and Cassie, too; their veils were effective, yet less definite, softer and more amorphous—again, a reflection of their characters. While Lucasta undoubtedly possessed an iron will and a spine of steel—how else had she coped with the vicissitudes of fate over all these years?—of her three daughters, Edwina was the most alike, possessing a similar, pliable yet invincible, feminine strength.

That truth had dawned on him two nights before—and brought with it another ripple.

When he'd set his sights on Edwina, he'd assumed the Delbraiths, a ducal family, would be conventional, conservative, if anything rather stuffy. Instead, he'd discovered they were hiding a secret, one so outrageous and potentially socially catastrophic that it was crystal clear that in terms of being *un*conventional, the Delbraiths could give the Frobishers a run for their money.

Lucasta was a very far cry from the tradition-obsessed dowager he'd taken her for. As for Edwina…

His view of a predictable, ordinary, orthodox marriage had evaporated.

The lady he had married had an entirely different character from the lady he'd assumed he would take to wife.

Her small hand rested on his sleeve; he could feel the light pressure as if a bird perched there. Yet her presence held him so securely, captivated him so thoroughly, that he barely heard the comments of others enough to respond with the appropriate remarks. He wasn't interested in those who gathered around them; he was interested only in her.

She'd explained that it was necessary for them to appear in society to "establish themselves." He wasn't sure exactly what she meant by that, but clearly she had some goal in mind. Being as inexperienced as she was experienced in this sphere, he hadn't yet figured out precisely what her ultimate goal was, yet he understood and accepted that she had one...

And *that* said something all by itself.

It was a reflection of that ripple he'd only recently recognized: His delicate, fairylike wife had a decisive and definite mind of her own.

She formulated goals and planned campaigns—then executed them. She spoke of what amounted to strategy and tactics.

He was now fairly certain she would also harbor a definite view of how their marriage would work, but he'd yet to gain any insight whatsoever into what her view of that critical issue was. Were her putative rules of engagement ones he could smile at, accept, and fall in with? Or...?

As of that moment, he had no idea what their future on that front would bring. Yet he'd married her, and he wouldn't change that for all the gold in the world. Having her as his wife had been his principal goal, and now she was his.

He glanced at her and saw her eyes sparkle, her face lighting with animation as she charmingly accepted congratulations on their marriage from some other couple.

All in all, he was beyond pleased over having her as his wife. The part he had yet to define was what it was going to take to be her husband.

Edwina stood by Declan's side with her smile in place and her eyes firmly fixed on her prize. She, her mother, and her sisters had agreed it was vital that she and Declan present themselves to the ton in exactly the right light. How the ton viewed them, now and in the future, would depend entirely on the image they projected over these critical first weeks. That tonight, more or less from the moment they'd arrived, they'd remained fixed in the center of the room with a constant stream of intrigued guests jockeying to join their circle testified as to just how highly the ton now ranked them as acceptable acquaintances.

A sense of triumph rose within her; her first goal as a married lady was all but attained.

When Lady Holland stopped to chat and, when introduced to Declan, deigned to smile approvingly, Edwina had to work to keep her delight from too openly showing and her relief from showing at all. The ton could be a highly censorious sphere, but the blessing of such an august hostess was the ultimate seal of tonnish approval; they had, in ton terms, *arrived*.

Of course, Lady Holland had always had a soft spot for charming and handsome gentlemen.

Slanting a glance at Declan, Edwina allowed her gaze to dwell on his chiseled features—the distinctly aristocratic line of his brow, the long planes of his lean cheeks below high cheekbones, the firmness of his mobile lips, and the definitely masculine cast of his chin. The crinkling around his sky-blue eyes, set beneath angled slashes of brown brows, and his perennially tanned complexion spoke of long months at sea. His light brown, sun-kissed hair completed the image, appearing fashionably windblown with the bright streaks and tips burnished by the sun highlighting the effect.

The combination of his height and his broad-shouldered stance, the very way he held his long frame, both upright and yet fluid, always perfectly balanced and ineffably confident and assured, set him apart from well-nigh every other gentleman in the room.

As Lady Holland moved on, Lucasta touched Edwina's sleeve, drawing her attention. "My dear, I see Lady Marchmain holding court by the wall. I believe it would be wise for me to join her and ensure she comprehends all the pertinent facts."

Edwina followed her mother's gaze to a coterie of older ladies gathered around a chaise. She nodded. "Thank you, Mama. We'll come and find you when we're ready to leave."

Lady Marchmain was one of her mother's bosom-bows and also one of the most active ladies in the ton; if one had a message to deliver to the upper echelons of society at large, then Lady Marchmain was an excellent courier.

Returning her attention to the gratifying number of ladies and gentlemen eager to make Declan's acquaintance, Edwina wondered how much longer they needed to stay. Neither she nor her mother had made any estimation of how many evenings it might take to establish her new position as a married lady and, more critically, establish Declan as a member of recognized society, but their assumption had been that it would take considerably more days and nights—more at-homes, morning and afternoon teas, luncheons, balls, and soirées—to achieve their aim. They'd arrived in town only a week ago; they'd been waging their campaign for a mere six days. They hadn't expected to succeed so soon.

Regardless, she was exceedingly glad that matters had gone as well as they had. Spending her evenings standing beside Declan—handsome, attentive, and suavely engaging as he'd been— had proved far less of a trial than she'd expected. She had thought she would have to rescue him from social traps, yet that hadn't been the case; he'd seen the snares and sidestepped adroitly all by himself. For someone who had rarely moved within the ton, he'd handled it well.

While she continued to exchange comments and the usual social banter with those gathered about them, as with every word the reality of their social success was confirmed and sank in, she was increasingly aware of rising impatience. Given they'd succeeded on this front, it was time to advance to the next stage in forging their marriage into the union she wished it to be. And for that, she and Declan needed to be elsewhere—anywhere but in the middle of the ton.

Declan was quite happy to depart Montgomery House. At Edwina's suggestion, together with Cassie, they crossed to where Lucasta was conversing with several older ladies. The dowager rose and introduced him to her friends. Once the inevitable exchanges were complete, the dowager settled her shawl, and together their party took leave of their hostess, then made their way downstairs. Somewhat to Declan's relief, Cassie offered to take Lucasta up in her carriage, leaving him and Edwina to their own company as they traveled the short distance to Stanhope Street.

The instant the carriage door was shut upon them, Edwina's social veil vanished. During the drive, she chattered, animated and intense, reviewing the comments made by several of those they'd met, explaining the significance of this observation or that connection. Her insights proved illuminating; he was struck by how familiar the moment seemed. As they rattled over the cobbles, he realized it was very like a debriefing after one of his covert missions.

The more he thought of it, the more apt the analogy seemed.

Edwina capped her comments with the statement "It appears that Mama had the right of it." Through the shadows, she met his eyes. "She was quite sure that, when it came to our marriage, the ton would take its cue from me—from how I, and Mama, and Millie and Cassie and their husbands, too, reacted. Mama was convinced that all I had to do was to keep you beside me and openly show my delight in being your wife, and all would be well." She sighed happily. Facing forward, she settled back beside him. "As usual, Mama was correct."

He debated several questions, then voiced what to him was the most pertinent. "And are you truly delighted?"

Her small white teeth flashed in an ebullient smile. Through the enfolding shadows, she glanced at him. "You know I am." She slipped one small hand into his and lightly squeezed. "I couldn't be more happy over being your wife."

Confident sincerity resonated in the words; he drank it in and couldn't help a satisfied smile of his own.

The carriage rolled around a corner, tipping her against him.

She glanced up as he lowered his head.

Their eyes met; their gazes held.

He raised one fingertip and gently, slowly, traced the lush fullness of her lower lip.

Her lids lowered, screening her eyes as she tipped up her face, and he leaned closer.

The carriage slowed, then halted.

Her eyes opened wide. From a distance of mere inches, she studied his, then beneath the pad of his finger, her lip curved.

He heard the footman drop down from the rear of the carriage, and with a sigh, he straightened. "I believe, my lady, that we've reached our home."

"Indeed." Even through the dimness, he saw desire gleam in her eyes. As the footman opened the door, she murmured, "I suggest, dear husband, that we go inside."

Anticipation flared between them, tangible and hot. With one last wanton look, she turned to the door. He rose and descended to the pavement, then handed her down.

Retaining his hold on her fingers, he escorted her up the town house steps.

The door opened before they reached it. Humphrey, their new butler, bowed them inside. "Welcome home, my lady. Sir."

"Thank you, Humphrey." Edwina slipped her fingers from Declan's clasp and headed straight for the stairs.

He prowled in her wake.

Humphrey closed the door. "Will there be anything else, sir? Ma'am?"

"I think not." Declan didn't shift his gaze from his wife's curvaceous hips, sleekly cloaked in pale blue satin. "You may lock up. Her ladyship and I are retiring."

Without glancing back from her steady ascent, Edwina said, "Oh, and please tell Wilmot I won't need her tonight."

Wilmot was her lady's maid. Declan smiled.

Edwina reached the door to the bedroom they had elected to share, opened it, and sailed through. On her heels, he crossed the threshold, paused to shut the door, then, his gaze locked on his prize, continued his pursuit.

Before she reached the foot of their bed—a large four-poster draped in blue silks—she abruptly swung around. One step from her, one stride from him, and they met.

Her head barely reached his shoulder; coming up on her toes, she wound her arms about his neck, pressed close as his hands fastened about her tiny waist, and raised her lips as he bent his head.

Their lips touched, brushed, then settled.

The kiss deepened, their lips effortlessly melding. She parted hers in wanton invitation, and he sent his tongue questing. Conquering and commanding.

She'd been a virgin on their wedding night, yet she'd been anything but reticent; she'd plunged into the whirlpool generated by their avid, greedy, too-long-denied senses with an eager enthusiasm that had stunned him. Her open and ardent desire to learn *everything* about passion had claimed him. Her utterly fearless adventurousness in this sphere continued to captivate him.

Comprehensively enslaving him.

He didn't mind, not in the least. As he steered her back toward the bed, the sole remaining thought in his head was how to most effectively enjoy the fruits of his surrender.

Edwina felt awash on a sea of triumph. She wanted to celebrate what ranked as a minor victory—successfully establishing their union as entirely acceptable and, more, as distinctly desirable in the eyes of the ton.

Joy and delight bubbled and fizzed inside her. Effervescent

excitement gripped her as she felt the bed at her back, then Declan's fingers found her laces, and she sent her own hands seeking, nimble fingers deftly dealing with the large buttons of his waistcoat. He paused only to shrug off both coat and waistcoat, letting them fall where they would, and she eagerly set her fingers to the small, flat buttons closing his shirt.

This was one arena within their marriage in which she'd felt utterly confident from the first, and she knew she had his passion, his understanding, his honesty, and his expertise to thank for that. His own inner confidence in his manly attributes, too. He'd been so focused on her, so openly desirous, and so unwaveringly intent on claiming her—so committed and caught up in the moment—that he'd shown her all.

All he felt for her.

All she meant to him.

She'd sailed into passion with a questing heart, buoyed by confidence in her own desirability.

No woman could have asked for more on her wedding night.

And from that night on, they'd embarked on a joint exploration of what engagements such as this could bring them.

She'd devoted herself to learning all he would teach her and all she might of her own volition learn. And every night, although the destination remained blessedly the same, the journey was different, the road subtly altered, the revelations along it fresh and absorbing.

His lips supped from hers, his tongue teasing hers. She responded, using all she'd learned to tempt and lure. She hauled his shirt from his waistband and freed the last button closing it. Anchored in the kiss, in the heat and the passion that rose so strongly—with such reassuring hunger—between them, she blessed him for his innate elegance, which ensured he used a neat, simple knot in his cravat. The instant she unraveled it, she drew the long strip of linen free. With gay abandon, she flung it away.

Finally clear of obstacles, she pulled his shirt wide, set her hands to the sculpted planes of his chest and joyfully—greedily—claimed, then she pushed the garment up and over his shoulders. He refused to release her lips but broke from the embrace enough to shrug off his coat and waistcoat. Then he opened the shirt's cuffs, stripped the garment off, and let it fall to the floor, and she fell on him, fell into his embrace, and gave herself up, heart and soul, to learning what tonight would bring.

Shivery sensation. Heat.

Knowing touches that claimed and incited, that excited and lured and drew them both along tonight's path.

The whisper of silk. The rustle of the bedclothes.

Fingertips trailing over excruciatingly sensitive skin.

Muscles bunching and rippling, then turning as hard as steel.

Incoherent murmuring.

Naked skin to naked skin, body to body, they merged and, together, fingers linked and gripping, lips brushing, heated breaths mingling, followed the path on.

Journeyed on through the enthrallments of desire, through passion's licking flames, faster and faster they rode and plunged, then surged toward the glorious end.

To where a cataclysm of feeling ripped through reality and sensation consumed them.

Then ecstasy erupted and fractured them, flinging them into oblivion's void…

Until, at the last, spent, hearts racing, blinded by glory, they sank back to earth, to the pleasure of each other's embrace, to the wonder of their discovery.

When her wits finally re-engaged and she could again think, she found she was still too buoyed on triumph—on multiple counts—to, as she usually did, slide into pleasured slumber. She wasn't sure Declan was sleeping, either; wrapped in his arms, her head pillowed on his shoulder, she couldn't see his face—

couldn't be sure if he was sleeping or not without lifting her head and disturbing them both.

In that moment, she was at peace, sated and safe, and felt no need to converse. And, it seemed, neither did he; the slow rise and fall of his chest beneath her cheek soothed and reassured.

Her mind wandered, instinctively cataloguing—where they now were, where she wished them to go.

The path she wanted them to follow—the marriage she was determined they would have.

Her assumption that it was up to her, her responsibility to steer them in the right direction, wasn't one she questioned. She had her parents' marriage and that of her late brother as vivid examples of how terribly wrong things could go if a lady didn't institute and insist on the correct framework. And putting that correct framework in place was much easier if one acted from the first, before any unhelpful habits became ingrained.

She knew what she wanted; she had several shining examples to guide her—her sisters' marriages, Julian and Miranda's marriage, and, more recently, what she'd seen of the relationship between Declan's parents, Fergus and Elaine.

That from his earliest years Declan had been exposed to such a marriage, one that was founded on a working personal partnership—that he would have absorbed the concept, seen its inherent strengths, and, she hoped, would now expect to find the same support in his own marriage—was infinitely encouraging.

Throughout their teens, she and her sisters had spent hours in their parlor at Ridgware discussing the elements of an acceptable-in-their-eyes marriage. Both Millie and Cassie, each in their own way, had set out to achieve that ideal in their marriages and had succeeded. Both Catervale and Elsbury openly doted on their wives, were strong and engaged fathers to their children, and shared everything; they included their wives in all areas of their lives.

Edwina was determined to have nothing less. Indeed, with

Declan, she suspected she wanted more. Compared to Millie and Cassie, she was more outgoing, more curious and eager to engage with life and actively explore the full gamut of its possibilities.

She wanted their marriage to be a joint venture on all levels, first to last.

With their position within the ton now established and their physical union so vibrantly assured, she could now turn her mind and energies to all the other aspects that contributed to a modern marriage.

On the domestic front, she had all in hand. Together, she and Declan had chosen this house to rent for the Season, and perhaps longer, but he'd ceded the tiller entirely to her with respect to selecting and hiring their staff. She'd been lucky to find Humphrey, and Mrs. King, their housekeeper, and the new cook were settling in nicely. The small staff met their needs more than adequately; other than deciding menus, she needed to do little to keep everything running smoothly in that sphere.

Which left her with one outstanding issue, that of how to merge the rest of their lives—how to align their interests, activities, and energies when they weren't in the bedroom, or at home, or socializing within the ton.

All the rest.

Thinking the words brought home just how little she knew of the details of Declan's business—how he occupied himself, what role he played within his family's shipping empire, or any particular causes he espoused. He'd told her he didn't expect to sail again until July, or perhaps later; that left her with plenty of time to question and discover all she needed to learn so that she could work out the details of how he and she were going to work together. How she could and would contribute to his career.

A working partnership such as his parents had was what she wanted, one where she contributed as she could, where appropriate—a partnership that allowed her to understand the demands made on him and the pressures those brought to bear.

Despite her predilection for active engagement, such a partnership didn't necessarily require her to be actively involved in each and every facet, but rather to always be in a position to understand what was going on. She was immutably convinced that such an arrangement was critical to them having the marriage she was determined they would have.

Sleep drew nearer; her already relaxed muscles lost what little tension they'd regained.

Even as she surrendered to slumber's insistent tug, she sensed a nascent swell of eagerness, optimism, and determination. She was free to start her campaign to create the marriage they needed first thing tomorrow morning.

Declan didn't succeed in summoning his wits—in being able to think worth a damn—until Edwina finally fell asleep. Until then, caught between worlds, he knew only the tumultuous emotion that welled and swelled within him. It had flared to life on their wedding night; he had assumed it would fade with time, that exercised daily—nightly—it would gradually lose its power. Instead, it had burgeoned and grown.

But, at last, the soft huff of Edwina's breathing deepened, and she sank more definitely against him, and his senses finally ceased their fascination, withdrew from their complete and abject focus on her, and allowed his wits to resurface.

And that overwhelming emotion subsided, but the effects lingered, leaving him unsettlingly aware of just how much she now meant to him. He dwelled on that reality for a moment, then buried the understanding deep. The only consequence he needed to consciously grasp was that, now, putting her—or allowing her to put herself—in any danger whatsoever was simply not on the cards.

For several moments, the potential conflict between that consideration and her as-yet-undefined unconventionality—underscored by their recent activities—and how that might impinge on the way their marriage would work cycled through his mind. His only clear conclusion was that establishing the practical logistics of their marriage was shaping up to be significantly more complicated than he'd assumed. He would need to establish boundaries to keep Edwina separate from the other side of his life, to keep her safely screened from it.

He tried to imagine how he might achieve that, especially given the understanding that niggled deep in his brain—that given his own character, it was her adventurous soul that had from the first drawn him.

Yet adventuring of any sort invariably led to danger. How was he to suppress that aspect of her personality while simultaneously preserving it?

He fell asleep before even a whisper of a suggestion of a plan bloomed in his mind.

Two

The following morning, her marital challenge in the forefront of her mind, Edwina swept into the breakfast parlor to find her handsome husband frowning over a letter. She halted. "What is it?"

He glanced up. His gaze rested on her for a second, then he shook his head. He folded the letter and tucked it into his coat pocket. "Just a note calling me to a meeting. Company business."

The tip of Edwina's tongue burned with the urge to press him for more; for a second, she flirted with the idea of offering to accompany him just to see how he would react. But… It was too early for that. Frontal assaults rarely worked with men like Declan; they instinctively resisted any pressure, which later made convincing them to change their stance all the harder. She needed to pave her way.

She turned to the sideboard, sent a smiling nod Humphrey's way, and accepted the plate he handed her. As she sampled the various delicacies in the chafing dishes, then went to the table and slipped into the chair Humphrey held for her, she reflected on her glaring lack of knowledge of her husband's business. While she might not yet be in a position to demand to know the details of an upcoming meeting, there were other questions it was patently time she started asking.

She reached for the teapot, poured herself a cup, then lifted it and sipped. Looking over the rim, she studied Declan; he appeared absorbed with making inroads into a mound of scrambled eggs. "I know you captain one of your family's vessels, but

I don't know what you actually do." When he looked up, she caught his eyes and arched her brows. "For what reasons do you sail? What tasks do you accomplish for Frobisher and Sons?"

Declan regarded her. He was happy enough to answer that query, if only to distract her from those facts he didn't wish to share. Rapidly, he canvassed his options to most effectively—engagingly and distractingly—satisfy her. "In order to do that, I have to explain something of the structure of the family's fleet."

When she opened her eyes wide, indicating her interest and that he should continue, he smiled and complied. "The fleet has two principal arms. The first is comprised of traditional cargo vessels. They're larger—wider, deeper, and heavier—and therefore slower ships that carry all manner of cargo around the globe, although these days, we concentrate on Atlantic routes. At present, our farthest port on routes to the east is Cape Town."

He paused to fork up the last bite of his scrambled eggs, seizing the seconds to consider his next words. She took the chance to slather jam on her usual piece of toast, then lifted the slice to her lips and took a neat bite. The crunch focused his gaze on her mouth; he watched the tip of her tongue sweep the lush ripeness of her lower lip, leaving it glistening...

Quietly, he cleared his throat and forced his wayward mind back to the issue at hand. After remarshaling his thoughts, he offered, "It's the other arm of the family business in which my brothers and I are actively engaged. We each captain our own ship, and it would be accurate to say that we still carry cargo. But our ships are by design faster and also, again by design, newer and better able to withstand adverse conditions."

With a soft snort, he set down his knife and fork and reached for his coffee mug. "You might have noticed that Royd is somewhat obsessed with our ships' attributes and performances." Royd—Murgatroyd, although no one bar their parents ever dared call him that—was his eldest brother and, these days, more or less in charge. "He's constantly redesigning and updating. That's why *The Cormorant* has been out of commission over these past weeks. She's been in dry dock in the shipyards at Aberdeen while Royd fiddles, implementing his latest ideas, which I'll eventually get to test."

Declan paused to sip, then wryly acknowledged, "I have to admit that the rest of us are usually very grateful for his improvements." Often those improvements had tipped the scales between life and death, between freedom and captivity.

"When you say 'the rest of us'"—Edwina brushed crumbs from her fingers—"who precisely do you mean?"

"The four of us—Royd, Robert, me, and Caleb—and several of our cousins. Still other cousins captain several of our merchantmen, but there's a group of family captains, about eight all told, who sail for the other side of the business."

"Last night, some gentleman mentioned a treaty your family had assisted with. Was that an undertaking you were involved with?"

"No. That was Robert. He tends to specialize in meeting the more diplomatic requests."

She frowned slightly. "What is the nature of this other side of the business? What sort of requests, diplomatic or otherwise, do you undertake?"

Declan considered for a moment, then offered, "There are different sorts of cargoes."

She arched her brows. "Such as?"

Fleetingly, he grinned. "People. Documents. Items of special value. And, most valuable of all, information." He paused, aware that it would not be wise to paint their endeavors in too-intriguing colors. "It's a relatively straightforward engagement. We undertake to transport items of that nature quickly, safely, and discreetly from port to port."

"Ah." After a moment of consideration, she said, "I take it that's the motivation behind Royd's obsession."

He set down his coffee cup. He hadn't consciously made

the connection before, but... "I suppose you could say that the fruits of Royd's obsession significantly contribute to Frobisher and Sons being arguably the best specialized shipping service in the world."

She smiled. "Specialized shipping. I see. At least now I know how to describe what you do."

And that, he thought, was as much as she or anyone else needed to know.

Before he could redirect the conversation, she went on, "You said that you only sail for about half the year. Do you sail at any time, or are your voyages always over the same months each year?"

"Generally, our side of the business operates over the summer and into the autumn months, when the seas are most accommodating."

"But you don't expect to set out on *The Cormorant* before July or thereabouts?"

He nodded. "There was no"—*mission*—"request falling between now and then that I, specifically, needed to handle. The others took it upon themselves to cover for me." He grinned and met her eyes. "I believe they thought of it as a wedding gift."

"For which I am duly grateful." She set down her empty teacup.

Before she could formulate her next question, he swiveled to glance at the clock on the mantelpiece above the fireplace at the end of the room. As he had hoped, she followed his gaze.

When she saw the time, her eyes widened. "Great heavens! I have to get ready for Lady Minchingham's at-home."

He rose and drew out her chair. "I've this meeting to attend, then I think I'll call in at our office, purely to keep abreast of what's going on in the world of shipping." The Frobisher and Sons office was located with many other shipping companies' offices near the Pool of London.

Distracted now, she merely nodded and led the way from the room. "I'll see you this evening, then."

She stepped into the hall, then paused. "I had planned for us to attend Lady Forsythe's rout, but I rather feel we've moved beyond the need." She glanced at him and smiled, one of her subtly appraising—and frankly suggestive—looks. "Perhaps a quiet evening at home, just the two of us, might be a better use of our time."

He saw nothing in that suggestion with which he wished to argue. Halting on the parlor's threshold, he smiled into her wide blue eyes. "A quiet evening spent with you would definitely be my preference."

Her smile blossomed with open delight. She stretched up on her toes, and when he dutifully bent his head, she touched her lips to his.

He locked his hands behind his back to rein in the impulse to catch her to him and prolong the caress; aside from all else, both Humphrey and the footman were within sight.

If the commiserating quality of her smile as she drew back was any guide, she'd nevertheless sensed his response; while the look in her eyes suggested she shared the temptation, her expression also stated that she approved of his control. She lightly patted his chest, then turned away. With an insouciant wave, she headed for the stairs.

He remained where he was and watched her go up. Once she'd passed out of the gallery in the direction of their room, he reached into his pocket and drew out the folded note that had been burning a hole there. His smile faded as he reread the simple lines of the summons. They told him little more than that he was expected at the Ripley Building as soon as he could get there.

Glancing up, he saw Humphrey waiting by the side of the hall. "My hat and coat, Humphrey."

"At once, sir."

As Humphrey helped him into his greatcoat, Declan reflected that his summoner wasn't a man it was wise to keep waiting. Seconds later, his hat on his head, he walked out and down the steps. Lengthening his stride, he headed for Whitehall.

From Whitehall, Declan turned into the Ripley Building. When he presented himself to the sergeant on duty, he wasn't surprised to be directed into Admiralty House. He was, however, surprised to be directed not downward to some undistinguished office on the lower level but upstairs to the office of the First Lord of the Admiralty. Then again, the war was long over, and as far as Declan knew, the gentleman who had summoned him was no longer actively engaged in managing their country's defenses; presumably, he no longer maintained an official office to which to summon his minions.

A harried-looking secretary asked Declan's name; on being supplied with it, the man immediately escorted him to an ornate door. The secretary tapped, then opened the door, looked in, and murmured something; he listened, then speaking more loudly, he announced Declan, stepped back, and waved him through.

Very much wondering into what he was strolling, Declan walked into the room.

As the door closed silently behind him, he scanned the chamber. Two men waited for him.

The Duke of Wolverstone—Declan's summoner—had been standing by the window looking out over the parade grounds. He'd acceded to the title of duke shortly after the war, but Declan still thought of him as Dalziel, the name he'd used throughout the years he'd managed the Crown's covert operatives on foreign soil—and on the high seas. As Declan walked forward, Wolverstone turned and came to greet him.

If becoming the duke, marrying, and having several children had in any way blunted Dalziel's—Wolverstone's—lethal edge, Declan couldn't see it. The man still moved with the same predatory grace, and the power of his personality had abated not one jot.

Declan glanced at the only other occupant of the large room—Viscount Melville, current First Lord. Declan recognized him, but they hadn't previously met. A heavy-boned, slightly rotund gentleman with a round face, a florid complexion, and the dyspeptic mien of a man who liked order but who was forced to deal with the generally disordered, Melville remained seated behind his desk, fussily gathering the papers on which he'd been working and piling them to one side of his blotter.

Literally clearing his desk.

The sight, indicating as it did Melville's interest in meeting with him, did not fill Declan with joy. He was supposed to be on his honeymoon. His brothers and cousins had worked to clear his schedule.

Unfortunately, it appeared that the Crown had other ideas.

"Frobisher." Wolverstone held out his hand. When Declan grasped it, Wolverstone said, "I—we—apologize for dragging you away from your new wife's side. However, the need is urgent. So urgent that we cannot wait for any other of your family to reach London and take this mission." Wolverstone released Declan's hand and waved him to one of the pair of chairs angled before Melville's desk. "Sit, and his lordship and I will explain."

Although Declan had been too young to captain a ship during the late wars, through the closing years of the conflict he'd sailed as lieutenant to his father or one of his uncles, and had experienced firsthand, as had his brothers and cousins—those currently engaged in the other side of the business—the workings of the largely unwritten contract that existed between the Crown and the Frobishers. Alongside straightforward shipping, their ancestors had been privateers; in reality, those sailing for the other arm of the company still operated as privateers—the company's Letters of Marque were active and had never been rescinded. In return for the company continuing, on request, to provide certain specialized and usually secret services to the Crown, Frobisher and Sons enjoyed the cachet of being the preferred company for the lucrative shipping contracts the government controlled.

The symbiotic link between the Frobishers and the Crown had existed for centuries. Whatever the request Wolverstone had summoned Declan to Melville's office to hear, there was not the slightest question that Frobisher and Sons would, in one way or another, oblige.

Exactly how they responded, however, was up to them—and, it seemed, in this instance, the decision was in Declan's hands.

He subsided into one chair. Wolverstone sat in the other.

"Thank you for answering our call, Mr. Frobisher." Melville exchanged nods with Declan, then looked at Wolverstone. "I haven't previously had reason to invoke the Crown's privilege and call on your family for assistance. However, Wolverstone here assures me that, in this matter, asking Frobisher and Sons for help is our best way forward." Melville's brown eyes returned to Declan's face. "As His Grace is more experienced than I in relating the facts of such matters, I will ask him to explain."

Declan looked at Wolverstone and faintly arched a brow.

Wolverstone met his eyes. "I was at home in Northumberland when word of this problem reached me." Declan was aware that Wolverstone's principal seat lay just south of the Scottish border. Wolverstone continued, "I immediately sent word to Aberdeen. Royd replied, reluctantly naming you as the only Frobisher available. He wrote that he was dispatching your ship, *The Cormorant*, with a full complement of crew south at the same time as he sent his reply. Your ship should be waiting for you at the company berth in Southampton by the time you're ready to leave." Wolverstone paused, then said, "Again, let me offer our—and your family's—regrets over disrupting your honeymoon. Royd, I believe, would have answered our call himself, but your father and mother have left on a trip to Dublin and are not available to take the company's helm."

Declan recalled his mother mentioning the trip.

"Robert, meanwhile, has recently set sail for New York and is not expected back for some weeks—and, as mentioned, our matter is urgent. Likewise, none of the others are immediately available"—Wolverstone's lips twisted wryly—"while courtesy of your honeymoon, you are already here, on our doorstep in London."

Resigning himself to the inevitable, Declan inclined his head.

"Royd also wrote that, as the mission involves our West African settlements, you are unquestionably the best man for the job."

Declan widened his eyes. "West Africa?"

Wolverstone nodded. "I gather you're familiar with the ports along that coast and have also gone inland in several locations."

Declan held Wolverstone's gaze. Royd might have mentioned Declan's knowledge of the region, but his eldest brother wouldn't have revealed any details, and Declan saw no reason to regale Wolverstone, of all men, with such facts. "Indeed." In order to avoid further probing, he added, "Royd's right. Assuming you want something or someone found in that area, I'm your best hope."

Wolverstone's lips curved slightly—he was far too perceptive for Declan's peace of mind—but he obliged and moved on. "In this case, it's information we need you to find."

Leaning over his desk, Melville earnestly interjected, "Find— and bring back to us."

Wolverstone flicked the First Lord a faintly chiding glance, then returned his dark gaze to Declan's face. He imperturbably continued, "The situation is this. As you no doubt know, while Freetown is presently the base for the navy's West Africa Squadron, we also have a sizeable detachment of army personnel stationed at Fort Thornton, in support of the governor-in-chief of the region, who is quartered there."

"The governor's currently Holbrook." Melville caught Declan's eye. "Do you know him?"

"Not well. I've met him once, but not recently."

"As it happens, that's advantageous." Wolverstone went on, "An army engineer from the corps at Fort Thornton disappeared four months ago. As far as we've been able to learn, Captain Dixon simply vanished—he was there one day and not the next. Apparently, none of his colleagues have any idea of where he might have gone or that he'd been planning any excursion. Although relatively young, Dixon was an experienced engineer and well regarded. He was also from a family with connections in the navy. At those connections' request, Melville authorized a lieutenant from the West Africa Squadron to investigate."

Wolverstone paused; his gaze held Declan's. "The lieutenant disappeared—simply vanished—too."

"Bally nonsense," Melville growled. "I know Hopkins—he wouldn't have gone absent without leave."

"Indeed." Wolverstone inclined his head. "From what I know of the Hopkins family, I would agree. Subsequently, Melville sent in another lieutenant, Fanshawe, a man with more experience of investigations and the local region. He, too, vanished without trace."

"At that point," Melville stated rather glumly, "I asked for Wolverstone's advice."

Without reaction, Wolverstone continued, "I suggested a gentleman by the name of Hillsythe be sent to Freetown as an attaché to the governor's office. Hillsythe is in his late twenties and had worked for me previously in covert operations. His experience is sound. He knew what he had to do, and, once there, he would have known how to go about it." Wolverstone paused, then, his voice quieter, said, "Hillsythe has disappeared, too. As far as we can judge, about a week after he'd arrived in the settlement."

Declan absorbed what it said of the situation that one of Wolverstone's own had vanished. Imagining what might be going on, he frowned. "What does the governor—Holbrook— have to say about this? And the commander at Thornton, as well. Who is that, incidentally?"

"A Major Eldridge is the commanding officer at Thornton. With respect to Dixon, he's as baffled as we are. As for Holbrook…" Wolverstone exchanged a glance with Melville. "Holbrook appears to believe the, for want of a better term, local scuttlebutt—that people who vanish in that manner have, and I quote, 'gone into the jungle to seek their fortune.'" Wolverstone's gaze locked on Declan's face. "As you are someone who, if I'm reading between Royd's lines correctly, has walked into those same jungles in search of fortunes, I'm curious as to what your opinion of Holbrook's assessment might be."

Declan returned Wolverstone's steady regard while he considered how best to reply. Given he would be contradicting the stated opinion of a governor, he chose his words with care. "As you say, I've been into those jungles. No man in his right mind would simply walk into them. The roads are mere tracks at best and are often overgrown. Villages are primitive and few and far between. The terrain is difficult, and the jungles are dense and, in many places, impenetrable. While water is, in general, plentiful, it may not be potable. It's entirely possible, if not likely, that you will meet hostile natives." He paused, then concluded, "In short, any European venturing beyond the fringes of a settlement would need to gather a small company, with significant supplies as well as the right sort of equipment, and assembling all that isn't something that can be done without people noticing."

Melville humphed. "You've just confirmed what Wolverstone's been telling me. That we—meaning the Crown—can't trust Holbrook, which means we can't trust anyone presently

on the ground in Freetown." Melville paused, th⟋
and looked at Wolverstone. "We probably shouldn't ʋ.
one in the fleet, either."

Wolverstone inclined his head. "I believe it would be wise
not to do so."

"Which," Melville said, returning his gaze to Declan, "is why
we have such urgent need of you, sir. We need someone we can
trust to go out to Freetown and learn what the devil's going on."

Wolverstone stirred, reclaiming Declan's attention. "We
should clarify that, in part, our urgency is fueled by wider considerations." Wolverstone caught Declan's gaze. "I'm sure you'll
recall the case of the Black Cobra, which ended with a public
hanging just a year ago." When Declan nodded—who hadn't
heard of that episode?—Wolverstone continued, "The Black
Cobra cult, controlled by a trio of English subjects, caused significant harm to our colonial peoples. That the cult was able
to spread so widely, and act for as long as it did, was an indict-
ment on the British government's ability to manage its colonies."
Wolverstone's lips thinned. "The government—the Crown—
does not need another similar incident raising further questions
about our ability to rule our empire."

Declan didn't need further explanation. He now fully understood that the pressure on Melville to find out exactly what
was going on in Freetown, to resolve the matter and re-estab-
lish appropriate order, was coming from a great deal higher up
the political pole. "Very well." He glanced at Wolverstone. "Do
you know when *The Cormorant* is due to reach Southampton?"

"Royd said it sailed…it would be the day before yesterday."

Declan nodded. "They most likely left late, so the earliest into
Southampton would be tomorrow morning, but allowing for
the winds and the tides, it'll probably be later. The crew will
need a day to fully provision the ship from our stores there. I'll
use the next two days to see what information about doings in

Freetown I can glean from the London docks, then I'll leave for Southampton the following day and sail on the evening tide."

"How long do you think it'll take you to reach Freetown?" Melville asked.

"With favorable winds, *The Cormorant* can make it in fourteen days."

"There's one thing both Melville and I wish to stress. Indeed," Wolverstone said, "you can consider it a part of your orders—an instruction not to be ignored."

Declan arched his brows.

"The instant you learn anything—*any fact at all*—we want you to return and bring that fact back to us." Wolverstone's voice had assumed the rigid tones of absolute command. "We cannot afford to lose more men while continuing to have no idea what is taking place down there. We need you to go in, winkle out a first lead—but we don't, specifically *do not*, want you to follow it."

"We need you to come back and tell us," Melville reiterated.

Declan didn't have to think too hard to understand that the political pressure for some answers, any answers, would be mounting by the day.

Wolverstone's tone was dry as he remarked, "I realize that, as a gentleman-adventurer, you would prefer not to operate under such a restriction. That is, however, what is needed in this case. The instant you learn anything—and especially if, subsequently, you sense any opposing reaction—you are to leave immediately and bring that information home." He paused, then, in a quieter tone, added, "We've lost too many capable men already, and for nothing. That cannot go on."

Although he hadn't personally received orders directly from Wolverstone before, Declan knew enough of the man's history to know that last stipulation was a very un-Dalziel-like stance. The man had been renowned for giving his operatives objectives as orders, allowing said operatives to execute their missions largely as they saw fit. Dalziel had always shown an appreciation for flexibility in the field. And an expectation of complete success.

Which, more often than not, had been met.

That he was being so very cautious—indeed, insisting on such rigid caution—Declan suspected was more a reflection of the seriousness of the situation rather than any indication that the leopard had changed his spots.

He didn't like the caveat, the restriction, but... "Very well." If all he was required to do was learn one fact, that would probably take him no more than a day. In effect, his unusual orders would reduce his time away from Edwina; he decided it behooved him to be grateful rather than disgruntled. He glanced at Melville, then looked at Wolverstone. "If there's nothing else...?"

"I've penned a letter giving you the authority to call on the West Africa Squadron for any assistance you might need," Melville said. "It's with my secretary—you can pick it up as you leave."

As Declan rose, Wolverstone, too, came to his feet. "Short of a compelling need, however, I would suggest you keep that letter to yourself. Use it only as a last resort." He met Declan's eyes. "Were I you, I would trust no one. Not with the details of your mission. Not with anything they do not need to know."

The cool incisiveness in Wolverstone's words told Declan very clearly that neither Wolverstone nor Melville trusted Governor Holbrook or Major Eldridge, or Vice-Admiral Decker, presently in command of the West Africa Squadron. And if they didn't trust them, they didn't trust anyone.

There was something rotten in Freetown, and it had spread and sunk its roots deep.

Declan exchanged a nod with Melville.

Wolverstone extended his hand, and Declan gripped it and shook.

"We'll expect to see you in a month or so." Wolverstone

paused, then, releasing Declan's hand, murmured, "And if you're not back inside six weeks, I'll send Royd after you."

Declan grinned at the threat, which was no real threat at all; he and his big brother might butt heads all too frequently, but he couldn't think of any man he would rather have at his back. "I'll return as soon as I can."

With a salute, Declan made for the door, already thinking of the preparations to be made—and the news he now had to break to his wife.

Three

Knowing that Edwina would already have left the house for her morning's engagements, Declan went on to the Frobisher and Sons office, located off Burr Street between St. Katherine's Docks and the London Docks. There, he set in train various inquiries, dispatching several of the company's retired sailors to quietly ask questions in the inns and taverns scattered about the area. He doubted they would hear anything specifically relating to his mission, but if there was some wider scheme afoot that might impinge on it, he would prefer to know of any potential complication before he set sail from England's green shores.

The rest of his day went in gathering all the information he could about the current state of commerce and industry in the West African colonies from those in the office, as well as from his peers and contacts in the nearby offices of other shipping companies.

He was an adventurer at heart. As he was going to West Africa anyway, he might as well be alert and aware of any emerging possibilities.

He returned to Stanhope Street in the late afternoon. Taking refuge in the small library, he waited for Edwina to return. He spent the minutes pacing before the fireplace, rehearsing the words and phrases with which to excuse and explain his sudden and impending departure.

When he heard Humphrey's heavy tread cross the front hall, then Edwina's voice greeting the butler as she swept into the house, Declan drew in a deep breath and walked to the door. He opened it and looked out.

Edwina saw him and halted.

Going forward, he reached for her hand. "If you have a moment, my dear, I have some news."

She surrendered her hand. Her eyes searched his face. Whatever she saw there sobered her. "Yes, of course." She handed her bonnet to Humphrey and allowed Declan to usher her into the library.

After shutting the door behind them, he led her to the space before the fireplace. Unable to resist, he drew her to him and bent his head for a kiss. Stretching up, she met him in her usual eager fashion. She tasted of honey-cakes…

Before the engagement could spin out of hand, he broke the caress, then released her and waved her to the small sofa facing the hearth.

She glanced at his face, then, in a rustle of silk skirts, complied. He remained standing to one side of the hearth—instinctively assuming the stance of a captain addressing his crew. He was conscious of the nuance, but as the stance gave him confidence that he knew what he was doing and would accomplish the task before him, he pushed the question of its appropriateness from his mind.

She sank onto the sofa and locked her gaze on his face. "Don't keep me in suspense. What is it?"

He'd debated how to phrase his news and had decided that brevity would serve them best. "I've been called on to do a short run to the capital of the West African settlements. It won't take long—I'll only be away for a few weeks—but for business reasons, the voyage has to be made immediately. None of my brothers or cousins is available. They're at sea and not due back in time or, in Royd's case, unable to set sail due to other commitments."

For several silent seconds, she stared up at him. Then in a

perfectly equable tone, she asked, "How dangerous is this voyage likely to be?"

"Not dangerous at all—or, at most, only minimally so." Given his orders to cut and run the instant he learned anything, he couldn't imagine he would face any real danger. He didn't want her worrying. He summoned a reassuring smile. "I'll be home safe and sound before you know it."

"On that route, is the weather favorable at this time of year?"

"Generally speaking, yes. I don't expect to run into any storms."

Again, she stared at him as several seconds ticked by. Finally, her gaze fixed unwaveringly on his face, she stated, "In that case, I should like to accompany you."

His mind seized. His wits froze. Blindsided—knocked entirely out of kilter—he simply stared down at her.

Apparently not noticing his stunned state, she blithely rattled on, "Given we've accomplished the most important goal we came to London to achieve, and as all else here is running smoothly, there's really no reason I need to remain in town over the next weeks." Her eyes warmed and her lips curved with eager enthusiasm. "And I would so like to sail with you—to see the world by your side."

He finally managed to find his tongue. "No."

She blinked, then clouds gathered in her sunny blue eyes and a frown drew down her brows. "Why not? Is there some reason you haven't yet told me that makes it inadmissible for me to travel with you?"

Yes. He opened his mouth, then shut it. He couldn't tell her any details. She moved in circles that might easily include connections of the Holbrooks, Decker, or Eldridge; one loose word and she might unwittingly place him and his crew in danger— a danger they would not otherwise face. He couldn't tell her about his mission, and he certainly couldn't take her with him. *Lord above!* He'd only just recognized how incredibly precious to him she now was, how central to his future life, to his future happiness, and she wanted to accompany him on a flying visit to one of the roughest settlements in the empire?

"No—or rather, yes." He resisted the urge to rake his fingers through his hair. "There are any number of reasons that make it impossible for you to sail with me." His tone made the declaration unequivocal. "And I'm sorry, but I can't explain. It's entirely untenable for you to travel with me in this instance." Probably in any instance; he rarely traveled but for business, and his business was rarely without some risk.

Indeed, sailing on the high seas was never devoid of risk. Ships wrecked. He might survive, but she was so small and weak, he doubted she would.

Edwina's heart sank, but she told herself that this obstacle had always been lurking somewhere along their path. She'd already decided that it was time to move forward, time to focus on establishing the daily ins and outs of how their marriage would work. Here was her first challenge. They would have come to this at some point; there would always have been a first time for her to convince him to take her sailing with him.

That said, she hadn't expected this particular hurdle to appear quite so soon. Clasping her hands in her lap, she fixed her gaze on his face. "Declan, I realize we haven't specifically discussed this, but I knew you spent at least half the year on your ship when I accepted your proposal. I married you in the full expectation that however many months you spent on the waves, I would be able to spend, if not all of those months, then at least the majority of them by your side, on the deck of your ship."

She couldn't be sure but she thought his eyes widened; it seemed her revelation had come as a surprise. Yet surely he hadn't imagined that she was the type of lady to remain snug and safe at home by the fire, oblivious to whatever dangers or threats he might be facing halfway around the world?

She fought to stifle a snort.

Studying his expression, she frowned more definitely. "You cannot possibly be surprised by that. By the notion that I want to be a part of your life—all of it—rather than being relegated only to the land-based part." Leaning forward, she made her eyes, her whole expression, as beseeching as she could. "Please, Declan. I would so like to go on your ship and sail the seas with you."

For a moment, he held her gaze, then his chest swelled as he drew in a deep breath. For one instant, she hoped... But then his chin firmed; she saw his jaw harden.

"I have to admit that I did not quite appreciate your interest in sailing. If you like, I'll take you on *The Cormorant*, perhaps to Amsterdam, and then down the coast of France and Spain and into the Mediterranean when I return from this trip."

She considered the offer—clearly an olive branch of sorts—for half a minute before firming her own chin. "I would enjoy such a trip, but it fails to address the issue before us, which is that I wish to, and expect to, share all of your life and not just some of it."

He held her gaze; the sky blue of his eyes seemed somehow flatter, less alive—less open, his emotions screened. "I cannot, and will not, take you on this particular voyage."

She narrowed her eyes. "So I am to be allowed to share some of your life—the parts you deem appropriate—but I am to be excluded from those business ventures, those adventures, you wish to keep private, to yourself."

She paused to give him a chance to respond, but although his nostrils pinched as he drew in a long breath, he refused the unstated invitation to correct her.

Taking that as a sign—a negative one—she evenly continued, "I have already stated that such boundaries are not what I expected in our marriage—one I wish to be based firmly on the concept of shared enterprise. As I understand your mother has always sailed with your father, I had not realized that you might think I would be happy being left at home."

His lips thinned. "My mother's case is different."

She arched her brows. "How so?"

"She—" He stopped. His eyes remained locked with hers as his expression turned openly exasperated. "My mother is not you," he eventually stated, his tone clipped and hard. "She's my father's responsibility, and you are mine."

She returned a terse nod. "Indeed. Our marriage is as much your responsibility as mine. And I will go further and definitively state that I am not prepared to accept the restriction of not sailing with you, short of there being sound reasons and a compelling argument against it. I am not prepared to acquiesce to such a limitation being put on our sharing—on our marriage."

She'd concluded on a belligerent note. She knew what she wanted, what she needed, and she was as certain as she could possibly be that—granite-headed though he clearly was—he, too, would gain enormously from a sharing union. The entire point was to support each other through no longer being alone. By no longer having to face life and its challenges, threats, and dangers alone.

That meant they had to share their lives.

He could argue until he was blue in the face, but she was not going to back down.

Declan looked into her face, saw the stalwart determination infusing her features, and understood that, entirely unexpectedly, he stood on very thin ice.

He wished it was otherwise—wished he'd comprehended her vision of their marriage before they'd reached this pass, so that he might have known which way to tack to better avoid cutting across her bow. He wished he could convince himself that this was a temporary whim of hers, that she couldn't possibly be truly serious, that her statements of direction and intent were not rooted in sincere belief...but he couldn't. She was the least whimsical female he'd ever met. And while he hadn't foreseen her direction regarding their marriage, he had unshakeable faith in her honesty, especially when it came to what lay between them.

That was why wooing her had been so damned easy. She'd wanted him as much as he'd wanted her, and she hadn't been backward about letting him know.

While such emotional honesty—such emotional clarity—had been a boon earlier, it made what he had to do now very much harder.

He hauled in an unsettlingly tight breath, held her gaze, and quietly, evenly, said, "I regret, my dear, that in this instance, I cannot take you with me. I would if I could—I would lay the sun, the moon, and the stars at your feet if that was what you wished and it lay within my ability. While not fraught with danger, this journey is not one I can allow you to share."

He paused, then—deciding that he might as well be hung for a wolf as a lamb—he added, "There will always be some voyages like this. With others…perhaps we can reach some agreement when I get back. However, for now, my decision stands. I am the captain of *The Cormorant*, and I have absolute authority over who boards my ship. I cannot, and will not, take you with me."

He expected her to erupt, although, truth be told, he'd never yet seen her lose her temper. He'd seen her annoyed, irritated, but never truly furious. But he now comprehended that this issue meant a great deal to her, and he knew she was stubborn, someone who would fight for what she believed… Instinctively, he braced for her anger.

It never came.

Instead, she studied him through narrowed eyes, glinting an unusually hard, bright blue from beneath her fine lashes. Gradually, her expression grew pensive.

After several moments of fraught silence—of him waiting for some high-flown denunciation—in a relatively normal tone, she asked, "Is that because, despite you saying there'll be no real danger for you, you fear exposing me to even that low level of danger?"

He blinked. "Freetown—the capital of Sierra Leone—is no Bombay, or Calcutta, or Cape Town. It's basic in every sense of the word and definitely no place for a duke's daughter."

"And that's where you're going?" When he nodded, she said, "I see. So your decision is driven by wanting to protect me."

"Yes." *Exactly.* He didn't say the word but was quite sure she read his exasperation in his eyes. Why else would he deny her?

She studied him for a moment more, then—to his complete surprise—she gave a little nod, more to herself than him, and rose. "All right. That I can accept."

Suddenly, he felt oddly unsure, as if some unexpected wind had blown up and was steadily pushing him off course. He tried to study her face, but she was looking down and shaking her skirts straight. "Just so I have this issue clear, as long as my intention is to protect you, then you'll accept whatever decisions I make?"

She raised her head, met his eyes, and smiled—gently, reassuringly. Then she stepped closer, came up on her toes, and lightly touched her lips to his. Drawing back, her hand on his chest, she stated, "I accept that, in seeking to protect me, you will make such decisions."

Sinking back to her heels, she watched him for a second, then her smile deepened. "Now." She turned and walked toward the door. "As we discussed last night, we're having dinner here, just the two of us, and then spending a quiet evening in the drawing room."

He followed as if drawn by invisible threads.

At the door, she turned and, smiling, arched her brows. "Unless you would prefer to attend more events?"

"No, no." He quelled a shudder. Reaching past her, he opened the door. "I'm looking forward to spending a whole evening in which I don't have to share you with anyone else."

Belatedly, he realized what he'd said—which word he'd used—but she only smiled sweetly and led the way out.

Feeling very much as if he'd avoided a cannonball to his mainmast, yet having no clear idea how he'd accomplished the feat, he followed at her heels. They'd got over that stumbling block and peace and harmony had—somehow—been maintained. He told himself to be grateful.

The evening following Edwina's discussion with Declan in their library, she stood by the side of Lady Comerford's ballroom and pretended to pay attention to the various gentlemen surrounding her. A few ladies were scattered among the ranks, but to Edwina's dismay, for some ungodly reason, a sizeable cohort of gentlemen seemed intent on vying for her attention.

Even though the group included several she'd heard spoken of in hushed whispers by the racier of her peers—the young matrons of the ton—and even though she recognized the attraction several of those gentlemen possessed, she had no attention to spare even for such potent distractions.

Declan had informed her that he would be departing London sometime the next day; he had begged off accompanying her to this ball on the grounds of having to deal with last-minute preparations. Given she'd already declared their purpose in appearing together at such major ton events achieved, she'd had to accept his decision with a gracious smile. She'd hidden her welling consternation; she had yet to decide how best to respond to his decision to leave her safely in London.

She understood his motives, but equally, she knew that they would have to start somewhere—that at some point, she would have to press her case to accompany him on his business trips. In the circumstances, it was difficult to find a reason not to commence as she intended to go on. If she bowed to his fear for her now, if she gave it credence on what he'd assured her was an as-near-as-made-no-odds dangerless voyage, his attitude would only grow more entrenched, making her ultimate battle to change his mind that much harder.

On them both.

As she was beyond determined that, ultimately, she would prevail and would routinely accompany him on his voyages, then letting his decision stand, even this once, seemed an unwise path to take.

Outwardly gay, she attempted to respond to the banter and comments directed her way sufficiently well to camouflage her distraction. Meanwhile, the better part of her brain revisited the options she'd identified over the past twenty-four hours. She wasn't the sort to fret and fume, to argue and shout; over the years, she'd found that the most effective way of overcoming hurdles was to ignore them and act as she believed she should. However, this situation was complex and complicated, affecting not just her but Declan, and also impacting and potentially shaping the foundation of their marriage.

She'd thought about seeking advice, but there were precious few whom she might ask, and even fewer with what she deemed the requisite experience and understanding to whom she might consider listening. There were few ladies in the ton whose husbands were adventurers. The closest comparison she could think of was her brother, Julian, and with respect to his marriage, it had, indeed, been Miranda who had acted to make their marriage happen; if she hadn't taken a decisive step against Julian's clear direction, the joyful marriage she and Julian shared would simply not have been.

Impulse, observation, and contemplation all urged Edwina to act. If she truly believed—as she did—that her accompanying Declan on this voyage was critical for their marriage to succeed, then it behooved her to make that happen for their joint greater good.

That was a nice, clear, unequivocal conclusion. All she needed to do was convince herself that it was, indeed, the right one.

She was still mentally debating, still absentmindedly fending off subtly worded advances when, across the ballroom, a gilded head of light brown hair caught her eye. She was too short to see the face beneath, but that color, that recklessly windblown style…

Seconds later, the crowd thinned, and she glimpsed Declan moving purposefully in her direction. Her pulse sped up; she ignored all those about her—she had eyes only for him.

It appeared he felt the same way about her; although several ladies attempted to intercept him, and although he cloaked his responses in superficial civility, his gaze barely diverted from her.

And then he was there, smoothly taking her hand and raising it to his lips while his gaze held hers. "My dear, I apologize for my tardiness. Matters took longer than I'd anticipated." Tucking her hand in the crook of his arm, he raised his gaze and allowed it to travel over the group of over-attentive gentlemen.

Declan smiled, coldly, on the group of, at least to him, unwelcome admirers who had had the temerity to gather about his wife. He didn't like the looks of any of them. An unsettling thought rose in his mind—that with him absent on the Crown's business, she would have no one to send them packing. "Do introduce me to your"—*cicisbeos*—"friends, my dear."

Several of said friends all but deflated.

He managed not to bare his teeth and managed to respond with passable civility to the introductions Edwina was quick to make.

This was the first night he hadn't accompanied her into the ton, and he was going to be away for at least a fortnight, possibly longer…

He squelched the impulse that rose within him; this was not a venue in which snarling was acceptable.

The introductions were barely complete when the small orchestra at the end of the room put bow to string, and the introduction to a waltz rose above the chatter. He fell on the opening.

Closing his hand over hers, he smiled into the widening eyes she turned his way. "I do hope you've saved this waltz for me."

She blinked several times, then somewhat carefully said, "Yes—that is, I believe I might chance it."

He gave her a quizzical look, but he wasn't about to argue; she'd accepted and given him the opportunity to remove her from the horde surrounding her. He flashed a smile he fought not to allow to be too overtly possessive around the group, made their excuses, and drew her away.

The open space of the dance floor was only two paces distant; as he turned her into his arms and stepped out, he arched a brow at her. "What was that all about?"

She sighed. "I claimed to have a twisted ankle so I could avoid all their invitations to waltz."

Happiness bloomed. He grinned. "Clever girl."

She pulled a face at him. "I feel I should point out that you've just shown me to be a liar."

He arched his brows, considering, then offered, "Most of them probably knew you were lying."

She snorted. After two brisk revolutions, she admitted, "Most likely."

That was the last word they exchanged about her court of would-be admirers. Declan set himself to entertain her and not-too-subtly monopolize her time. He saw her mother, her sisters, and several of the older ladies noticing and commenting, but he'd be damned if he was going to leave anyone, gentleman or lady, in any doubt that Edwina was his—and that he intended her to remain so.

As the evening wore on, he took a leaf out of the Delbraith ladies' book; working on the principle that the most effective way of discouraging any would-be lovers was to demonstrate just how happy he and Edwina were in each other's company, how steeped in each other they had already become, he did something he'd never imagined he would do and openly wore his heart on his sleeve—and encouraged her to do the same.

What followed was the most enjoyable evening they had spent in the ton since their wedding. He kept his attention locked on her, and hers remained locked on him; the rest of the guests were merely a colorful backdrop for their play.

Gradually, his possessively protective tension faded, soothed by her laugh, her smile, and the openly loving light in her eyes. Earlier in the day, he'd taken time from his search for information to hunt up Catervale and Elsbury and alert them to his impending absence. Both Edwina's brothers-in-law had readily agreed to do what they could to shield her from any unwanted advances. Of course, it went without saying that both would have to rely on her sisters to alert them to any need for action.

Foreseeing the weakness in that plan, Declan had hailed a hackney, traveled to the house overlooking Dolphin Square, and spoken to her brother. Julian and his wife might not circulate within the ton, but as Neville Roscoe, he had eyes and ears everywhere. Once Julian had shaken off his surprise that Edwina had agreed to remain in London, he'd undertaken to watch over her while Declan was at sea.

Declan had taken every precaution he could. Given that Edwina wasn't a silly female prone to taking unnecessary risks, when they finally departed Comerford House and settled in the shadows of their carriage to rattle over the cobbles to Stanhope Street, he felt more settled than he had since he'd learned of his mission. Assured that while he was away, all would be well with her, and relieved he'd managed to navigate his way through the marital shoals caused by his unexpected voyage.

Having her seated beside him with one small hand tucked into one of his and her soft shoulder pressing against his arm set the seal on his peace.

As the carriage turned a corner, she glanced at his face. "Do you know at what hour you'll be leaving the house?"

Her tone was even, the question simply that.

"As soon as I receive the reports I'm expecting, but I suspect it'll be after midday. Regardless, I'll have to leave before midafternoon in order to make Southampton before the evening tide."

"So your ship will sail on the evening tide?"

He nodded. "If we don't get out then, we'll have to wait until the next day, and time is of the essence."

"I see." A moment ticked by, then she said, "I once went sailing on a yacht in the Solent and saw some of the larger ships pass by. Is it possible for a ship like yours to sail out into the Solent and then wait for people to be ferried from the port before going further?"

"If we weren't in a hurry, yes. But we need to catch the tide to get out of the Solent itself, and once we're in the Channel, there's no turning back—not until the tide turns again."

She fell silent as if digesting that, then she leaned closer, her head resting against his shoulder, and gently squeezed his hand. "Tell me about your ship. Does Frobisher and Sons have a particular wharf at Southampton? You have that in London, don't you?"

He returned the pressure of her fingers. "We have two wharves in London—one in St. Katherine's Docks, the other in London Docks. The office is more or less between them. But in Southampton, all our ships come into one section of the main wharf."

"What about *The Cormorant* itself? Describe it."

He did. As they rattled along the night-shrouded streets, he painted a picture drawn from fond memories, his words colored by emotion, by the joy he always felt on the waves, with the creak of the sails, ropes, and spars above his head, the slap and shush of the waves caressing the hull, and the pitch and roll of the deck beneath his feet. He opened his heart and shared it all with her.

When the carriage drew up outside their town house and

he helped her from the carriage and escorted her up the steps, he realized he wanted this evening—this last night they would have together for weeks—to be perfect. For the pleasure they'd rediscovered in each other to remain unmarred by any discord, by any jarring note.

She seemed to have the same agenda. They climbed the stairs to their bedroom, closed the door on the world, and gave themselves up to each other.

Somewhat to his surprise, she took the lead—demanded it. He ceded the reins readily, intrigued as to what she had in mind, only to discover that she'd decided that he should remember this night...vividly.

Her small hands were everywhere, stroking his skin, caressing, then clutching, nails sinking in evocatively when he struck back and ravaged her mouth. But she drew breath and came back at him; with lips and tongue, with her curves clothed in silken, heated skin, with her breathing ragged and her lids at half mast, she seized the tiller of their passions and orchestrated a wave of need, greed, and delirious wanting that all but overwhelmed him.

Then she took him into her mouth and drove him to madness. Her tongue artfully stroked, then she suckled, and he thought he would lose his mind.

Blue eyes bright beneath passion-weighted lids, she played, joyous and bold—more confidently assured in this sphere than he'd ever seen her. Than he'd ever imagined she might be; the sight sent a lustful wave of sheer, prideful possessiveness surging through him.

That she was his had never been in question—not here, like this, with them naked and writhing in their bed. But tonight, she went a step further. Tonight, she lavished a devotion to his pleasure upon him—a commitment so intense, so deep and absolute, it left him giddy.

Giddy and glorying that he had found her, that she had accepted him and consented to be his.

When she finally rose above him and took him into her body, that appreciation, that bone-deep thankfulness thudded in his blood.

Joined, their senses fused, their fingers linking, they set off on their journey, on the long, rocking ride up and over the pinnacle of their desire, straight into the molten heat of their passion.

They raced on through the flames, gasped and clung and shuddered through the intensity, then as one, they surrendered to the final conflagration that cindered their senses and propelled them headlong into ecstasy.

Up, through, and on, ultimately to fall into the oblivion beyond.

Wrapped together, their hearts thudding in unison, they sank back to reality, back to the earthy pleasure of each other's naked embrace, back to the tangled sheets of their bed, the quiet rasp of their breathing, and the shadows of the night.

She had collapsed on top of him. When she finally stirred and rolled to his side, he drew her closer, tucking her against him. Blindly, he searched, found the sheets, wrestled, and drew the silk over their cooling bodies.

Then he lay back, surrendered, and let satiation have him.

Despite his looming departure, all was well between them. He was, he felt, an extremely lucky man. And if she'd intended to bind him to her with her unrestrained passion, she'd succeeded beyond her wildest dreams. For this, for her, he would walk through fire. No sea, no storm, no danger on earth would keep him from returning to her side.

Tucked against her husband's solid heat, somewhat to her surprise, Edwina discovered her mind crystal clear and her decision made—definitive, final, and resolute. The events of the evening had only underscored the value of what they already had, what they already shared. Contrary to her assumption on embarking on their lovemaking, she hadn't been driven by the thought of fresh insights and new explorations; instead, her actions had been a recommitment—something that had welled from deep inside her, an instinctive and powerful response to their current situation.

To their current need.

She'd recommitted to protecting what they already had and to moving ahead and securing the marriage she wanted them to have—the marriage that would best benefit them both.

She now knew what she had to do—the essential elements were clear in her mind. Courtesy of the past day, she had a vague notion of how she might accomplish the crucial first step.

Tomorrow, she would act. Tomorrow, she would take the first step in forging the marriage she—and he—needed to have.

Regardless of all else the evening had wrought, she sensed—felt, could all but touch—a solid certainty that now dwelled at her core. She was not giving up—she never would give up—on her dreams.

Four

Declan dallied at the breakfast table the next morning until Edwina breezed into the parlor.

They exchanged comfortable, knowing, richly private smiles, then she turned to the sideboard. He seized the moments while she filled her plate to drink in the sight of her, her trim figure displayed in a day gown of blue-and-white-striped cambric. Her pale golden hair was drawn up into a knot at the top of her head, from where it cascaded in a glory of bouncing curls that framed her face and brushed her nape.

Then she turned, and he rose and drew out the chair to the right of his. Once she'd sat, he resumed his seat at the table's head.

Her gaze had gone to the various letters and notes piled beside his plate. "Have you had news?"

"Yes." He flicked a finger at the missives. "Most of the reports I was waiting for have come in. I'll need to go to the office for the last of them, but other than that…" He caught her gaze. "It appears I'll be leaving immediately after luncheon."

She stared at him blankly for half a minute, then she grimaced. "Damn." She threw him an apologetic glance. "I have a luncheon, followed by an event, and I simply cannot cry off from either." Her expression turned downhearted. "I'm so sorry. I had wanted to be here to wave you away, but…" She gestured, signifying resignation, then she shrugged and returned her attention to her plate, to the slice of toast she was slathering with jam. "Still, given the urgency of your trip, you must leave, and that's that. I can't even be sure exactly when I'll get back—the event is on the outskirts of town. In Essex."

Essex. On the other side of the capital from the road to Southampton; he couldn't even arrange to turn aside and meet her... "So this is the last time we'll see each other until I get back."

She nodded. "Sadly, yes. I have an at-home this morning, and after that I'll go on with my sisters to the luncheon."

Declan told himself that the disappointment he felt, its oppressive weight, was entirely uncalled for. She was behaving exactly as a lady of her ilk should when faced with the situation he'd foisted on her; she wasn't railing at him, crying, or enacting any scenes. He should be grateful for her attitude.

He had no grounds on which to feel that it lacked a certain something.

He squashed the sense of dissatisfaction deep, but the feeling didn't leave him.

He dallied over his coffee until she'd finished her toast and tea. Then he rose, slipped his missives into his pocket, and drew out her chair. Together, they strolled into the front hall.

"Well, then." Facing him, she donned a bright—patently superficial—smile. "It seems this is farewell." She gripped his arm, stretched up, and placed a peck on his cheek. "Adieu, my darling. I'll be here when you return."

Before he could respond, she whirled and strode briskly to the stairs.

In something close to disbelief, he watched her ascend... That was it? His grand farewell wasn't even a proper kiss?

He stared after her until she disappeared around the gallery, then he shook himself—and called his errant thoughts, and his uncalled-for emotions, to order. What had he expected? He was leaving her to live her life here in London and heading off on a voyage, and if he was honest, he would admit the unknown, the potential for danger, for adventure, called to him.

Edwina was adventurous, too.

"True. But she's a woman." A vision of his cousin Catrina—Kit—who captained her own ship in their fleet, swam across his mind, and he amended, "A lady. A noble lady."

And she was his and now meant far too much to him for him to even contemplate putting her at risk—not of any sort or of any degree.

He had to go and sail and investigate, and she had to remain safely here.

That was all there was to it.

Feeling the weight of the missives in his pocket, he considered, then waved at Humphrey to fetch his coat.

A minute later, his expression set, he strode down the front steps and headed toward the Frobisher and Sons office and whatever last dregs of information his searchers had gleaned from the ships currently bobbing in the Pool of London. The more information he had before he sailed, the less time he would need to spend on the ground in Freetown—and the sooner he could return to re-engage with his wife and, in light of the separation, re-examine how their marriage should work.

He hadn't in the least expected it, but deep down in his gut, he wasn't at all satisfied with leaving her behind.

Edwina stood at the window of their bedroom and watched Declan stride away from the house. The instant he turned the corner and disappeared from her sight, she swung around and beckoned to her maid, Wilmot, who'd been packing the last of the clothes Edwina had selected into a small portmanteau. "Quickly—help me out of this gown."

Wilmot hurried to Edwina's side. As she set deft fingers to Edwina's laces, the severely garbed middle-aged maid anxiously murmured, "Are you sure about this, my lady?"

"Absolutely definitely." Shrugging out of the loosened gown and letting it fall, Edwina added, "You needn't worry. I'll be perfectly safe." Wilmot had been with her since her come-out; she was an excellent maid, but rather timid.

"If you say so, my lady." Wilmot clearly remained unconvinced, but she held her tongue as she helped Edwina into a dun-colored carriage dress.

As soon as all the tiny black buttons at the back of the dress were secured, Edwina waved Wilmot to the last of the packing and headed for her dressing table. In short order, she stowed her brushes, combs, and a handful of hairpins into a large traveling satchel. From a drawer, she drew out a wad of banknotes. She tucked some into a small purse that she placed in a black traveling reticule, then secreted the rest of the notes in a pocket sewn into the lining of the satchel. When she turned, Wilmot was securing the straps of the portmanteau.

Edwina slipped the reticule's ribbon over her wrist, settled the satchel's strap on her shoulder, picked up the bonnet Wilmot had left ready, then waved the maid to the door. "Remember what I told you. Go down the back stairs, and you'll be able to slip out of the house while I'm talking to Humphrey in the front hall. I'll see you in just a few minutes."

Still looking worried, Wilmot hefted the portmanteau, bobbed a curtsy, then hurried out of the door.

After one last glance around the room, Edwina followed, closing the door behind her.

She descended the main stairs. When Humphrey joined her in the front hall, she smiled brightly at him. "I require a hackney, Humphrey. Please summon one for me."

"Of course, my lady." Humphrey hesitated, then somewhat diffidently said, "If you're sure the carriage will not suit?"

"Sadly, it won't." Tugging on her gloves, she went on, "For this particular excursion, a hackney is what I need."

Humphrey bowed. "I'll summon one immediately, ma'am."

Edwina waited in the front hall while Humphrey opened the front door and stepped out onto the porch. She heard a shrill whistle; half a minute later, the clop of hooves informed her that her carriage had arrived. Calmly, she walked out onto the porch and down the steps. Humphrey held open the hackney's door; he gave her his hand to help her into the carriage.

After settling on the thankfully clean seat, she nodded to Humphrey. "Thank you, Humphrey. I'll see you anon."

The jarvey said something, then Humphrey looked at her. "The direction, ma'am?"

"Oh—Eaton Square."

Humphrey shut the carriage door and conveyed her instruction to the jarvey. A second later, the carriage jerked into motion.

Edwina felt her eyes grow round, felt excitement tempered by apprehension grip her. "I'm off on my journey," she murmured to herself.

She waited until the carriage slowed at the corner, then stood and rapped sharply on the trapdoor set into the hackney's ceiling. When it opened and the jarvey said "Yar?" she called up, "When you turn the corner, you'll see a woman in a black gown holding a portmanteau. Please pull up beside her."

The jarvey paused, then said, "'Ere—this isn't one of them scandalous elopements, is it?"

"No. Not at all."

"Huh. Pity." The jarvey flicked his reins, and his horse stepped out. "I always wanted to drive someone setting out on one of those."

Edwina shut the trapdoor and sank back onto the seat, a very large smile spreading over her face. She wasn't escaping to marry some unsuitable man—she was escaping to be with the entirely suitable gentleman she'd married.

She was still grinning when the jarvey drew up alongside the pavement where, as she'd arranged, Wilmot stood waiting with the portmanteau. Even as Edwina opened the carriage door and took the portmanteau, Wilmot was darting anxious glances in every direction.

"Don't worry," Edwina reiterated. "Now, don't forget to give Humphrey those letters I left with you. They're important, and it's also important you don't hand them over until six o'clock this evening."

She'd written letters to her mother, her sisters, her brother, and to Humphrey and Mrs. King, explaining where she'd gone and how long she expected to be away. Given her destination, she couldn't see that they would worry; she'd be just as safe as she would be in London. Possibly safer, given Declan would be with her.

"I won't forget, my lady." Wilmot bobbed a last curtsy. "I don't know how you'll manage with your hair, but I pray that you'll take care."

Edwina smiled. For all her nerves, Wilmot was a dear. "I will. And we'll be home before you know it. Now hurry back before you're missed."

Wilmot bobbed again, whirled, and plunged into the narrow lane that ran along the rear of the houses in Stanhope Street.

Edwina shut the carriage door, then sat back with a satisfied sigh. She'd managed to leave the house, luggage and all, without anyone but loyal Wilmot knowing.

The trapdoor opened, and the jarvey asked, "So are we still headed to Eaton Square, mum?"

Edwina shook herself to attention. "No. I wish to go to Mr. Higgins and Sons' establishment in Long Acre."

"Right you are." The trapdoor fell closed. An instant later, the carriage rocked into motion.

"And now," she murmured, "I really am off—off on a true adventure."

Declan strode up *The Cormorant*'s gangplank as sunset was streaking the sky.

He'd been held up at the London office when one of his searchers was late getting back. Subsequently, he'd delayed at

Stanhope Street as long as he could, hoping that Edwina might return before he absolutely had to leave, but she hadn't. Then on reaching the office here, he'd found more men waiting with verbal reports on the current conditions in Freetown.

He'd hoped that somewhere amid all the information, he might have found some glimmer of a clue as to why four men—Captain Dixon, Lieutenant Hopkins, Lieutenant Fanshawe, and Hillsythe—had vanished, but no. Instead, the news from Freetown was entirely benign, with not even a hint of disturbance among the natives.

On gaining *The Cormorant*'s railing, he paused to look across the harbor at the forest of masts set against the bright orange and scarlet hues in the palette the westering sun had flung up. Such sights never failed to steal his breath; there was beauty in the sky and in the promise of the ships bobbing at anchor, of the journeys they would make and the far-flung places they would visit before they returned to this port.

His gaze moved on to the billowing sails of the ships sliding majestically out of the harbor and into the Solent beyond. Soon *The Cormorant* would be joining the line.

His sailing master, the principal navigator, was waiting, smiling, at the head of the gangplank. As he stepped down to the deck, Declan acknowledged the master's crisp salute with a nod and a matching smile—one of anticipation. "Mr. Johnson. How is she?"

"Shipshape and ready to sail, Captain."

"Excellent." With a nod, Declan acknowledged the salute of his quartermaster—Elliot, a burly Scotsman who was waiting by the wheel—then stepped aside to allow a pair of sailors to bring in the gangplank.

Grimsby, the bosun, bowlegged and barrel-chested, supervised the stowing of the gangplank. He grinned at Declan and saluted. "Good to have you aboard again, Capt'n."

After replying to that and other greetings from his crew, all of whom had sailed with him before, Declan made a quick circuit of the deck, instinctively noting the ropes and sails, the set of the spars, and checking for anything not precisely as it should be. But everything appeared in perfect order; his ship stood ready to get under way.

Finally, he climbed to the poop deck, located over the stern, and joined his lieutenant, Joshua Caldwell, by the wheel. "Right, Mr. Caldwell. Shall we get under way?"

"Aye, Captain—ready and waiting at your command."

Declan grinned; he and Caldwell had sailed the world for years, and those words had become a habit between them. "It's good to be on the waves again."

"I can imagine." Caldwell raised his voice and called for a jib to be set. "There's enough wind, I think, to get us out with just that."

Declan nodded in agreement. He waited while the ropes were cast off and the ship slowly slid away from the wharf; under Caldwell's careful steering, *The Cormorant*'s bow came around, and the ship eased into the channel leading out of the harbor basin. "So what did Royd do this time?"

His older brother was constantly tinkering with this and that, trying one thing, then another, to improve the performance of the Frobisher fleet. His favorite test subjects were his own ship, *The Corsair*, Robert's ship, *The Trident*, and *The Cormorant*. Whenever any of those vessels docked at Aberdeen, the chances were good that Royd would have them out of the water.

"He had the hull refinished in some new varnish—he claims it has less resistance, so the ship should cleave through the water more cleanly and therefore go faster. He also changed the set of the rudder, so be warned. It feels different—reacts a little differently."

"But…?" Declan prompted.

Caldwell grimaced. "As much as it pains me to admit, Royd's 'improvements' usually work. Wait until you take the wheel and see how you find it, but for my money, the altered angle, or whatever he did, gives us a touch more definite control."

"Hmm. Greater speed, better control. I'll take it."

Caldwell chuckled.

Declan grinned. He left Caldwell to his steering and walked to the stern rail. Gripping it, he stood and looked back at the receding town—in his mind, he looked further still, all the way to London. He wondered what Edwina had planned for the evening. Would she stay at home by the drawing room fire and think of him?

Would she miss him?

Or would she go to some ball with her mother and sisters and be surrounded by gentlemen who were drawn to her scintillating beauty like moths to a flame?

His hand tensed on the railing; his knuckles showed white. He noticed and eased his grip, and told himself he could have faith in her if in no one else.

In an effort to refocus, he filled his lungs. The wind ruffled his hair; the tangy scent of salt and the sting of spray flooded his senses. The tilt and roll of the deck beneath his feet was comforting, so familiar, yet...

Something was missing. Not in the atmosphere around him but inside him.

For a moment, he dwelled on the hollow sensation engulfing his heart.

He pushed away from the rail. He flung "I'll be back to take over once we're into the Solent" at Caldwell, then went down to pace the main deck.

Useless, really—he couldn't run away from his feelings. He didn't understand how it had happened, how it could be so, but already he missed her. This situation—him on a voyage with her remaining in London—was precisely how he'd imagined their wedded life would be, yet now he knew that couldn't be. This wasn't going to work.

Yet what they might do about it, what other options they might have, eluded him.

As matters stood, this was how things had to be.

Wasn't it?

He was halfway down the length of the ship when Johnson came up from one of the companionways.

"Ah—just who I wanted to see." Johnson fell in beside Declan. "Is Freetown proper our destination, or do you want to stand off in one of the other bays?"

Like Declan, Johnson had sailed into Freetown before; he knew of the many other bays that lay to either side of Kroo Bay, on the shores of which lay the port of Freetown, along with its Government Wharf.

Clasping his hands behind his back, Declan continued to stroll while he considered his orders and his mission. Then he grimaced. "I haven't yet decided exactly what my plan will be. Let me think about it for a few days. Meanwhile, I want you to have us on the fastest course possible for Freetown."

Behind them, Caldwell called for the mainsail on the mainmast to be raised. Nearly at the bow, Declan and Johnson halted and looked back, watching as the sailors hauled on the ropes, hoisting the sail, but, under the bosun's directions, keeping it reasonably taut. The wind filled the canvas, and *The Cormorant* surged, but almost immediately settled to a steady, if faster, clip.

Declan looked up at *The Cormorant*'s three towering masts. Like all the Frobisher ships that sailed for "the other side of the business," *The Cormorant* was a full-rigged ship, fitted to carry maximum sail. To Johnson, he said, "We'll be going to full sail as soon as we hit the Channel. From there on, we'll take whatever speed we can capture from the winds."

Johnson nodded. "I'll check the charts and plot a course accordingly."

"Without checking, what's your best guess?"

Johnson wrinkled his nose in thought, then offered, "Thirteen days—but I'm factoring in the effect of whatever Royd did to the hull. We made the trip from Aberdeen three hours faster than I expected."

Declan heaved a put-upon sigh. "Looks like I'll owe my annoying big brother another case of whisky when I get home." That was the standing arrangement between the brothers—Royd's way of inducing his siblings to allow him to tamper with their ships. If Royd's tinkering worked, then whoever's ship benefited—Robert, Declan, or Caleb—owed Royd a case of his favorite Highland whisky. If the improvement did nothing, then he owed them the same, but if the improvement resulted in any loss of performance, Royd had to put it right, and his debt doubled.

It said something for his eldest brother's inventiveness that Royd was knee-deep in cases of whisky.

"Odd that's his choice—I've never heard of him ever being drunk."

Declan shook his head. "It's like some sort of guilty pleasure—he only imbibes in very small quantities." Despite Royd having a reputation as the hellion to beat all hellions, not even Robert, the next oldest, could recall ever seeing Royd even tipsy, much less drunk. Declan snorted. "At the rate he drinks the stuff, it's going to take the rest of his life for him to drink what he's already got in his cellar."

Johnson humphed.

Declan stood with Johnson close by the bow until the ship passed into the Solent proper. Then Johnson disappeared below deck, and Declan made for the bridge.

He took over the wheel as the winds strengthened, bringing with them the first scent of the wide open sea. The tide was running strongly, and as they'd exited the harbor well back in the line of ships waiting to get away, there were masts and sails aplenty dotting the run between them and the Channel. From lumbering East Indiamen, to swift schooners, to smaller private yachts, every ship was tacking, looking for the wind and an opening in the hulls ahead of them, yet few had the power *The Cormorant* could command.

Declan had steered vessels of all sorts out of Southampton harbor more times than he could count; he knew the way the winds clipped the surrounding hills, understood the differing levels of power hitting his topsails and topgallants compared to his mainsail. He kept the jib up, but as he steered a path between the heavier, slower vessels, he successively called for more sail.

Finally, he had a clear run, and the open waters of the Channel lay ahead. He looked up, considered the tautness of the sails, then said to Caldwell, standing alongside, "Hoist the royals—foremast, mainmast, and mizzen. And tell Grimsby to fly the staysails once we're out in the open—his call."

Caldwell stepped to the railing to relay the orders.

Declan held the wheel steady as the sails unfurled, then caught the wind, and the hull all but lifted onto the waves.

Caldwell returned, whistling through his teeth. "We really are in a hurry."

"Indeed." His eyes on the sails, Declan called adjustments. Once they were in the Channel proper, he called more orders, then turned the wheel, sending the ship into a wide, sweeping arc, eventually straightening with the bow cutting cleanly southwest, heading for the deeper, darker waters of the Atlantic.

Satisfied, he handed the wheel back to Caldwell. Grasping the smooth wood and retaking control, Caldwell asked, "So—did you feel it?"

Declan paused to think, to compare, then nodded. "Yes, damn him. It's a definite improvement—the steering's tighter in some way."

Caldwell nodded. "Yes—exactly." He cast a knowledgeable glance up at the yards. "What? No skysails or moonrakers? I thought you wanted speed?"

Declan laughed. "I'm saving them for the open sea. Don't call them early and risk my masts."

Caldwell made a rude sound.

Still grinning, Declan swung down the stairs to the main deck. For a moment, he paused by the rail. He was standing at the widest part of the ship; looking forward, he could see the way the hull sliced through the waves. From experience, given the waves, given the winds, if he'd set his sails correctly, he knew exactly how that peeling wake should appear. Satisfied that all was exactly as it should be, he pushed away from the rail, opened the door to the aft companionway, and went quickly down the steep stairs, dropping into the corridor leading to the stern cabins.

His verbal exchanges with his friends and his time spent at the wheel had calmed him. He was still aware of that new emptiness within, but there was nothing he could do about it—not until he returned to London and Edwina's side.

So he would concentrate on getting to Freetown with all speed, learning what Wolverstone and Melville needed to know, then racing home as soon as he could.

His cabin stretched across the width of the stern. Before he reached it, he came upon Henry, the ship's steward. "What ho, Henry! A lovely evening for starting a new adventure."

"Aye, sir." Henry beamed. "You have that right. Pleasure to have you back aboard, Capt'n." Reaching back, Henry opened the door of Declan's cabin and waved him in. "I was wanting to ask if you needed anything more in here. If not, I'll make a start on the meal."

Declan halted in the center of the cabin, drew in a deep breath, then slowly exhaled. He'd spent more nights here than anywhere else in the world, even his room at Frobisher Manor.

Before him, the wide windows that ran the full width of the stern showed him the tumbling wake of his ship, the darkening evening sky over a pewter-gray sea, with the southern cliffs of

England a distant smudge on the northern horizon. He glanced to his right, to where his large captain's desk was bolted to the floor, surrounded by various chart-lockers and cupboards for journals. A large ship's globe sat anchored beside the desk. His sextant and other instruments were housed in a glass-fronted cupboard attached to the paneled wall.

The entire cabin was encased in oak paneling; the curtains currently tied back from the windows were crimson velvet.

All appeared exactly as it should. He glanced fleetingly to his left, to where a four-poster bed was built into the cabin's corner, with a washstand and commode closer to the door.

He was turning back to assure Henry that he had everything he needed when his mind registered what his eyes had actually seen. He swung to his left. Frowning, he pointed to the large traveling trunk set at the foot of the bed, with his own smaller and distinctly battered sailing trunk beside it. "What's that?"

Even as the words left his lips, even as he glimpsed the puzzled look his steward sent him, premonition rose and rolled over him.

Henry looked at the traveling trunk. "Isn't it yours?"

"No. Where did it come from?"

"It was delivered to the ship this afternoon. The porters said as it was yours and was supposed to be put in your cabin."

Declan didn't know what he felt. A panoply of emotions were clamoring for prominence, shoving his wits into complete disarray. He stared at the trunk.

She was his.

Surely not. She wouldn't.

Would she?

From where he stood, he could see that the trunk had a complicated latch—not one that would easily open—but it didn't appear to be locked. He strode across the cabin, shifted aside his sailing trunk, then bent, studied the latch, then swiftly undid it.

The instant the latch fell loose, he drew in a shallow breath, held it, and raised the lid.

He looked down—into Edwina's face as she blinked her eyes wide.

Then she focused on him. On his face. He had no idea what she saw there, but her chin remained firm—her expression determined—and her first words in no way surprised him.

"Please tell me that we're too far from the harbor for you to turn back."

Declan raised his gaze to the stern windows, to the soft sea mist that was closing in, cutting them off from the very last sight of England. He looked down at his wife then looked back at the sea.

He couldn't even decide if he wanted to swear.

Five

Declan raked his hands through his hair, then halted and fixed Edwina with a frustrated, exasperated glare. "I ought to put you off at Bordeaux. Hire some guards and send you back home."

The look she returned—one that clearly stated she couldn't comprehend why he was wasting time pretending—was one his mother could not have bettered. "You know perfectly well you won't. If you're truly concerned with my safety"—she held up a hand, forestalling his protest—"and I fully accept that you are, then, of course, you'll keep me with you."

Seated in one of the visitors' folding chairs before his desk, she calmly went back to consuming the soup Henry—on hearing she hadn't eaten all day—had rushed to lay before her. "This is excellent soup. I expected something more along the lines of gruelly broth and hard biscuits." With a tip of her head, she indicated the bowl placed before his admiral's chair. "You should have yours before it grows cold."

Declan stared at her for several seconds, then flung up his hands. He'd been fuming and ranting for over half an hour; much good had it done him. She was determined. And he couldn't shift her.

Just as his father couldn't shift his mother when she was set on some particular course. As he'd heard his father mutter more than once, sometimes females got their rudders jammed and were impossible to bring around.

Fully aware that the action constituted a surrender of sorts, he rounded his desk and dropped into his admiral's chair. The soup did smell appetizing. So did Edwina. Her expensive perfume, the honeysuckle and rose of her soap, and the scent of sunshine in her hair all contributed to the particular fragrance he associated with her; it teased his senses and positively lured.

He picked up the soup spoon and addressed the less dangerous of his hungers.

The mundane act of eating soup allowed his mind to calm, allowed him to step back and reassess. He realized there was much he didn't know. He glanced across the cabin at the trunk in which she'd arrived. "Where did you get that?" When she glanced at him, he nodded at the trunk.

It was new, and had small holes for ventilation neatly concealed in the ornate metal banding the upper rim. The latch–cum–lock was a neat piece of engineering; she could have released it from the inside. Given her lack of height and girth, the trunk had been large enough for her to lie comfortably; she'd made a bed of her clothes and, he gathered, had been reasonably cushioned and protected.

"A luggage maker in Long Acre has been supplying the Ridgware household for years. He was quite taken with the challenge. He already had the trunk made up, so he only had to put in the breathing holes and replace the latch."

"When did you arrange all this?"

"This morning. I left the house immediately after you did and went to Long Acre."

He frowned. "And the staff just waved you off?"

"They knew nothing of my plans, but you needn't worry. I left letters for Humphrey and Mrs. King, and also for my mother, sisters, and brother, so everyone knows I went to Southampton to sail with you."

So she'd covered her tracks—and, he suspected, his opposition—completely.

A tap on the door heralded Henry, followed by both cabin boys—Ginger and Cam—bearing the rest of a substantial meal.

Declan sat back and allowed Henry to clear the soup plates and lay out the next course. He normally ate with his crew in the galley, but occasionally, usually when in port, he had reason to entertain dignitaries; Henry had broken out the good china and wine goblets. Fleetingly, Declan wondered what his crew thought of Edwina's presence, of her stowing away. If the bright eyes and beaming smiles of Henry and the boys as they responded to her comments and praise were any guide, his hardened crew would be no match for a duke's daughter taught from the cradle to charm.

In dealing with others, he'd yet to see her stumble, and he doubted she would do so now. She seemed to have a sixth sense over how to connect with others, how to induce them to view her as a friend and confidante through just a few minutes of innocent conversation. More, those she so effortlessly drew to her seemed bespelled into wanting to please her.

When Henry and the boys withdrew, her gracious thanks apparently making their day, Declan picked up the decanter, poured wine into both their goblets, then sat back and sipped.

Edwina picked up her cutlery and started to eat. He studied her expression; he could almost see her shaping the questions with which she would all too soon start to pepper him.

Setting his goblet down, he picked up his knife and fork, cut into the prime roast beef, and turned his mind to the question of *what now?*

And discovered that an unnerving, distinctly unexpected idea had already taken root in his brain and was growing.

After a moment, without looking up, he said, "You're not going to go home, are you? Even if a ship and captain I trust were to pass us going the other way, you won't consent to change ships and go back."

She didn't look up from her plate either; she just shook her head. "No." She paused, then went on, "I came to share this voyage with you. To learn about and share your business life, to learn how I can contribute to it. I can't do that in London."

When he didn't respond, she glanced at him; he felt her gaze like a touch on his face. But then she looked down at her plate again.

After a moment, she ventured, "I know you might not yet understand this, but my traveling with you is important—to me, to us. Most definitely to our marriage. I might not be able to travel with you always, but whenever I can, I need to do so."

He raised his gaze in time to see her lightly shrug.

"This voyage is your first since we wed, and as you said it didn't involve any real danger—" A second passed, then she looked up and met his eyes. "Is that true? That there is no real danger? Or did you just say that to assuage my wifely fears?"

He held her gaze for a heartbeat, then fleetingly grimaced. "What I told you was a reasonable assessment. It's unlikely there will be any real danger involved—but, of course, danger is always a possibility."

She studied his eyes. A frown slowly formed in hers. "What is the purpose of this voyage? I can't recall you ever mentioning that."

He looked into her blue eyes—and the unexpected, distinctly unconventional idea that had bloomed in his brain took on form and shape.

Why not? The question reverberated through his brain. Unconventional it might be, but the Frobishers were the definition of unconventional, and her family could give his lessons.

There would be risks involved, true, but he could ensure they remained minimal, and the potential gains could be enormous.

He was an adventurer at heart—who knew the heart had adventures all its own? He certainly hadn't, but if any man was going to take such a plunge, surely it should be him.

Apparently sensing he was debating some major decision, she'd waited, patient and watchful. Even when the silence continued to stretch, she didn't prod.

"What I am about to tell you is in the nature of a trade secret." His gaze unwaveringly locked on her face, he told her of the Frobishers' relationship with the Crown.

Unsurprisingly, she found it intriguing. Even exciting. Eyes alight, she asked, "So this voyage?"

"Is not about trade." In broad strokes, he outlined his mission. While one tiny part of his mind gabbled in horror, aghast at what he was doing, most of his conscious mind and all of his instinctive self were now fully committed to his new direction.

He'd been separated from her for no more than a few hours before he'd realized he needed to change the tack he'd assumed was the correct one for their marriage. Through her reaction to Wolverstone's urgent need of his services, she'd opened up a new route; his adventurer's soul was always ready to explore unexpected paths simply to see where they led.

In this case, on several levels, the gains could be significant.

By the time Henry and the boys returned to clear the main course and lay out a cheese board, fruit, and nuts, Declan had divulged all he'd learned of the situation in Freetown.

Aware of the change in the way the ship was riding, he glanced at Henry. "Who has the helm?"

"Master Johnson."

Declan nodded. "Tell him I'll be up later to review the sails." "Aye, Capt'n."

Edwina waited only until the door closed behind Henry to ask, "What do you know of the people—Governor Holbrook, Major Eldridge, and Vice-Admiral Decker?"

He was unsure what she was asking and let that show.

She looked at him as if her tack should be obvious. "Are they married? Are their wives with them? What sort of men are they?"

Ah. "Holbrook is typical enough for a governor—a genial

man, but bureaucratic at heart, very much given to dotting i's and crossing t's. He's married—governors generally are—and I believe his wife is by his side in Freetown. I've only met Holbrook once, at a gentlemen-only business dinner—I've never met his wife."

"You haven't heard anything about her?"

He met her gaze. "Men don't usually gossip about other men's wives—certainly not at business dinners."

She arched her brows. "How odd. Women gossip about their husbands and other women's husbands all the time."

He snorted, then refocused and continued, "I don't believe I've ever met Eldridge—he wasn't there, or at least not in charge, the last time I was in Freetown. As for Vice-Admiral Decker, he's not married and is a rigid old stick, but I know of nothing against him, any more than the others. Decker knows me and the family—he disapproves of us, although I gather that has more to do with him disapproving of those he considers dilettantes having better-equipped ships than the navy."

He paused, then went on, "Regardless, I doubt we'll run into Decker while we're there, and I'm going to do my best to avoid Eldridge, too."

"Because Wolverstone and Melville don't trust them?"

"In part. But given we'll be in Freetown for only a few days, there's no reason to invite Decker's or Eldridge's notice. No need for us to take any unnecessary risks. Holbrook, unfortunately, we can't avoid. His office will be informed immediately we enter the port. Unless we're there for less than a day, we'd be wise to call—if we don't, we're likely to attract more interest."

Edwina nibbled on a fig and allowed herself a moment to wallow in what was transforming into a significant victory, and to appreciate how very pleased she was. She supposed she was technically a stowaway, but after his initial shock and inevitable rant, Declan had calmed and accepted the situation she'd created, taken the bit between his teeth, and moved forward. He'd tacitly acquiesced to her continuing presence and taken her into his confidence over what was afoot—to her, that stood as a major triumph. Even more, to her very real delight, this wasn't simply a boring business trip but a secret mission for the Crown.

She could barely believe her luck. She'd always wanted to have an adventure, and this was shaping up to be simply perfect— exotic, intriguing, but unlikely to be physically dangerous and, best of all, with her husband as her partner.

The entire situation was *beyond* perfect in terms of forging the sort of relationship she'd set her heart upon.

Turning her mind to that task, she mused, "Is there…well, *society* in Freetown?" She met Declan's eyes. "Do the ladies gather together and have teas, and host dinners, and so on?"

He arched his brows. "I don't really know, but I assume they do. There's certainly little other entertainment to be had in the settlement."

"In that case, I think we can be certain that there will be a social circle operating."

"Why is that significant?"

She blinked at him. "Because if gentlemen have gone missing—from the army, navy, and most recently from the governor's office—then the ladies are sure to know something. Or, at least, have opinions. And, of course, once I convey that I'm bored and looking for distraction, they'll fall over themselves to regale me with every last bit of gossip."

Frowning, he studied her. "How can you be sure they'll be so accommodating?"

She grinned. "I'm a duke's daughter. I seriously doubt there are many such rattling around Freetown."

His brows flew as he considered that, then he acknowledged the point with a tip of his head. Relaxed now, asprawl in his admiral's chair, he popped a nut into his mouth and chewed. Then he swallowed and refocused on her. "I've been wondering how to explain my appearance in Freetown to Holbrook.

And indeed, all the others, given *The Cormorant* isn't exactly a vessel one can hide. Once they spot her in the harbor, many there will know I'm in town—and the first question to arise in everyone's minds will be *why*. Normally, the answer would be business—some specific cargo or some deal to be negotiated. But given how small the business community there is, it won't take long for people to ask around and realize that nothing's been arranged and no one's expecting me. If I then start asking questions about the missing men…" He shook his head. "I need a believable tale to excuse my—our—presence."

Holding his gaze, she arched her brows. "Easy enough, I would think—now that it's *our* presence and not just yours."

His lips twitched, but his gaze remained steady on hers. "Now that you're here, and given we still qualify as newlyweds, we could say this is a part of our honeymoon."

She nodded and asked, "Where are we planning on sailing on this honeymoon voyage of ours? And why have we chosen to stop at Freetown—which, from your description, isn't the sort of place a couple looking for romantic moments would go?"

"No, indeed. But if we were sailing to Cape Town—perhaps to visit some connection of your family there—then if I'd heard some rumor about, for instance, some new gold strike outside Freetown, then, given we were already passing, no one would be surprised if we put into the harbor for a few days for me to investigate that rumor." He thought, then nodded. "Rumors abound on the London docks, so that, I think, would pass muster quite nicely."

"You'll still need to be careful over asking questions about those four men."

"True. But if we're passing through on our honeymoon, then it's not such an oddity if I think to look up some gentleman I know, perhaps from school or university—perhaps to pass on a message from his family, or even in pursuit of my rumor." He raised his goblet and sipped, then looked at her. "You'll still need to avoid asking about the gentlemen—it would be odd if we both were known to be asking about the same men."

Cradling her goblet, she shook her head. "I don't plan to ask at all. I won't have to. If gentlemen have disappeared, then I'm sure that will feature in the local gossip, and if I manage things correctly, the Freetown ladies will readily volunteer everything they know."

She could see in his eyes that he doubted the ladies would know anything to the point, but the proof would be in the pudding, and if his underestimating the power of local gossip circles allowed him to more readily accept her pursuing that source, so be it.

They each took a sip of the remarkably pleasant wine.

In the silence that followed, one not entirely free of tension, she sensed he was, if no longer ambivalent, then not yet entirely at ease over her presence on this voyage—as if he was still gaining his sea-legs where she was concerned. As if he was still a trifle off balance and unsure of his footing. In all honesty, she felt the same; she'd forced the issue, and now the die was cast, and her joining him on this voyage-cum-secret mission could not be changed, they each needed to adjust to the new situation.

Despite her determination to press her point and join him on the journey, she hadn't, in her heart, been certain how he would respond. She'd hoped, but she hadn't known. She'd tried not to think about it—about the possibility that he might not respond as she wished—but beneath her driving confidence, she'd been just a little trepidatious.

She needn't have feared. After that initial eruption, he'd come around and, indeed, had gone much further than she had hoped. Then again, she hadn't known about his secret mission.

He drained his goblet, then glanced at hers, still cradled between her hands. "I need to go on deck. Would you prefer to stay here or...?"

She brightened and set down the goblet. "I would love to get some fresh air."

He snorted and rose. "It'll be chilly, what with the wind. You'll need a shawl—a warm one if you've packed one."

"As it happens, I did." She rose and crossed to her trunk.

He followed and opened the heavy lid for her, then held it while she rummaged. "I still can't quite believe you did that—stowed away in a trunk."

She found her knitted shawl and straightened, shaking out the folds. "It was the only way I could think of to get onto your ship without having to involve anyone else."

He lowered the lid. As she flicked the shawl about her shoulders, she asked, "What about a bonnet?"

He met her gaze. "Not unless you want to lose it. We'll shortly be passing into the Atlantic, and the winds will pick up." He waited while she knotted the shawl, then held out a hand. "Are you game, Mrs. Frobisher?"

She slipped her fingers into his and beamed. "If you're involved, dear husband, always."

He tried to keep a straight face, but failed. Instead, he shook his head at her, then led her to the door, opened it, and ushered her through.

Edwina decided that the deck of a ship like *The Cormorant* was an exhilarating place to be.

Together with Declan, she'd completed a circuit of the main deck, during which he'd made known to her all the ship's crew they'd encountered. Finally, they'd climbed to where the huge wheel stood, and he'd introduced the ship's master, Mr. Johnson, then relieved the master navigator of the wheel.

Johnson, clearly curious, had lingered to chat for a few moments before heading down for his evening meal.

Edwina remained beside Declan, gripping the rail to one side of where he stood before the heavy spoked wheel; she looked down the length of the ship, then looked up at the masts soaring high above and at the huge kite-like sails. Finally gazing out and around, she felt engulfed by nature's power, by the sheer immensity of the sky and the sea, the force of the wind and the waves. In that moment, she understood why Declan would never give up sailing—would never give up the chance to experience elemental moments like this.

Eventually, curious, she reached out and placed one hand on the wheel, a little below where Declan held it. To her wonder and delight, through the tension and vibration in the wood—caused, she realized, by the forces pushing against the rudder—she could sense the power of the sea running beneath the hull.

His eyes narrowed against the whip of the wind, Declan glanced, somewhat searchingly, at her. "I forgot to ask, is this your first time at sea?"

She shook her head, glorying in the tug of the wind on her curls. "Julian loves to sail. When we were younger, before George died, Julian used to take me on his yacht—we sailed on the Irish Sea." She lifted her face to the wind. "I used to think that was thrilling, but this...this is nature's power made manifest."

Declan heard the sincerity in her tone, saw the wonder in her face; if he hadn't already fallen in love with her, he would have fallen then.

They remained as they were, side by side, and she seemed content to be there—watching, seeing, absorbing.

After some time, entirely without preamble, she said, "You understand why I had to do it, don't you?"

He took a moment to ask himself whether, in fact, he did, then answered truthfully, "Yes."

Her actions had been reckless, yet at the same time well thought-out and neatly executed—and entirely in keeping with what he now understood to be her overriding goal. Somewhere deep inside, he recognized that, and at some equally deep level, he'd come to realize that he wanted—wished to attain—the very same goal.

And he wasn't the sort of man to cut off his nose to spite his face.

She'd done what she had because she'd believed she had to—that it was necessary for him and for her. She'd done it because she was committed to their marriage—wholeheartedly and without reservation.

By acting as she had, she was—perhaps not intentionally but in effect—challenging him to be equally committed—to their marriage, to her, to what might be.

How could he not step up and face that challenge with her?

She didn't say anything more, but in the same way that he was starting to understand her, he was increasingly aware that she was starting to understand him. Already, she seemed able to pick those moments when to push and when to let him find his own way through the maze.

And when she and he didn't need to say anything more to grow a little bit closer.

Eventually, he broke the spell that the night, the sea, and the stars had cast over them. "I need to stay at the helm until we pass into the Atlantic proper. We need to turn onto a south-south-westerly heading, and for that we'll need to change the set of the sails. It might get rough. If you want to go down to the cabin, Grimsby"—he nodded to the bosun, who stood on the deck below the wheel—"will help you down the stairs."

Catching and holding back her whipping hair, she leaned nearer and yelled over the wind, "Will it bother you if I stay?"

He thought of the familiar chaos of a course change; she might well enjoy the excitement. "No. Just as long as you stay close—here, by the wheel—and promise to hang onto the railing."

She grinned. "All right."

So she was by his side when *The Cormorant* cleaved through the rolling turbulence that marked the mouth of the Channel, then surged and plunged into the deeper swells of the Atlantic. He called sail changes, and Caldwell—who had come up on his other side—relayed them to Grimsby, Elliot, and Johnson, each overseeing one of the three masts from the main deck. For a good twenty minutes, the air was thick with instructions and orders as the sails were reset, then trimmed.

In between, *The Cormorant* pitched and steadied, then pitched and steadied again. As she had promised, Edwina clung to the railing; Declan was relieved to see that she was sensible enough to use both hands.

Finally, the ship was riding—almost gliding—through the waves once more, their speed swift, their course steady, and all was silent on the main deck, all eyes on the sails as they creaked and settled.

Further along the rail, Caldwell arched a brow Declan's way. "Are we going for broke?"

Declan felt Edwina's questioning look. He grinned. "Mr. Grimsby—skysail, if you please."

"Aye, aye, Capt'n!"

Seconds later, the skysail on the mizzen mast unfurled, snapped once, then caught the wind.

"Oh, my!" One hand holding back the hair over her forehead, Edwina gazed up, up, to where the second highest sail bloomed white against the black sky.

On seeing the look of wonder on her face, Declan smiled. When she glanced at him, he mouthed, "Just wait."

Once the ship had stabilized, he called for the skysails on the mainmast, then the foremast.

Then, once the effects of those changes to the ship's handling had been adjusted for and absorbed, he called for the moonrakers—foremast, mainmast, then mizzen—to be unfurled.

"Oh, my Lord!" Edwina stared upward, her expression one of unrestrained awe. "I can't believe how high up those are! Much less what it must feel like to be up so high."

Although absorbed with calling adjustments, he realized she was watching the sailors nimbly swarm over the spars, adjusting lines, bringing the sails taut to his relayed specifications. When she glanced his way, her mouth still ajar, he grinned. "Now you know why they're called moonrakers."

Edwina remained utterly fascinated with everything she saw. Despite her earlier engaging and absorbing experience with Julian in his yacht, she'd nevertheless had no idea that sailing in the likes of *The Cormorant* would be so much more—that it could be so enthralling. The speed alone stole her breath; she'd never traveled so fast in her life. The sense of power—from harnessing the forces of nature, from being allied with them and somehow linked—was all but overwhelming.

"It's a thrill," she murmured. "This is the epitome, the definition, of a thrill."

To her senses, at least. The drama and action of the course change and associated sail changes had effortlessly captured and held her attention. The interaction of the sailors, the orchestration and teamwork involved, had been engrossing to watch. As for the unfurling of the pair of sails at the very top of each of the three masts—the skysails and moonrakers—that had been truly awe-inspiring.

Excitement and exhilaration still bubbled in her veins when Declan finally handed the wheel to Mr. Johnson and came to escort her back to their cabin.

She led the way in, but he paused on the threshold, the door-knob in one hand.

When she looked questioningly at him, he said, "I normally do one last circuit of the deck, just to make sure everything's exactly as it should be." He nodded toward the bed. "Make yourself comfortable. I won't be long."

The implication that they would be sharing the bed—that he wasn't going to attempt to make any silly stand against that—gave her the confidence to smile at him. "I'll be waiting."

He went still for a second, then he nodded, stepped back, and closed the door.

Her smile widened. Turning, she strolled toward the bed.

I'll be waiting. Declan shook his head as he took the stairs up to the main deck two at a time. He'd told the truth about always doing a last circuit, but he was grateful to be able to seize a few moments away from Edwina's distracting presence.

When he'd called for the moonrakers, he'd realized that he hadn't, until that moment, known precisely where the moon was. Although he'd immediately rectified that oversight, he hadn't noticed whether the sky was completely clear or whether they were running under light cloud. He did know that there were no storms imminent, but that relied on gut-feeling rather than the use of his eyes. Still, since when did he not know the state of the sky?

Since he had his distracting wife standing alongside him.

Gaining the deck, he strolled slowly up the port side to the bow, listening as much as looking. Experience told him exactly how *The Cormorant*'s spars and lines should sound in any situation; all the tiny creaks and groans reassured him everything was correctly set. His ship was perfectly balanced and running fast before a nicely brisk wind.

For long moments, he stood in the bow, simply absorbing the joy of being once more on the sea. But, for once—indeed, for quite the first time in his life—that joy failed to snare him, to hold him.

His mind drifted, shifted, and realigned.

The lure of the sea couldn't compete with the lure of what he knew was waiting for him in his cabin.

Surrendering to the compulsion, to the need he could no longer stand against, he left the bow, continued his perambulation down the starboard side, then nodded to Grimsby, currently at the wheel, and walked to the companionway. Hauling open the door, he went quickly down the stairs.

At the end of the corridor, he paused before his cabin's door and drew in a fortifying breath. Then he turned the knob, opened the door, and stepped inside.

Taking that cautionary breath had been wise. The sight that met his eyes made his lungs seize.

She was sitting in the bed, his large pillows at her back, the crimson silk covers and ivory sheets modestly drawn to just below her bare shoulders. The small bed lamps were lighted; their soft glow cast a pearlescent sheen over every delectable square inch of her skin. She'd let her hair free of its usual top-knot; it fell in a cascade of rippling curls, framing her face and draping over her shoulders and arms, playing peekaboo with that tempting skin he knew was satin to the touch.

To his touch. In that instant, he realized that she was his re-ward, his prize for having consented to walk the path that had brought them to this moment. His to savor; his to delight in. She, her body, was a gift given—in trust, in desire, in knowing, and in entirely deliberate passion.

She'd been reading a slim novel, but had looked up as he'd stepped into the room. She let her eyes rove over him as she smiled.

In open welcome.

Deliberately, she shut the book and reached to place it on one of the shelves in the bed's headboard.

He remembered how to breathe, drew in another, tighter breath, and shut the door. With his gaze locked on her, he slowly crossed to the bed, drawn by a force he could not have resisted.

Not that he tried.

His mind was already avidly fixed on what he would find be-neath the covers—nothing but satin skin, soft curves, and sup-ple limbs. Nothing but lush flesh waiting to firm at his caress, to heat and burn him.

He halted by the bed, shrugged out of his coat, and tossed it toward his trunk, now neatly stowed beyond the foot of the bed.

He noticed the eager glint in her eyes—very blue in the soft lamplight—and slowed his movements. He took his time releasing the silver buttons of his waistcoat before sending it to join his coat. He removed his shirt to the same lazy, languid rhythm and saw impatience spike in her eyes.

Eyes that slowly narrowed as he continued the teasing performance.

The instant he tossed his breeches aside, she reached for him—caught his hand and, with a tug stronger than he'd anticipated, tumbled him down to the bed.

To her.

To her hunger. To her need.

Before he could even catch his breath, her small hands framed his face, and she kissed him. Kissed him with an incitement, an elemental wanting it was impossible to mistake—and utterly impossible to resist.

He answered her call and kissed her back and plundered, then he let desire loose, let passion reign—and she did the same.

Between them, they wrestled the covers away, then hands found skin and they rejoiced.

Kisses, caresses, gasps, and soft moans became their currency; with lips and mouths, teeth and tongues, with palms and fingers they drove each other on.

Limbs tangled, pressing close, then shifting away, effortlessly rearranging in a dance they both knew well.

Yet something had changed.

Despite the familiarity, this, tonight, was different—a new exploration of a previously traveled landscape.

For several heated heartbeats, he searched for some guidepost, some frame of reference. It seemed nonsensical to him to feel lost and adrift in this sphere.

Then he had it.

Just as, an hour ago, he'd changed *The Cormorant*'s course, he and she were changing course and taking a new tack in their joint life; in the same way as he'd reset his ship's sails, what he sensed was them making the consequent adjustments to allow their marriage to run smoothly over life's waves.

Once he'd grasped that reality, he steadied, then gave himself over to the task. To joining with her in discovering what, in this sphere, they might do to adjust and strengthen what already existed between them.

That fundamental connection neither wanted to damage, much less lose.

In the heated whirl of the moment, their gazes occasionally meeting from under heavy lids, with hot breaths mingling, with lips and mouths trailing over desire-dewed skin, they tried this, then that, searching for, reaching for, a connection on a level they hadn't previously breached.

Never before had he thought of using passion to speak—to communicate. With no other woman had he even thought of passion in that way, yet tonight...with his hands and body he spoke to her, stated and questioned, and she replied.

Awareness peaked; sensitivity overflowed.

It was a give and take, not of words but of feelings.

He showed her his thankfulness that she was there, that regardless of his previous stance, he delighted in her company, in the joy of having her with him, of having the chance to share this side of his life with her. And she reciprocated with elation, with effervescent delight in his acceptance of that challenge; she showed him how thrilled she was that he had bent, adjusted, and consented to explore this different tack with her.

Need built; the passion they'd unleashed whipped them on.

As he surrendered to the irresistible tide, one last revelation gleamed through the sensual fever overtaking his mind.

Layers. Everyone had them. It was how she and her family managed the ton, by donning another layer over their already complex personalities. But knowing someone, revealing oneself to another, sharing oneself with another, demanded that those layers—of civility, of defense, of self-protection—be peeled away.

Tonight, fingers twining, only to clutch tight as desire peaked, bodies joined and straining, merging and fusing to the heated beat as they pushed each other on and up passion's peak, amidst the sensual maelstrom, they each knowingly stripped another layer away and stepped onto a new level of closeness.

A new level of intimacy.

One step further—from where they had been to where they now were. One more step along the road to where they wanted and needed to be.

Joy in that moment, acknowledgment of what was, and hope for the future—all were encapsulated in the mingled breath each drew before the final moment of passionate cataclysm.

And then they were there. Fused anew, forged anew as ecstasy claimed them. She valiantly tried to muffle her scream; he buried his face in the pillow by her head and groaned long and deep.

Then he slumped atop her, and she wrapped her arms about him and held him close.

Together, they wandered oblivion's shore, more deeply linked than they had been before.

Six

Thirteen days later, Declan stood beside Edwina at the starboard railing of *The Cormorant* and watched the buildings of Freetown draw near. They'd been lucky, and the winds had remained favorable for the entire journey; they'd raced across the mouth of the Bay of Biscay, rounded the northern tip of Spain, then continued south well out from the Spanish and African coasts until they'd finally swung west and sailed into the estuary of the Sierra Leone river. The settlement of Freetown had grown up around one of the bays on the estuary's southern shore.

Courtesy of the benign conditions, they'd been able to maintain full sail for much of the journey. Given the need for speed, Declan had chosen to do so. The amount of canvas they'd been flying had attracted attention from other ships out on the Atlantic roads and had, no doubt, caused some raised eyebrows.

The only Frobisher vessel they'd passed had been the one Declan would have preferred not to meet. Caleb had been sailing north in *The Prince*, returning from ferrying a merchant delegation to Cape Town, and of course, the number of sails Declan had been flying—and, indeed, that *The Cormorant* had been at sea at all—had piqued his younger brother's interest. The brothers had long ago devised their own private flag-based language; on spotting *The Cormorant*, Caleb had all but immediately flown "What's going on?"

Declan had pretended not to see. He felt sure he could rely on Royd to keep Caleb busy elsewhere. The last thing any of the family would want was for the youngest Frobisher—he who had yet to learn the meaning of the word fear—to learn about Wolverstone's mission. It was just the sort of situation that would appeal to the daredevil in Caleb; he would race in, eager to engage regardless of any danger to himself or anyone else.

Although he was only three years younger than Declan, Caleb was considered the baby of the family by all—someone who still needed to be protected for his own good. That was the reason Royd rarely consented to make the same improvements for speed and agility he made to his own, Robert's, and Declan's ships to Caleb's *Prince*. If a grown man could pout, Caleb pouted, not that that affected Royd in the least.

Still, Declan would have felt happier had Caleb not seen *The Cormorant* racing south under full sail.

Relegating his younger brother to the back of his brain—he had more than enough to deal with in what lay before him—Declan refocused on the bustling wharf drawing ever nearer.

They'd sailed into Kroo Bay at daybreak and had anchored farther out in the harbor. He'd dispatched Henry and two crewmen in the tender, their task to secure suitable accommodation in the town. Henry now waited on Government Wharf, having sent the crewmen back with the news of a bungalow that was available for rent in the middle of the wealthier part of the town.

Had Edwina not been with him, Declan would have used the ship as his base for his excursions and investigations in the settlement. But the notion of confining Edwina on board had occurred only to be dismissed; quite aside from the fact that wouldn't have fitted with their new direction, he hadn't forgotten his father's words. Edwina and her family possessed talents he and his lacked. She remained confident that she would be able to glean information from the ladies of the town. In the circumstances, he would be a fool to deny her the opportunity to utilize and, if the chance was there, capitalize on her innate skills.

The house and her appearance in local circles would also bolster their claim of being on their honeymoon; the more he'd thought of it, the more he'd realized that such a heaven-sent cover for his investigations might well prove critical.

He glanced at Edwina. *His wife.* Throughout the past thirteen days, she'd reopened his eyes in so many ways. Through familiarity, he'd forgotten so many of the delights of ocean sailing, but experiencing them again through her—the dolphins, the whales, the albatrosses and the wheeling gulls, the sunrises and sunsets, the sharp tang of the whipping breeze, the brilliance of the constellations in the black skies of midnight, and so much more—had given them, their impact, back to him.

Now, amused and, truth be told, a touch reassured, he took in the eager enthusiasm in her face as she drank in the sights and sounds—to her, no doubt exotic—of the hustle and bustle of the Freetown wharves. The area teemed with the usual assortment of sailors and navvies, with colorful locals and a sprinkling of uniforms and more formal coats mixed in. It was a polyglot place, with countless races brushing shoulders, the color of skins ranging from the paleness of the Scandinavians, through every shade of brown, to the near blue-black of the Africans from the interior. Hairstyles were equally varied, and the clamor was well-nigh deafening, a babel of hundreds of voices raised in dozens of different tongues, punctuated by the raucous cries of the ever-present gulls. The stench of fish, rotting seaweed, and brine was pervasive, but today was alleviated by a freshening sea breeze.

Declan glanced back at the bridge. He'd left Caldwell to bring the ship in to the wharf; looking up at the sails, he approved the changes his lieutenant had called, then he turned his attention back to Edwina and to what awaited them once they disembarked.

Over the past thirteen days of untrammeled sailing, they'd spent more hours together—truly together without having to think of the expectations of others—than they ever had. Stitch by inch, touch by all-but-imperceptible shift, they'd continued reshaping the framework of their marriage, consciously, and at times unconsciously, adjusting to each other's needs.

Defining the path that would keep his needs, her wants, and their shared life aligned.

In balance.

He was confident that, for now, they were on a firm footing, as if the deck of their joint life had settled on an even keel.

The bagged side of the ship bumped up against the wharf; ropes in hand, his crewmen leapt to the wharf fore and aft to secure the ship.

The gate in the rail rattled back, then the gangplank rumbled out and thumped down on the worn timbers of the wharf.

He turned to Edwina. When, all but jigging with impatience, she swung to face him, he asked, "Are you ready?"

Given the light in her eyes, the eagerness that lit her whole face, the question was entirely redundant.

She gripped his sleeve and, tugging him into motion, shifted to walk by his side. "This is all so exciting!" From beneath the rim of her bonnet, she cast a laughing glance up at him. "I daresay you're jaded, but this is all new to me."

He smiled and refrained from pointing out that having her there was new to him, too. He offered his arm, and when she took it, he led her to the gangplank and escorted her down.

It was now midafternoon, and the tropical warmth was oppressive, yet in her lightweight green-and-white-striped day gown, with her pale golden curls peeking around the rim of her bonnet, she was a splash of brightness, a delicious spectacle that attracted and fixed the interest of damn near every man on the wharf.

Government Wharf was the primary commercial wharf in the harbor and also the wharf the naval squadron used. At that time of day, the long stretch of weathered timbers was crowded, male bodies milling everywhere, yet all but magically a path opened up for them as men noticed Edwina and stopped to stare.

Declan's smile didn't waver; that she knew exactly how to respond and "manage" the male admiration she inevitably drew was another thing he'd learned on the voyage. Watching her deal graciously—with understanding and gentleness—with his unexpectedly bashful and tongue-tied officers and his even more starstruck crew had been an education in her abilities and an assurance his male pride hadn't been slow to recognize.

He stood in no danger whatsoever of losing her—other than, possibly, by overreacting and overreaching or, worse, doubting her.

In this instance, as they strolled along the wharf, she didn't ignore the stares but rather behaved as if the attention was nothing out of the ordinary. Merely what anyone might expect.

And, he realized, that was precisely the right tack to take. With no overt reaction from either her or him to further fuel interest, the multitude looked, then went back to their tasks. They strolled on unimpeded to where Henry waited by the steps leading up to the street.

As they neared the steps, Edwina leaned closer and murmured for his ears alone, "I really don't think we'll need to advertise our arrival."

His lips quirked. "No, indeed. The news will be all over town by sunset."

Edwina continued to drink in all she could see without overtly staring. She felt thrilled, buoyed on a wave of delight and anticipation beyond anything she'd expected to feel. Eager excitement bubbled from deep inside her. Until now, she'd assumed her true sphere was the ton, that, as for her mother and sisters, London society would provide the stage on which the important events in her life would be played. Now, however, walking by Declan's side into a distinctly foreign place on a secret mission, she finally understood where, for her, true satisfaction lay. Joining with him and aiding him in this quest would require all her talents—all her social skills plus the exercise of every wit she possessed.

She couldn't wait to get started.

They halted before Henry, and he snapped off a salute. "The agent swears the house he has will be exactly what you want." Henry tipped his head up and back to where tiled roofs rose in irregular terraces up the side of a hill. "It's in the right quarter. He's waiting there to show you and her ladyship around."

"Did you mention my title?" she asked.

"Aye." Henry nodded. "And just like you said, he couldn't find the key fast enough."

She smiled approvingly. "In that case, I'm sure this bungalow will suit."

Several crewmen and both cabin boys had followed them from the ship, toting her trunk and Declan's, as well as various bags and satchels of their own. Henry would act as their butler in town, and three sailors and the cabin boys would be their household staff. The sailors would also double as guards; having now glimpsed the nature of the settlement, she had no fault to find with that arrangement.

In a group with Henry leading, they climbed the steep steps, then walked up a short unpaved street to where it joined what was clearly the main thoroughfare. "Water Street," Declan informed her. "It runs east to west, parallel with the shoreline, more or less from one side of the town to the other."

Henry had a hired carriage and a cart waiting. One of the sailors, Dench, took the carriage horses' reins and climbed up to the box. Henry held the door; Declan handed her inside, then followed. After shutting the door, Henry climbed up beside Dench, and they set off, leaving the cart with the other sailors, the cabin boys, and their luggage to follow. The carriage rolled very slowly over the rutted street, then turned south onto another street that wound up the hill.

The carriage was old, but clean, reasonably sprung, and the

seats still had some stuffing. Edwina peered out through the windows, studying the areas through which they passed. Water Street was lined with largely single-story buildings housing businesses of one sort or another. As they climbed the hill, the businesses gave way, first to what appeared to be the local equivalent of terrace houses, built cheek-by-jowl on both sides of the road; from what she glimpsed through open front doors, each house appeared to be home to several families. As they climbed higher, the abodes changed to individual houses, each set on their own block of land. By the time they reached the higher levels of the hill and turned onto a road that ran across the hillside, the houses had grown to larger bungalows in their own gardens, with stone walls set with heavy gates surrounding them.

They rolled past a very English-looking church.

"This is, for want of a better term, the European quarter." Declan ducked to look up the hill, then pointed. "That's Fort Thornton. The garrison quartered there has responsibility for keeping the peace throughout British West Africa, which extends much farther than Sierra Leone. In reality, the peace is kept by the chiefs of the local tribes, and the garrison stands more in support of the governor's authority with those chiefs."

She digested that, then asked, "And the navy—the West Africa Squadron—assists with that?"

"No." Declan sat back. "The West Africa Squadron's principal task is to enforce the anti-slavery laws, at least on the high seas—if anything, the garrison at Fort Thornton is supposed to act in support of them. However, finding slave caravans or slavers' camps in the jungle in this region is well-nigh impossible, not unless you know exactly where to look. It's much easier for the navy to pick off the slavers' ships, and over the years, they've had considerable success." He looked out of the window. "That said, there are still slave traders in this region, and some ships do get through the blockade."

"Hmm. So we'll have naval officers as well as army officers in town?"

"Not at the moment. From the hulls in the harbor, most of the squadron is presently at sea."

After a moment, she said, "So that letter to Vice-Admiral Decker is unlikely to be of much use."

Declan snorted. "I would have to be desperate to use it, anyway. Quite aside from Wolverstone's warning, the notion of appealing to Decker to come to my aid... Let's just say that I would really rather not."

The carriage slowed and halted. Declan reached for the door handle. "Let's see what this bungalow is like."

He stepped out and looked around, then gave her his hand and helped her down to the dusty roadway.

She shook out her skirts, then looked around herself. All she could see were stone walls lining the street, some trees draping over the tops, a dray rumbling by, and a lone donkey tied up by a gate further down the street.

When she looked at Declan, he grinned. "Yes, this is the best residential street in town."

With a light shrug, she reached for his arm, and they turned to the gate in the wall.

The garden beyond was lush with trees and bushes she didn't recognize, creating a cooler oasis in which the house sat. A tessellated front porch ran the length of the house and was draped with a vine carrying small, white, highly scented flowers. The walls of the house were of whitewashed stone, and the windows and doors looked to be mahogany.

They passed through the open double doors into the front hall and found the local agent waiting.

At the sight of them, he bowed obsequiously. "My lady, Mr. Frobisher. Welcome to Freetown. I believe this house will fill your needs perfectly."

Declan glanced at her. She met his gaze, then smoothly took

the lead in an inspection of the house's amenities. While the wooden ceilings were lower than those to which she was accustomed, the rooms were spacious, and all had multiple windows and French doors opening to terraces or garden nooks; the drift of air through the house eased the otherwise oppressive atmosphere. The house came fully furnished; somewhat to her relief, the pieces were all European in style and in excellent condition.

When she remarked on that fact, Wallace, the agent, mentioned that the house was often rented by visiting ambassadors and similar dignitaries.

On returning to the front hall, she smiled graciously upon him. "Thank you, Mr. Wallace. This will do very well."

Declan reclaimed her hand. "We'll take it for a week—at least initially." To Wallace, he said, "Mr. Henry will settle the account."

"Thank you, sir." Wallace bowed deeply. "And if there's anything further with which I might assist you, please feel free to send to my office."

Declan nodded a dismissal and led Edwina into the drawing room.

As soon as Wallace departed, his rental fee in hand, they all joined in to assist with unpacking and settling in.

When, an hour later, Edwina returned with Declan to the drawing room, she was surprised to see nothing but blackness outside. "Great heavens! I hadn't realized it was so late."

"It's not." Declan waved her to the sofa, waited until she sat, then sprawled in a nearby armchair. In response to her puzzled look, he explained, "We're almost on the equator, so night comes earlier than you might expect, and the darkness falls swiftly. Very swiftly. Don't imagine you'll have the sort of twilight you're used to at home. Here, it goes from daylight to deepest night in less than half an hour."

She arched her brows. "So we have day and night, and not much in between?"

"Precisely."

"Very well." She leaned back. "So we're here. What's our next step?"

He smiled. "Dinner."

As at that very moment, Henry appeared in the doorway to call them to the table, she bided her time. Henry, the cabin boys, and the three sailors ate in the kitchen, leaving the long table in the dining room to her and Declan. She was grateful that Henry had set her place to Declan's right and not at the far end of the long board.

Declan was clearly hungry, and to her surprise, she discovered she was, too; they left aside the matter of his mission to deal instead with a savory stew. She asked about spices and the odd vegetables in it, and wasn't entirely surprised to find that he knew the answers. He was almost as naturally curious as she.

Finally, however, once they'd finished their desserts of some sort of piquant fruit even Henry couldn't name, Declan pushed aside his plate, folded his arms on the table, and looked at her. "All right. I know what I need to do, which is to rather carefully make inquiries and see if I can pick up any leads as to where the four men who've disappeared have gone. If they all met the same fate, which is what Wolverstone and Melville fear, then it seems reasonable to suppose that they all went somewhere, or contacted someone, in common. I'll start with Dixon, given he was the first to disappear and the others were sent to follow him. If I can get some idea of where he might have gone or if he spent time with anyone in particular, I can then check that against where the others went or who they visited before they vanished, too."

She nodded. "Indeed. Meanwhile, I'll see what the local ladies can tell me, both about those four men and also about anything else that might have a bearing on the disappearances." She frowned. "At this point, I don't imagine I will need to entertain, to host any social events, in this house. Certainly not at this early stage—no one will expect that. I suspect that all I will need to do is"—she gestured airily—"contact one of the established ladies in town, drop my title, and let matters evolve from there."

"As to that, I believe we can set your ball rolling very easily. Remember I mentioned I would need to call on Holbrook, a courtesy visit to confirm my presence and trot out our excuse for being here?" When she nodded, Declan continued, "It's too late to call on the Holbrooks tonight. I suggest we call at the governor's house tomorrow morning, at whatever time you think it most likely that Lady Holbrook will be available to meet with you while I talk to her husband."

She beamed. "Excellent." After a second's consideration, she stated, "Ten-thirty. Unless things are very different here, that should prove the perfect time."

Declan nodded. "Ten-thirty it is, then." He hesitated, then said, "While I'm out trawling the streets of Freetown, there might be times you wish to go out and join the local ladies. The carriage will be here, at your disposal. That said, I brought Dench, Carruthers, and Billings with us for a reason. I don't want you going anywhere alone. Dench will drive you in the carriage, and at least one of the others will tag along as a footman of sorts. In reality, they are your guards. This is not the sort of town in which a lady such as you should ever walk alone."

He paused, holding her gaze, reading in it that she wasn't about to argue or resist his orders. Her calm acceptance persuaded him that it was safer to be entirely open. "While it's unlikely there are any slave traders operating within the settlement, one can never be sure. On top of that, the fact that you're blond—especially blond of such a shade—makes you an especially attractive target. That's the one thing I would ask of you while we're here—please, never risk getting plucked off the streets."

She reached for his hand and squeezed. "I won't. And please promise me that wherever you go, you will also take care."

"Fair enough." He turned his hand and gripped her fingers. "I promise."

Like so many things about this unexpected, unprecedented partnership of theirs, that had proved easier than he'd expected. He seriously doubted she would face any danger while visiting with any ladies, but her safety while traveling from house to house was less certain. Consequently, he'd put thought into ensuring her protection; he'd chosen Dench, Carruthers, and Billings as their on-shore support because the three men were all experienced fighters and had the scars to prove it. All three had served with him for years, and all three were quick with their knives. As for Henry—who looked like someone's genial uncle—he was a devil with a blade, had uncanny hearing, and possessed a sixth sense for trouble. With those four on hand and their sojourn in Freetown likely to last no more than a week, he had decided against hiring local help, even local women. When it came to Edwina, he simply couldn't entrust her safety to anyone he didn't know and trust implicitly himself.

He was increasingly confident they would pull this off—that he would succeed in his mission, whatever success in that respect might mean, while simultaneously having Edwina by his side and sharing even this side of his life with her.

What surprised him was that he now actively wanted that—specifically desired that level of togetherness. Perhaps because she was, as he'd always sensed, as much of a questing soul as he; if one considered the basis of the link between husband and wife—what it was that made one the complement of the other, the right person to make the other whole—his newfound desire to join his life with hers even at this level possibly made sense.

Regardless, he felt as if he was simply *more* purely because she was beside him.

As if she'd guessed the direction of his thoughts, she lightly gripped his fingers and shook them to reclaim his attention. When he refocused on her face, she arched her brows. "As there's nothing more we need to do tonight, perhaps we should retire?"

He didn't reply, not in words. He rose, drew her to her feet, tucked her hand in his arm, and led her to their room on the other side of the house.

Two hours later, Edwina lay slumped on the rumpled sheets of their bed. She was physically wrung out and deliciously sated.

Beside her, Declan lay softly snoring.

Peace enveloped them. In the quiet and calm, her wits slowly re-engaged.

Everything to do with his mission was decided. There was nothing more she needed to consider, not tonight. Tonight was, indeed, a hiatus of sorts—they were there, they knew what steps they wished to take next, but there was nothing more they could achieve and no more to think about tonight.

Which left her wits free to pursue wider thoughts. To consider and analyze where they—he and she—now were.

In that respect, she was still having trouble believing her luck. Not just because they'd found each other, not just because he'd wanted her as his wife every bit as much as she'd wanted him as her husband, but because they had managed to travel so far into togetherness already. While achieving true togetherness remained her ultimate goal for their marriage, she hadn't anticipated succeeding so well so quickly.

Or so easily.

Today had been one long succession of happenings, of vignettes of action each illustrating their continuing growing together. And their recent interlude had set the crown on her day. The big bed with its exotic netting—he'd explained it was to prevent them being bitten by nighttime insects—had been the perfect stage for yet another extension to their private interaction.

Yet another new horizon in their bedtime play.

While she'd heard about what a man could do with his mouth, nothing had prepared her for the reality of that particular brand of ecstasy; she'd literally thought that her heart would give out, but it hadn't.

Then, of course, she'd had to return the favor—and that had proved yet another novel experience that had filled her mind and extended their sensual landscape. She'd never truly comprehended just how powerful holding him—her husband and lover—at her mercy could make her feel.

Confident, assured—and oh, so very certain.

Of him, and of herself. Of them and their togetherness, and that they would, in time, attain her ultimate goal.

"Thank God I stowed away." She whispered the words into the night, then let her lips curve, let her lids fall.

Compared with remaining in London as they'd planned, sailing with Declan and joining him on his mission was proving over and again to be a much more exciting—and infinitely more effective and satisfying—honeymoon for them both.

Seven

"Socially speaking, it might be to your advantage that the governor and his lady are currently residing among the civilians." Declan glanced out of their carriage as it rolled further along the street that ran roughly parallel to theirs, one level further up the hill overlooking Kroo Bay.

"Indeed." Seated beside him, Edwina was peering out of the window on the carriage's other side. "I imagine the local ladies would feel rather intimidated by having to go into the fort to call on Lady Holbrook. I'm sure they'll feel much freer to drop by now that they don't have to pass by the guards."

Earlier that morning, Henry had gone down to the market and had returned with the news that the governor and his lady were living temporarily in a large bungalow at one edge of the fashionable quarter while the governor's residence inside the walls of Fort Thornton was rebuilt in stone.

Edwina squinted ahead. "We must be nearly there."

"Henry said it's the last house on this street."

Almost immediately, the carriage slowed.

Declan looked at Edwina. When, sensing his gaze, she glanced at him, he met her eyes. "I know you're adept in society, and Lord knows, you and the females of your family know more about keeping secrets than Wolverstone himself, but please promise me you'll exercise all possible caution when asking after our four missing men."

For a second, she studied him, then she smiled and patted his hand. "If you like, I can go one better and promise that their names will at no point pass my lips."

He blinked. "Can you promise that?"

"Yes. Quite easily."

Supreme confidence rang in her tone. As she turned back to the window, he decided he'd gently been put in his place; he had to accept that she knew what she was doing—and he'd already decided to trust her in this.

The carriage swung in a wide arc, then halted parallel to a high stone wall running across the end of the street and enclosing what appeared to be quite a large compound. A heavy gate with a barred opening was the only entrance from the street; Dench had drawn the carriage up directly before it.

After alighting, Declan handed Edwina down, then gave their names to the solitary soldier standing on guard by the gate; earlier, he'd sent word to the governor's secretary of his and Edwina's intention to call. Apparently, the solider had been warned of their likely arrival; he swung open the gate and waved them through.

Edwina entered first; as Declan stepped past the guard, the man tugged a handle dangling from a chain on the inner wall. Somewhere in the house, a bell jangled.

Taking Edwina's elbow, Declan paced beside her as they walked unhurriedly up the garden path. The house before them was similar to theirs, but older and roughly twice the size. The garden, which appeared to surround the building on at least three sides, was mature and dense, the trees gnarled, their boles thick and twisted, their large-leaved branches interlocking overhead; even with the sun beaming down, the garden remained cool and laced with shadows.

On reaching the front steps, they ascended and were met on the front porch by an earnest young gentleman. "Mr. Frobisher. Lady Edwina. It's a pleasure to welcome you to Freetown. I'm Satterly, the governor's principal aide." Satterly stepped back and waved them to the open front door. "Please come in. Governor Holbrook and Lady Holbrook are expecting you."

Declan caught the glance Edwina threw him; she was transparently looking forward to interrogating the governor's wife. He followed her into the house.

The sound of their footsteps on the tiles of the front hall brought Holbrook from his office.

"Frobisher! I didn't expect to see you back here anytime soon, but"—while offering Declan his hand, Holbrook shifted his gaze to Edwina and his smile widened—"I understand congratulations are in order."

Declan returned the hearty handshake. "Indeed." He followed Holbrook's gaze; it took no effort at all to make his own gaze proudly proprietary. Edwina had donned a summer gown of sky blue with silver piping; with her hair tumbling in artful curls about her face, she looked delicious enough to eat. He pushed such thoughts out of his mind and stated, "Lady Edwina and I were married some weeks ago, and nothing would do for it but that I must take her on a voyage to all my old haunts."

Seeing Holbrook and hearing his voice again brought Declan's previous memories of the man into sharp focus. Holbrook was a large-boned, bluff, and rather blunt sort of gentleman, a type found inhabiting local manors over the length and breadth of England. His distinguishing trait was a somewhat pedantic fussiness over the workings of his office. Despite Wolverstone's and Melville's reservations, Declan found it difficult to see Holbrook as a man likely to be involved in anything unsavory; he was simply too straightforward a character.

Edwina threw Declan a droll look as she offered Holbrook her hand. "The sadly mundane truth," she said, as Holbrook bowed suitably low over her fingers, "is that we are on our way to meet with some connections of my family in Cape Town, and my dear husband persuaded me to call into your town for a few days while he pursues one of his infernal rumors."

"A rumor, heh?" Holbrook straightened and released Edwina's fingers. "Dashed rumors abound in a place like this, y'know. Never can tell what's real and what's not."

"Too true," Declan replied. "But with some rumors, it's simply too risky not to seek clarification."

Holbrook's brows rose. "Like that, is it?" A glimmer of speculation crossed his face, but then he shook his head. "I sometimes wonder what it might be like to go traipsing into the jungle, but I fear I must leave such adventuring to you younger men." With a wave, he urged them toward an archway giving onto what appeared to be the drawing room. "My wife's entertaining some ladies over tea—" Holbrook broke off as a large lady of matriarchal mien came sailing out of the drawing room. "Ah—there you are, m'dear. I told you Frobisher and Lady Edwina would call, and here they are."

"Indeed." Lady Holbrook dipped a regulation curtsy to Edwina. "Welcome to Freetown, Lady Edwina." She exchanged nods with Declan. "Mr. Frobisher. Allow me to join with my husband in hoping your stay will be a felicitous one."

With graying brown hair drawn back in a neat bun, and a pair of shrewd gray eyes set in a soft-featured face whose lines suggested its owner spent much of her day smiling, combined with an ample, matronly figure, Lady Holbrook's appearance added to the couple's country-manor charm. "Dare I hope you can take tea with us, Lady Edwina? Several local ladies have called, and everyone is most keen to hear the latest news from London."

Edwina smiled brightly. "Yes, of course. I would be honored to take tea. We've come directly from London, as it happens—I would be delighted to share all I know."

"Wonderful." With a smile, Lady Holbrook waved Edwina on into the drawing room.

Holbrook took a step backward. "I believe, m'dear, that Frobisher and I should repair to the study. Business, y'know."

"Yes, of course." Lady Holbrook smiled indulgently. "Perhaps you might join us when you finish your discussions."

"Indeed." Looking at Declan, Holbrook tipped his head toward the door from which he'd emerged. "Shall we?"

Fleetingly, Declan met Edwina's eyes and saw eager anticipation glowing in their depths. With a slight nod to her, he turned to Holbrook. "Lead on."

He followed Holbrook into his office.

Holbrook waved him to a chair before the large desk. After shutting the door, Holbrook rounded the desk and sank into the chair behind it. "So you truly are here following some rumor?"

Declan gestured nonchalantly. "It may well be nothing—as you say, there are so many wild tales that do the rounds. But as we were sailing so close, the opportunity to make some inquiries was too good to pass up." He paused just long enough to make his next question seem reluctant, as if touching on a subject he would rather not openly discuss. "Have you heard of any others showing an interest in such prospective ventures?"

Holbrook's face clouded. "Sadly, just recently, there have been several men who should have known better who've fallen victim to the lure of jungle speculation." His tone and expression appeared more irritated than concerned. "Deuced inconvenient when they just up and leave, but you know what it's like, I warrant. Gold fever."

A heartbeat later, Holbrook's expression blanked, then he hurried to add, "Not that I meant to imply that you are subject to such foolishness. You're a businessman, and from all I hear you've considerable experience in explorations and the like. But these men who hear whispers of riches and have their heads turned and go wandering off in search of their fortunes—well!" Holbrook threw up his hands. "They let down everyone who relies on them. The worst of it is, we can't replace them, not unless we can prove they're dead, so we end shorthanded, and

you'll appreciate that's never a happy state of affairs in a settlement such as this."

"No, indeed." Declan waited, but after his outburst of disgruntled disapproval, Holbrook seemed to fall into a disaffected
reverie. Declan would have liked to probe further, but at this
juncture, questions naming the men who had vanished would
reveal his interest in them as specific—unwise given that Holbrook's trustworthiness wasn't guaranteed. After a moment,
Declan ventured, "Last time I was here, there was talk of setting
up a trade in native textiles. How's that developing?"

The question gave Holbrook an opening to extoll the improvements his administration had made and hoped to make in
the settlement. Declan sat back, folded his hands, schooled his
expression into one of earnest interest, and wondered how Edwina was faring with the ladies.

Seated in pride of place in an armchair in the drawing room,
Edwina set her teacup on her saucer and smiled at the eager
faces turned her way. "Indeed. Jellicoe's performance as King
Lear was quite extraordinary. I personally saw several grandes
dames moved to tears."

She'd allowed the assembled ladies, six in all, to quiz her on
fashionable events in London. She gave them a moment to sigh
and imagine what they'd missed experiencing, then moved to
refocus their attention; in the way of such exchanges, it was now
their turn to appease her curiosity. "But enough of London and
the ton. Tell me of what passes for excitement and entertainment
here." Before any could gather their wits and reply, she leaned
forward and, in a conspiratorially lower tone, said, "My staff have
heard whispers of gentlemen disappearing—simply vanishing into
thin air." Widening her eyes, she looked about the circle. "That's
not really the case, is it? The thought of Frobisher going out and
simply not coming back…" Melodramatically, she raised a hand
to her chest. "Why, the very thought gives me palpitations."

Rather than leap to assure her that such nonsensical rumors were mere gossip with no basis in fact, all six ladies shared long glances, as if none of them—not even Lady Holbrook—was quite sure how to reply.

Finally, the local minister's wife, a Mrs. Hardwicke, set her cup on her saucer, then she looked up and met Edwina's eyes. "Actually, there have been several disappearances lately."

"Really, Mona!" Lady Holbrook's tone was one of supreme unconcern with an underlying hint of censure. "You know there's nothing unusual in men going into the jungle to seek their fortunes. Misguided they may be, but these recent incidents are hardly the first. Why, men have been slipping away to venture into the jungles ever since the settlement was established."

With her steel-gray hair pulled tightly back from her face, leaving nothing to distract from her severe features, Mrs. Hardwicke inclined her head. "Perhaps. Yet these recent disappearances have not been limited to men. How can one explain the young women who have vanished as well—let alone the children?"

Lady Holbrook's lips curved gently, and she arched her brows. "I realize the explanation is not one that might instantly leap to your mind, Mona dear, but where men go, it's sadly true that women, young women in particular, often follow."

Mona Hardwicke stiffened; her features set even more rigidly. "And the children?"

Lady Holbrook waved dismissively. "As far as I've heard, the children presently unaccounted for are nothing more than ragamuffins who have doubtless run away from home. They'll return soon enough." Her ladyship bent a more openly chiding look on the minister's wife. "My dear, you don't want to give Lady Edwina the wrong impression of our little town. We're hardly a hotbed of crime, at least not as affects the Europeans. Why, I daresay we're safer walking the streets here than we would be in London."

Edwina wasn't about to argue that. She glanced at the other five ladies; while two—a Mrs. Quinn and a Mrs. Robey—were rather sycophantically nodding their agreement with Lady Holbrook's declarations, the other two—a Mrs. Sherbrook and a Mrs. Hitchcock—looked as if they would have liked to support Mrs. Hardwicke, but were too timid to speak up. Indeed, both looked troubled, as if each knew something pertinent to the disappearances to which the minister's wife had referred. Edwina resolved to speak with them later, preferably in a more private setting.

"But I believe Lady Edwina asked about our local entertainments." Lady Holbrook firmly steered the conversation into less troubled waters. "Sadly, we have no theaters as yet, and while a musical society has recently been formed, we have yet to gather players sufficiently talented to form even a chamber quartet. But we do have one quite esoteric entertainment—the services led by a local priest, one Obo Undoto."

"Indeed." Mrs. Sherbrook's face lit, and she nodded encouragingly. "Obo Undoto's services are all the rage. You must attend at least one—they're so very entertaining."

Mrs. Hardwicke sniffed. "I fear I cannot summon quite the same enthusiasm for Undoto's ravings. He might claim to have been ordained by some passing bishop and cloak his rhetoric in a veil of Christianity, but his sermons hold more theatrical bluster than piety."

"Now, Mona," Mrs. Quinn interjected, "you know we all attend your husband's sermons every Sunday, but there's no denying Obo Undoto's services fill a gap." Looking at Edwina, Mrs. Quinn explained, "In lieu of any other form of theater, it's no surprise that we make do with Undoto."

"Many of the Europeans in town—certainly the ladies—flock to his events." Mrs. Robey, a pretty younger matron, smiled at Edwina. "If nothing else, they always leave us with something to talk about."

"Indeed." Lady Holbrook set down her teacup and saucer. "If you have time while you're here, Lady Edwina, you really should catch at least one of Undoto's services. He's a very... charismatic man."

"He's quite handsome for an African," Mrs. Hitchcock allowed.

"And his voice!" Mrs. Quinn slapped a hand to her rather flat bosom. "Why, it quite gives one shivers."

Edwina wasn't surprised to hear Mona Hardwicke softly snort. Edwina smiled easily. "I'm unsure at present how long we'll be in town, but if time permits, perhaps I will attend."

"Undoto's services are irregular." Mrs. Robey exchanged a glance with Mrs. Quinn, then volunteered, "If you like, we could call and let you know when the next is scheduled, and perhaps you might like to accompany us."

Edwina let her smile brighten. "Thank you. That would be very kind."

While the priest's services were unlikely to have any connection with Declan's mission, the concept of church service as spectacle was curious enough to pique her interest.

Footsteps sounded on the tiles of the front hall, then Declan and the governor walked in. Introductions followed; Edwina couldn't help but notice that both Mrs. Robey and Mrs. Quinn preened rather girlishly under her husband's gaze.

When Declan suggested that they needed to leave, Edwina was content to fall in with his direction; she'd learned enough to be going on with, and caution urged her to think through what she'd learned before she pressed further. After exchanging farewells all around, they departed.

As he handed her into the carriage, Declan murmured, "Did you learn anything?"

She sat and settled her skirts. While Declan told Dench to take them home, then joined her in the carriage and shut the door, she allowed her mind to skate back over all she'd heard and, even more importantly, all the nuances she'd detected beneath the ladies' words.

When the carriage rocked into motion and she sensed Declan's questioning gaze on her face, she nodded. "I learned several things, but exactly what they mean—how to interpret them— I'm not yet sure. We'll be home soon—let me use the minutes to get my thoughts in order."

Facing forward, Declan was happy enough to give her the time; he had something he needed to ponder himself. From the moment back in London when he and she had argued over her accompanying him on this voyage, he'd realized that, where she was concerned, possessive protectiveness of a type he'd never harbored before—for anyone or anything else—would dog his every step were she with him.

Now she sat beside him, and those compulsive feelings simmered just beneath his surface, appeased for the moment given she was within arm's reach, unthreatened and patently unharmed. After an initial spike when he'd learned how she'd managed to stow away on *The Cormorant*, those unnervingly powerful instincts had settled; while she was on his ship, with him only yards away and surrounded by his loyal crew, she was safe, and both his conscious and unconscious mind accepted that.

Since their arrival in Freetown, he'd been diligent in keeping her with him; even inside their bungalow, whenever she was out of his immediate sight, he still knew where she was. He still monitored her safety.

The separation in the governor's house had been the first his possessive protectiveness had had to endure. He'd told himself that nothing could possibly threaten her while she was sitting with the governor's wife amid a bevy of local ladies. Regardless, as the minutes in Holbrook's office had ticked past, he'd grown itchy, instinct prodding him with a need to check on Edwina, to reassure those irrational yet overpowering instincts that she was safe and well.

The relief he'd felt when he and Holbrook had joined the ladies and his gaze had found Edwina transparently unharmed, focused and engaged, had been acute; given the circumstances—of course, she'd been safe—the feeling's intensity had left him wary.

He was accustomed to command; the role of captain fitted him like a glove, a natural consequence of his character. He expected to be in charge, not just of his men but of himself.

First and foremost of himself.

He didn't like, much less approve of, being subject to a compulsive, well-nigh overpowering need.

Especially one evoked by someone else.

To a man like him, that loomed as the ultimate weakness.

One he'd apparently invited when he'd married Lady Edwina Delbraith.

After a moment, he glanced at her.

She felt his gaze and turned her head to meet it. She searched his eyes, then she smiled and bracingly patted his hand. "Here we are."

The carriage halted; he looked out to see the gate of their bungalow.

He assisted her from the carriage, then he trailed behind her up the path and into the house. Henry met them in the front hall with the news that he had a cold collation ready for their luncheon.

Edwina cast Declan a questioning glance.

He waved her to the dining room. "We can share what we learned while we eat."

Once they'd settled at the table and helped themselves from the platters Henry arrayed before them, Declan stated, "I may as well go first, as I didn't get far. Holbrook is aware that several men have gone missing, but he clearly believes that they've gone venturing into the jungle in search of riches. I couldn't question him more closely without alerting him to our specific and particular interest."

"Hmm." Edwina had popped a section of fresh fig into her mouth. She chewed, swallowed, then said, "Lady Holbrook's reaction with regard to the missing men mirrored her husband's. Mrs. Quinn and Mrs. Robey echoed her stance, and given what I sensed of those two ladies, I suspect that means that view is the one to which most in local society subscribe. However, Mrs. Hardwicke—she's the minister's wife—was rather more forthcoming. I got the distinct impression that she, for one, doesn't agree with the generally held view—and not just with respect to the men's disappearances."

She caught Declan's eye and arched her brows. "Did you know that young women, and some children, too, have also gone missing? From what I gathered, missing in the same way as the men, without word, much less explanation."

He frowned. After swallowing a mouthful of roast kid, he asked, "Did you get any idea of how many women and children have vanished?"

"No." For emphasis, she prodded the air with the leg bone of a guinea fowl. "But I did get the impression that two of the other ladies—Mrs. Hitchcock and Mrs. Sherbrook—know more on that subject than they felt comfortable sharing in the face of Lady Holbrook's and the others' dismissiveness. I believe it would be helpful to speak with Mrs. Hitchcock and Mrs. Sherbrook in private, as well as with Mrs. Hardwicke. Being the minister's wife, she might well be my best source of information, and she was certainly less inhibited over speaking her mind."

He pushed away his plate and folded his arms on the table. "I have to admit to being rather surprised at the somewhat cavalier attitude toward the missing men. Then again, perhaps men do go prospecting in the jungle all too readily, and the local authorities have grown weary of reacting, much less sending out search parties." He paused, then added, "From Holbrook's attitude, I believe we can conclude that no attempt of any sort to locate the missing men has been made. Or, indeed, is likely to be made."

"So what's next?" Wiping her fingers on her napkin, she looked at him questioningly.

"At this point," he replied, "I suspect I should avoid asking questions of any of those on the governor's staff. Questions in that quarter are clearly going to lead to some level of consternation and possibly ruffled feathers. I rather think I'll get further faster by focusing on the first three men who disappeared—Dixon, Hopkins, and Fanshawe. Knowing the caliber of Wolverstone's agents, I doubt anyone here knew much of Hillsythe—certainly no facts on which I can safely rely. The other three, however, will have had friends and close acquaintances among their peers here. Someone must know something—Dixon might have mentioned what he was about, or Hopkins or Fanshawe might have mentioned where they intended to search for him." He frowned. "It would be truly bizarre if three men had vanished and none of them had left any trail."

Edwina tapped a fingertip on the polished surface of the mahogany table. "That young women and children have also gone missing, and that that, too, is being dismissed—just shrugged aside…" She met his eyes. "Lady Holbrook suggested that the young women had followed the missing men, presumably like camp followers. As for the children, it seems they hail from the lowest classes, and the consensus is that they're not really missing but have just run away and are somewhere in the settlement."

Lips firming, she held his gaze. "There seems to be something going on here that's rather more widespread than just four missing men. While you look for clues as to what's happened to them, I believe I should see what more I can learn about the women and children who've gone missing, too."

He—certainly his instincts—would be happier if she remained safely in the bungalow. Studying her face, seeing the determination in her expression, he asked, "How do you propose to go about that?"

"Mrs. Hardwicke, Mrs. Hitchcock, and Mrs. Sherbrook. They all know more about this situation, and I'm sure I can persuade them to confide in me."

"Perhaps you could invite them to tea." Here, where his men could keep a protective eye on her.

She tipped her head, considering it. "Perhaps. Or—"

A bell jangled loudly outside and was echoed from somewhere deeper in the house.

Startled, Edwina looked back and forth. "What's that?"

"I think it's the bell at the front gate." He pushed back his chair and caught a glimpse of Henry hurrying toward the front door. Declan rose and drew out Edwina's chair. "It seems we have visitors."

That proved to be an understatement. Arriving in twos and threes, sending Henry constantly scurrying for the gate, a small horde of ladies and gentlemen streamed into the drawing room. Together with Edwina, Declan found himself standing before the long windows leading to the terrace and effectively holding court.

Within ten minutes, they were besieged.

Edwina hadn't erred in thinking that her title would attract attention, but from the brief private glances she exchanged with him, it seemed that she no more than he had fully comprehended its impact. Ladies gushed and gentlemen jostled to be introduced, to bow over her hand. The noise in the drawing room escalated as those who had succeeded in gaining their objective gave way to those who followed and drew back to congregate in small groups to exchange speculation and comments.

Declan saw more than one assessing female glance travel down his wife's svelte figure, followed by eager exchanges behind raised hands. Luckily, Edwina seemed unperturbed by the attention; on looking more closely, he realized her social screen was back in place.

Initially, all he was called on to do was to stand by her side, smile charmingly, and return the customary polite greetings. However, once the first wave of ladies with their husbands in tow had flooded into the room, more gentlemen arrived. Associates from the past along with men whose interests competed with those of the Frobishers rolled up, and it was he they had in their sights.

"So what brings you back to this godforsaken place, heh?" Charles Babington eyed Declan shrewdly; his gaze shifted to Edwina, then returned to Declan's face. "Whatever rumor you're pursuing, it must be significant to divert you from what I understand is your honeymoon with the lovely Lady Edwina."

Others employed different words, but the crux of their inquiries was much the same. While Declan deflected their questions with noncommittal nonchalance, he inwardly cursed. He hadn't foreseen the implications of the juxtaposition of the two independent halves of their cover story; he hadn't realized what taking time out of his honeymoon with a beauty like Edwina would imply in terms of the spurious rumor he was supposedly pursuing. Now all those who knew him, even if only by reputation, had concluded that not only was his fictitious rumor true but also that it concerned some major find.

The last thing he needed was for his peers to start to trail him or, more likely, to send men to track his every step in the hope of learning what find he'd heard of and, if possible, beating him to it. But there was nothing he could do about that now. All he could do was grin and do his best to ameliorate the outcome.

Edwina hadn't expected anyone, much less such a crowd. While their number and the obsequious interest they displayed were no doubt flattering, she could have done without the interruption. As an hour ticked past, then another, she grew increasingly impatient.

Both Mrs. Sherbrook and Mrs. Hitchcock were present, having accompanied their husbands, who'd been eager to meet Declan as well as herself, yet courtesy of the crowd, she'd no opportunity to pursue her questions. Mrs. Hardwicke and Reverend Hardwicke had more recently arrived, but again, the setting wasn't conducive to private conversation.

Keeping her most gracious smile to the fore and deploying the polished manners she'd learned at her mother's knee, she drifted through the crowd, playing hostess. Henry had risen to the challenge, and he and the cabin boys, freshly scrubbed and in livery, moved through the gathering, offering beverages of various sorts.

At the end of the second hour of what had transformed into an impromptu afternoon-at-home-cum-soirée, she found herself back by Declan's side—just in time to face a fresh wave of callers.

As if sensing the question in her mind, he murmured, "The offices in town close at four o'clock—the newcomers will be either from some area in the administration or from one of the trading or shipping firms."

"So possibly more useful?" she murmured back. Letting her smile brighten, she directed her gaze to the couple approaching.

The man was in a red army uniform with epaulettes on his shoulders. He bowed low. "Major Winton, Lady Edwina. I'm in charge of the commissariat at the fort and also keep an eye on general supplies for the settlement. Permit me to introduce my wife."

Edwina drew in a fortifying breath, beamed, and concentrated on projecting the necessary image of a noble young matron with not a true care in the world.

She was grateful when, as the latest callers mingled, the earlier arrivals started to take their leave. Gradually, the outgoing stream grew larger than the incoming, and the crowd in the house started to thin. People had spread throughout the reception rooms, but as the numbers dwindled, they recongregated in the drawing room.

As she smiled and chatted, she increasingly appreciated the import of Declan's earlier comment; the later callers were those who made decisions, who could make things happen. They were the wielders of power in the settlement.

While the men presided over the settlement's management, their wives ruled local society. Yet even there, Edwina's nobility gave her an unassailable advantage, and in marrying her, Declan had, to some extent, donned a similar mantle. Certainly, in all the conversations to which Edwina was privy, Declan was accorded a degree of respect over and above what she sensed had already been his due.

Indeed, from all she saw, the older and wiser gentlemen had called precisely in order to reassess Declan and adjust their view of him in light of his marriage to her.

Navigating social shoals was a skill she'd been taught from the cradle; noting people's attitudes was second nature—as was knowing how best to manipulate the same to hers and now Declan's advantage. Consequently, she found herself engaging more actively with the later callers.

Finally, when the gathering had reduced to a mere handful of couples, all of whom seemed to know each other well, the oldest gentleman present—a Mr. Macauley, a large, heavily built, stoop-shouldered gentleman with sharp hazel eyes who was the local head of the trading firm of Macauley and Babington—imperiously rapped his walking stick on the stone floor.

When everyone, including Edwina and Declan, looked his way, Macauley focused on them and smiled a shark's smile. "My wife"—a handsome woman, she was standing alongside him—"and I would like to invite you all to dine at our house this evening." With both hands clasped on the head of his walking stick, Macauley inclined his head to Edwina. "We wish to honor Lady Edwina and to welcome her to our small town."

Macauley's gaze switched to Declan, and his smile deepened. "And I'd be greatly remiss not to congratulate one of old Fergus's sons on his marriage." Macauley looked back at Edwina. "I understand your stay here is likely to be short, hence I pray you'll excuse the precipitousness of our invitation." He arched one of his shaggy white eyebrows. "So what do you say, my lady? Dinner at eight?"

As Declan had seized a moment earlier to whisper in her ear that Macauley and Babington held the monopoly on trade between England and Freetown, and that there was a long history, there and elsewhere, between Macauley and Babington and the Frobishers, and that Macauley was something of an unpredictable terror, Edwina was in no way caught off guard. A serenely happy smile on her face, she exchanged a look with Declan—read the resigned message in his eyes—then turned back and beamed at Macauley and his wife. "What a lovely idea! We would be delighted to accept your invitation."

Eight

Macauley House stood on Tower Hill, only a few minutes from Declan and Edwina's rented bungalow. When, several hours later, they descended from their carriage and, garbed and gowned for the evening, walked through the well-tended garden and into the sprawling house, they discovered a select company gathered in the drawing room. All those who had been present when Macauley had issued his invitation were there and had been joined by three more couples, the most notable of whom were the Governor and Lady Holbrook.

Edwina exchanged greetings with Mrs. Macauley—"Do call me Genevieve, my dear"—then moved on to offer her hand to Macauley.

He grasped her fingers in a gnarled paw. "I hope you'll excuse me for not bowing, my dear, as I fear were I to attempt it, I would land in an ungainly sprawl at your feet. Most unsettling for us both." Releasing her, he grimaced. "Not as steady as I used to be, sadly. But allow me to congratulate you on your marriage, and to say how pleased I am that at least one of Fergus's offspring has been moved to tie the knot. Can't have the breed dying out, what? Regardless of our rivalry, England needs more men like me and Fergus—aye, and into the next generation, too. If the likes of us aren't around to make things happen, who knows what will become of the Empire, heh?"

Edwina couldn't help but grin. She detected no hint of hypocrisy or hidden agendas in Macauley's words. She judged that his personality combined with his age meant he no longer felt the need for obfuscation; he said what he thought, consequences be damned. Which, she reflected, as she parted from him and moved on to exchange hellos with the other guests, must make life in Freetown, in this circle at least, more interesting than it otherwise would be.

Soon, they were seated around a well-polished dining table, with silverware gleaming and crystal glinting in the light from a large chandelier. Seated in pride of place at Macauley's right hand, Edwina monitored all the conversations she could, but heard nothing more about any missing people—men, women, or children. She did, however, hear several comments from ladies extolling the delights of Obo Undoto's services. Only vaguely interested in the entertaining priest, she ignored such distractions and, instead, concentrated on absorbing all she could from Macauley and the others seated around her regarding the settlement and how it functioned.

On the journey to the house, Declan had explained what Macauley's position was and what that in turn meant. The conversations she overheard confirmed that, as head of the company holding the sole trading license to England, Macauley was closely involved in all major decisions. Holbrook, as governor, held ultimate authority, but it was Macauley who controlled the settlement's purse strings, and as in any other sphere, money talked.

Edwina debated mentioning the missing people just to see how Macauley reacted, but remembering Wolverstone's orders not to trust anyone in the settlement—and given the shrewd and sharp mind that lurked behind Macauley's hazel eyes—she held her tongue. First and last, Macauley was a businessman, and as they had no idea what was behind the disappearances, better not to alert him to their interest in even a vague way.

Finally, the covers were drawn, and Mrs. Macauley looked up the table. "Lady Edwina." She glanced to either side. "Ladies. Shall we retire?"

The gentlemen all rose and drew out the ladies' chairs, and

the company separated. The ladies dutifully followed Mrs. Macauley and Edwina back to the drawing room while the gentlemen rearranged themselves about the table, sitting in a group to either side of Macauley.

Being something akin to a guest of honor, Declan wasn't surprised when Macauley—damn the man's weathered hide—waved him to take the seat Edwina had vacated. As he'd expected, as soon as the decanters had gone the rounds, his host launched into an interrogation designed to lure him into revealing the details of his "rumor"—the rumor that had proved sufficiently alluring to make him turn aside from his honeymoon cruise.

All welcome aside, from Macauley's point of view, this was what the dinner had been about.

Macauley might be old, but he had a mind like a steel trap and the mentality of a battering ram. He probed, occasionally assisted by Charles Babington, who had claimed the chair on Declan's other side. Declan knew better than to let them rattle him or to rush into his replies. He took his time, returning answers that, on the surface, responded to their questions, but that in reality revealed nothing. Or at least nothing specific—nothing that would allow them to get any clear idea of the nature of what he was purportedly there to look for, or even in which direction his interest lay.

He'd played the same game countless times throughout his career; as the adventurer-explorer of the family, he was the one who ventured into the jungles and trekked the savannahs of the world, who plunged into all the wild and dangerous places in pursuit of nature's richest bounties. Gold, diamonds, emeralds, silver, and nickel—he'd found them all in his time, although he preferred the first two in terms of return.

Old Macauley and Charles Babington—currently the local representative of the other half of the company—knew Declan's history. Which, of course, was what had them so convinced that his fiction of being there in pursuit of a rumor of riches was true.

Somewhat to his surprise, he found himself enjoying the challenge of surviving their inquisition without being driven to concoct further details of his supposed find. If his rumor had been true, he wouldn't have felt anywhere near as entertained, and the secrecy Wolverstone and Melville had insisted upon for his real mission absolved him of any guilt over hoodwinking Macauley, Babington, and the other gentlemen about the table, all of whom, despite their occasional attempts at low-voiced conversation, were avidly hanging on his every word.

Finally, Macauley sat back and regarded him with a mixture of disgruntled disgust laced with respect. "Damn if you aren't more closemouthed than your father."

Declan considered that, then said, "Have you spoken with Royd lately?" His eldest brother had perfected the art of saying only what he deemed needed to be said.

Macauley's gaze grew distant, then he grunted. "Haven't seen him in years, but now you mention it, he might just trump you in that department." Suddenly, Macauley grinned. "Perhaps it's your mother's influence. Now *there* was a lass with fire. To this day, I'm not sure if Fergus was lucky to have won her, or if the luck was with the rest of us who escaped her eye."

Declan couldn't help but smile as he shook his head. "I'm sure I wouldn't want to venture an opinion."

"Huh!" Restored to good humor, Macauley pushed back his chair, gripped his walking stick, and got to his feet. "Right, then, gentlemen—I believe it's time we rejoined the ladies, or my good wife will have my head."

Chairs scraped as they all rose. The others stood back and allowed Macauley to lead the way. Declan dawdled until, together with Charles Babington, he ambled in the others' wake.

Babington was in many ways like Declan—similar height, similar build, but with fairer hair. Also like Declan, he was a younger son of a sea-trading family and captained his own ship, but for the last year or so he had been stationed in Freetown; as Declan understood it, his family had sent him there for the good of the joint firm to support the aging Macauley.

The parade ahead of them slowed as the gentlemen funneled through the door into the drawing room.

Pausing beside Babington at the rear of the group, Declan seized the moment to say, "I picked up a bit of talk on the wharf when we came in. Something about men—and possibly others—going missing." He glanced at Babington—and to his surprise, saw a ripple of emotion cross the man's otherwise uninforma-tive face. Pain? Declan frowned. "What is it?"

Babington stared at the backs of the gentlemen ahead of them. He hesitated, then he dragged in a tight breath and in a low voice murmured, "I know of a young lady who seems…to have van-ished." Confusion laced his tone, then he shook himself, raised his head, and more crisply said, "But you know what it's like out here—she may have left to go"—he gestured—"somewhere. Peo-ple are called away and leave in a rush all the time."

And Babington didn't believe a word of that.

But then the gentlemen ahead of them moved on into the room, and they followed. Declan looked around for Edwina. With a mumbled word, Babington left him and headed for Ma-cauley's side—the one place he could be reasonably certain Dec-lan wouldn't follow. After accepting that this was neither the place nor the time to further pursue whatever Babington could tell him, Declan located Edwina seated between Mrs. Macau-ley and Lady Holbrook on the sofa. He considered the sight for a full second, then he strolled to where several gentlemen stood by the open windows.

From the corner of her eye, Edwina saw Declan join the other men and was relieved he had chosen to leave her to her own devices. To her own investigative tack. While some of the ladies, including Mrs. Hardwicke, had risen and joined their husbands, there were six still gathered on the sofa and on the chairs angled before it.

Earlier, she'd tried steering the general conversation to the subject of the disappearances that were apparently plaguing the settlement, but, once again, had run into the wall of an "it's just something that happens in settlements like this" refrain. Mrs. Macauley had seemed genuinely unaware of anyone going missing, but from the ensuing discussion—which should have assisted Edwina's search for information, but had revealed nothing new—it appeared that the Macauleys were so absorbed with managing the complex trading in the colony that such things as the occasional missing person passed entirely beneath their notice.

That said, once Mrs. Macauley heard the dismissive reasoning put forward by the others, she accepted the situation as being "just one of those things."

Edwina was growing increasingly irritated by the ladies' constant "it's not something we need to bother our heads with" attitude, but she could see no benefit in openly dissenting. Instead, having noted that neither Mrs. Sherbrook nor Mrs. Hitchcock had joined in the dismissive refrain but, once again, had appeared distinctly self-conscious and uncomfortable, she set her sights on speaking privately with the pair, individually or together.

And the perfect opportunity had just fallen into her lap, at least with respect to Mrs. Sherbrook.

Edwina had continued to play the bored social butterfly, openly encouraging the local ladies to tell her all and everything about their lives in the settlement. Eventually, the talk had turned, again, to the local priest-cum-entertainer, and several ladies had exclaimed that they'd heard that he'd scheduled a service for the following day at noon.

Lady Holbrook and four others, including Mrs. Sherbrook, had immediately decided to make an excursion to the event.

Mrs. Quinn had turned and appealed to Edwina, "Do come with us, Lady Edwina. Obo Undoto's sermons are a real de-

Ten

An hour later, Declan returned to the bungalow, walked into the drawing room where Edwina was waiting, and slumped into an armchair. For several seconds, he stared unseeing across the room at the long windows open to the terrace, then he raised both hands and scrubbed them over his face.

Silk rustled as Edwina rose; he heard her footsteps on the polished floor, followed by the clink of crystal.

As he lowered his hands, she halted beside his chair. She held out a crystal tumbler with two fingers of whisky. "Here. You look like you need it."

He hadn't even told her where he'd been, much less what he'd seen. Gratefully, he took the glass. "Thank you."

While he took his first sip, she returned to her chair. She sat and clasped her hands in her lap. Her blue gaze traveled over his face. "So—where have you been and what did you learn?"

Her crisp tone helped him refocus. He took a larger mouthful, swallowed, and felt the burn all the way down his throat. The potent liquor hit his stomach, the warmth spread, and he felt a little better. He fixed his gaze on her face. "I've just come from the morgue."

She frowned. "Do you have reason to think the four men have been killed?"

"No. Quite the opposite." He cradled the glass between his hands and outlined the way he and his men had spent their day. "We found nothing to support the notion that any of the four men just up and went off to find their fortunes." He arched a light. Such passion! Such delivery. It's better than a Shakespearean play, which is why we attend well-nigh every event. Trust me." She waved at the others. "Trust us. You're sure to find the experience worthwhile."

Five pairs of eyes regarded her eagerly.

"It will be no difficulty to pick you up in my carriage as we go past," Lady Holbrook said. "At the very least, you will be diverted from the ennui of the day, although to be fair to the man, most of us consider our visits to Obo Undoto's church rewarding, and I'm sure you'll find the same."

Edwina hoped so. With nary a thought for the priest's performance, she smiled and inclined her head. "Thank you. If it's no trouble, I should like to accompany you."

Several hours later, Declan lay slumped on his back in the middle of their bed. One arm around Edwina, half-sprawled over him—despite the sultry warmth of the night, he craved the sensation of holding her close—with his other arm raised and bent and his hand behind his head, he stared up at the netting- and shadow-shrouded ceiling.

With his free hand, he found a lock of Edwina's hair and absentmindedly fingered the silk, letting it slide again and again through his fingers.

On the journey back from Macauley House, she'd told him of her plan to attend the local priest's service tomorrow. She intended to use the opportunity to seize a private moment with Mrs. Sherbrook, who, Edwina was convinced, knew something pertinent about the missing young women.

His initial reaction had been one of internal scrambling—not exactly panic but rather the impulse to rush to action in order to negate panic. The idea of her going out without his men to guard her had made his mind seize, his thoughts stall.

Then he'd reminded himself that she would be traveling to and fro in Lady Holbrook's carriage. If he couldn't trust Lady

Holbrook to keep a noble lady guest of hers safe, then who could he trust? Nevertheless, after several minutes—minutes in which Edwina's satisfaction with her plan and her determination to learn more about the troubling disappearances had flooded his awareness—he'd cleared his throat and said, "Perhaps, just for safety's sake, you could take Billings with you as your footman."

She'd softly snorted, a scoffing sound, no doubt at the thought of the long and lanky Billings as a fashionable footman.

Declan had tensed, anticipating having to argue for a concession that, having voiced it, he'd realized he truly needed, but to his surprise, after several seconds, Edwina had nodded. "All right."

She'd turned her head and, her blue gaze clear, had studied his face, searched his eyes; after a long moment, she'd given an infinitesimal nod and faced forward. "If it'll make you happier, I'll take Billings. Given I am the daughter of a duke, no one will question me feeling the need for additional routine protection."

He'd been so damned grateful—something he'd taken pains to communicate over the last hour.

Now, however, his thoughts had swung to Charles Babington.

It had been pain he'd glimpsed in Babington's face, but not just any pain. It had been the pain of loss—of having lost someone.

Babington had cared for the young woman who had vanished.

Declan had recognized the reaction because he understood it, all the way to his marrow. More, to his soul.

Instinctively, his arm tightened.

Edwina stirred.

He forced his muscles to relax, to ease.

Forced his senses to recognize that nothing had happened to her—and therefore to him.

Not yet.

He would do everything in his power to keep it that way. That was another fact he now knew to be immutable, set in stone, utterly ineradicable. If it ever came to it, he would fight to the death for her.

In the past, he'd actively enjoyed the edge danger had lent his excursions into the unknown. Now…he'd already started to consider how to rearrange his activities for Frobisher and Sons to minimize the dangers inherent in his quests so that she could travel with him. If not on all his voyages, then on most of them.

He knew it could be done, but he'd never before felt moved to protect even himself. He'd trusted in fate, in his luck and his wits, to keep him and his crew safe.

He wouldn't—didn't—trust fate, his luck, and not even his wits when it came to Edwina's well-being.

She now meant more to him than—meant *so much* more to him than—any frisson of excitement being in danger might bring.

Perhaps he'd simply grown older.

Perhaps, with her beside him, he'd seen a future beyond his recent past, a future so rosy, so alluring that he was now determined that future would be his. A home of their own—a family, children—with her forever by his side.

Both she and he had to live to make that happen.

Which was why he lay evaluating how much more information they needed to unearth before he fell back on Wolverstone's orders and took them racing home.

The four men who had gone missing were still missing, and no one seemed concerned, nor, as yet, had they found anyone who knew anything at all as to why, to where, or how the men had vanished.

In addition, it seemed young women and children were also disappearing—again without their disappearances raising any great furor.

What could possibly lie behind all these disappearances?

Everything hinged on that. If they could gain some inkling

of the reason behind the disappearances, learning the rest would be a great deal easier.

As sleep crept nearer, he reviewed their plans. Tomorrow, while Edwina extracted what she could from Mrs. Sherbrook, he would plunge into the investigations he'd intended to start that afternoon. He would amble up to the fort and see what he could learn about Captain Dixon and his movements prior to his disappearance. Meanwhile, he would send a few of his crew—those with experience in gathering information without triggering any alarms—to chat with the patrons of the taverns the navy officers frequented and see what they could learn about Lieutenants Hopkins and Fanshawe.

Once he left the fort, he might turn his attention to Hillsythe, although his instincts warned him away from inquiring at the governor's office. But Hillsythe must have billeted somewhere—in someone's house, most likely. Searching his room might turn up something.

Who knew? By tomorrow evening, they might have enough facts in hand to shake the dust of Freetown from their boots and be back on the sea, breathing in the bracing air.

The vision was so attractive, the last of his tension faded.

He hadn't even realized he'd closed his eyes when sleep rolled over him and dragged him down.

Nine

"What time is this priest's service?" Declan glanced across the breakfast table at Edwina.

"The service is at noon. I imagine Lady Holbrook will come by in her carriage sometime before that." Meeting his eyes, she pulled a face. "I didn't think to ask the location of Undoto's church, although given the number of ladies attending, I assume it's somewhere in the settlement."

"It would have to be." He sipped his coffee. "Immediately beyond the boundaries of the settlement, the jungle crowds in. In this area, the growth is dense, all but impenetrable except for the few tracks leading to outlying villages, and no European would venture that far, not without an armed escort."

Picking up her teacup, she nodded. "So it must be in town, which means it can't be far."

Declan glanced at Henry, standing by the sideboard and doing his best butler imitation. As usual, Declan had come down to breakfast before Edwina. Henry had seized the chance to whisper in his ear that he'd overheard enough about the local priest to have developed a curiosity to see Undoto's performance himself. Declan had—no surprise—given his permission for Henry to hire the local equivalent of a hackney and follow Lady Holbrook's carriage to the priest's church. Henry would watch the performance from the rear of the crowd, keeping a more distant eye on Edwina.

If there was any unexpected and potentially dangerous disruption at the event, Henry would be better placed to observe and to direct Billings, who knew Henry would be present, in how best to protect Edwina.

All in all, Declan now felt more comfortable over her plans for the day.

"So." Setting down her cup, she looked at him. "Where do you intend to start?"

"As we discussed yesterday, with Captain Dixon." He paused, then, frowning over his thoughts, went on, "I keep coming back to the fact that Dixon was the one who unexpectedly disappeared. The others were tracking him when they vanished, which suggests that following Dixon is most likely the reason they disappeared. But why did Dixon—he in particular—disappear? As I understand it, until he did, there had been no reports of soldiers or sailors going missing."

He stopped to think, then mused aloud, "I should check, but as far as I've heard, there have been no disappearances of soldiers or sailors other than Dixon and those sent after him."

For a full minute, silence reigned while they both thought through what they knew and what they didn't.

Eventually, Edwina refocused on his face. When he met her gaze, she stated, "Assuming Dixon didn't willingly leave the settlement, and assuming that some unknown entity is behind all these disappearances, then I can think of only two alternatives for why Dixon—he in particular—might have vanished. Either he was following the trail of someone else *he* knew had vanished—a young woman, for instance—and like those who followed him, got captured, too. *Or* he knew something, had some information perhaps, that our unknown entity wanted and actually needed for whatever they're doing, so they had to risk seizing Dixon, even though they've otherwise avoided taking soldiers and sailors—presumably because if enough of them got taken, the authorities would be forced to pay attention and, ultimately, act."

Declan replayed her words, assessed her logic, then inclined his head. "That's an excellent summation." He pushed back from the table and rose. "Let's see if I can turn up something today that will point to which of your alternatives is correct. I've already sent to the ship and set some of my crew to work through the taverns about the docks and see what they can turn up about Hopkins and Fanshawe."

Edwina rose, too, and came to meet him under the archway giving onto the front hall. "What about Hillsythe? He's the most recent of our disappearees. Won't information about him be freshest in people's minds?"

"Yes." He halted beside her and looked into her upturned face. "But please promise me you won't so much as breathe Hillsythe's name."

She studied his eyes and read the seriousness behind his request. "All right—I promise. But why?"

He hesitated, then inwardly sighed and said, "Because Hillsythe was one of Wolverstone's operatives"—she'd already known that much—"and Wolverstone's operatives aren't…"

When he paused, searching for the right words, she suggested, "Easy to overpower, much less capture?"

He nodded; he had reason to know. "And *that* says something about the people who accomplished that feat."

Studying the vibrant blue of her eyes, he wondered how much she comprehended, how much she'd guessed.

Wondered how much he wanted her to know.

But she surprised him by not questioning him further. Instead, she stretched up on her toes and pressed a kiss to his lips. He savored the sweet caress; for an instant, they both lingered.

Then she drew back, sinking down to her heels. "I imagine I'll return by midafternoon. I'll see you when you get back."

His fingers had found hers and twined, lightly gripping; slowly, he forced himself to let her go. "Be careful."

She met his eyes, her gaze direct. "You, too."

With that, she headed for their room. He watched her go, then regathered his wits, focused, and turned to the front door.

As per his plan, Declan went first to Fort Thornton. He approached the gates openly and, when challenged to state his business, transparently in no hurry he slouched against the guards' station and settled to chat with the pair on duty. He told them who he was, spinning his tale about why he was in Freetown and ultimately weaving a yarn of having agreed to ferry a message for a friend to the friend's cousin, a Captain Dixon presently stationed at the fort.

He asked to speak with Dixon.

Both guards shook their heads. "He's not here," one replied. "Don't know where he's got to, but he hasn't been around for months."

Declan feigned surprise. A second later, he frowned. "You mean he's just gone off? Are such unexplained absences common?"

Again, the guards shook their heads, this time with a certain grimness. One volunteered, "No one else has gone absent without leave—just Dixon."

A discussion of the lack of enticements in the neighborhood ensued.

Eventually, Declan straightened. "Is there anyone here—any other officer—who knew Dixon? Someone with whom I could leave this message I have for him in case he turns up?"

The guards chewed that over, then the older one said, "Don't actually know what his officer friends think of him vanishing as he has. We all know he's been gone for months, but although there've been plenty of opinions as to where he's gone, it's all just supposing. No one's come around asking official questions, like, so we've all been left to our imaginations."

His hands in his pockets, Declan shrugged. "Can't hurt to ask his fellow officers." He met the older guard's eyes. "If I learn anything definite, I'll let you know on my way out."

The second guard nodded. "As you say, can't hurt to ask."

Between them, the guards supplied several names and directed him to the officers' mess.

Declan dropped his slouch as he entered the building, resuming his normal captain's bearing. That, and his carefully presented story, got him introduced to the right group of officers in the mess, but as he quickly discovered, although they'd all been Dixon's peers, each officer had his own troop to manage; in reality, they spent only their off-duty hours in each other's company, and then only when those hours coincided.

Yet all were surprised, if not shocked, at Dixon's apparent desertion.

"Absolutely wouldn't have thought it of him," one junior lieutenant opined.

An older captain with graying hair shook his head. "Whatever happened to him, it's bad business all around."

The others rumbled agreement. Declan waited until the rumbles faded to ask, "Did Dixon have any particular expertise?"

"Sapper," the older captain replied. "Well, he was in charge of that company, not that they've had much to do out here. But if you wanted to tunnel under a wall, or bring down a wall or bridge, Dixon was your man. Built quite a reputation during the Spanish campaign."

Declan nodded his understanding. He bided his time, buying the men ales and playing up his connection to Dixon's supposed cousin. Finally, he succeeded in inveigling the older captain, Richards, into showing him Dixon's quarters.

The small room was scrupulously neat. At first glance, Declan discarded any thought of finding a clue there—then what he was looking at registered.

Dixon's brushes, his comb, and his shaving kit were neatly lined up on the top of the small dresser.

Frowning, Declan glanced at Richards; he waved at the dresser. "Are all his belongings still here?"

His expression grim, Richards nodded. "Everything. And if anyone were to ask me—not that they will—I'd say it was bleeding obvious that wherever Dixon went, he expected to return that day."

Declan let that sink in—both the observation and Richards's unvoiced implication—then he thanked the man and left.

The pervasive blindness of those in charge toward the disappearances was growing increasingly hard to excuse.

After spending another few minutes with the guards, reporting that no one, not even the officers closest to Dixon, had any clue where he'd gone, Declan headed down the hill to the harbor.

He'd arranged to meet Higgins, Martin, and Upshaw—the three experienced sailors he'd sent to scout in and around the dockside taverns—at one of the more reputable establishments.

They were waiting when he got there, gathered around a table in one corner.

"Anything?" he asked as he joined them.

All three rather despondently shook their heads.

Martin explained, "Most o' those who sailed with Fanshawe and Hopkins are out with the squadron, so those here only know what they've heard."

"Howsoever," Higgins said, "sounds like there's been plenty of grumbling going on. Both Hopkins and Fanshawe were respected and well-liked. None of the lads think either of 'em would've gone absent without leave, no matter what the higher-ups say."

Upshaw nodded. "Seems like even the other officers aren't too pleased about nothing being said or done—that it's simply been assumed that the pair went off just like that, no word to anyone and all their kit still in their quarters."

"Is that so?" Declan tapped his fingers on the table. "Dixon's belongings are also in his room. He obviously hadn't expected to disappear."

Higgins humphed. "Seems to me there's something havey-cavey going on when not one, not two, but three officers up and vanish, and no one bats an eye."

Declan agreed. He debated, then reluctantly revealed, "There's another man gone missing—name of Hillsythe. He was a relatively recent arrival attached to the governor's office. He was sent here to investigate the other three disappearances—Hillsythe's disappearance is what triggered us being sent from London to see what we can ferret out."

Upshaw's eyes rounded. "Gads! Hope we don't disappear, too!"

"Let's try to avoid that," Declan dryly returned.

After a moment's cogitation, he said, "I need to learn more about Hillsythe—I need to find where he was staying and check if all his things are there, too. It's not inconceivable that *he* didn't disappear, but that he's gone off following some trail..." He grimaced. "Possibly."

He thought, then he pushed away from the table. "Let's scatter and ask at the places a single gentleman might have gone to eat. Hillsythe wasn't with the army or navy, and he wasn't living with the governor and his lady, so he had to have found somewhere to dine."

Rising, he glanced at his men. "It's nearly midday—all the eateries will be open. Higgins, you take the docks. Upshaw and Martin—split up and cover the commercial district. I'll go to the streets higher up the hill. Let's meet here in two hours and see what we've managed to learn."

When Lady Holbrook's carriage finally rocked to a halt, Edwina looked out on a large, low, rectangular hall constructed around a framework of polished logs, with walls made up of panels of woven rushes, all topped by a roof of coarse thatch. The hall sat in a wide clearing bordered on all sides by rough dwellings; not far from the rear of the building, thick jungle pressed in, dark and faintly menacing.

It appeared that Obo Undoto's church lay almost at the edge of the settlement.

They'd traveled for about twenty minutes, heading east from the enclave of European settlers on Tower Hill and the commercial district around the harbor on Kroo Bay. Tower Hill, it transpired, was one of a range of minor mountains that ran parallel to the coast; they were now on the lower slopes of the next mountain to the east.

Lady Holbrook descended from the carriage first, handed down by Billings, who had traveled on the box with the governor's coachman. Edwina followed; she grasped the hand Billings offered and joined Lady Holbrook at the edge of the dusty forecourt in front of the hall.

Instinctively, Edwina looked north, toward the sea. Instead of the clutter of large ocean-going vessels that clogged Kroo Bay, she saw a motley collection of fishing boats bobbing on a gentle swell. There was no evidence of a commercial district here; a shantytown of crude dwellings filled the area between the church and the shore.

Mrs. Quinn and Mrs. Robey had also traveled in the Holbrooks' carriage. They, too, accepted Billings's help, climbed down, then shook out their skirts.

Lady Holbrook waved at the building. "Behold—Obo Undoto's church." She cast a smiling glance at Edwina. "While it's a far cry from St. George's, in terms of native churches, it's relatively luxurious." She started toward the building.

"The seats at least are comfortable." Mrs. Robey raised her hems, and she and Mrs. Quinn followed in Lady Holbrook's wake.

Edwina paused to take in the church's façade. The hinged woven panels that formed the main doors had been propped wide, creating a framed archway through which a steady stream of people, natives and Europeans both, was filing inside. Flanking the doorway, other panel sections had been lifted out of their frames in the walls, creating windows. It looked like a native meetinghouse—the equivalent of a town hall, perhaps; the only church-like feature was a large white-painted wooden cross set on the apex of the low-pitched roof.

After glancing around and failing to spot Mrs. Sherbrook, Edwina stepped out briskly to catch up with the other three ladies. Billings followed a respectful pace behind her; she was aware he was there, and as they merged into the press of bodies shuffling through the doorway and she clutched her reticule a little tighter, she owned to being glad he was.

Keeping her gaze trained on Lady Holbrook's gray head, Edwina followed the other ladies to one of the front pews to the left of the central aisle.

Lady Holbrook sat, then looked up, saw Edwina waiting to join them, and patted the space beside her. "Come and sit beside me, Lady Edwina. You'll have an excellent view of proceedings from here."

Edwina was happy to comply. As she settled her skirts, she looked around curiously. A raised pulpit, much as she might have seen at home in England, loomed directly ahead—doubtless the view to which Lady Holbrook had referred. A recognizable altar sat on a dais that ran across the width of the hall. The altar played host to a handsome silver cross and four candlesticks, yet behind the altar, where in most churches the main window would be, there was nothing but woven rushes.

Twisting in her seat, Edwina looked behind her. A phalanx of people in gowns, coats, and uniforms met her gaze. It seemed this half of the church was reserved for Europeans; the natives congregated on the other side of the aisle.

She spotted Billings. He'd tucked himself into the corner of the pew behind the one in which she sat; he was no longer behind her, but wasn't far away. She scanned the crowd, searching for Mrs. Sherbrook to no avail. The church was already quite full; the sounds of a multitude of chattering conversations filled the air.

Edwina was distantly following the conversation between Mrs. Robey and Lady Holbrook; she was starting to wonder if Mrs. Sherbrook had changed her mind about attending the event when, just as the congregation started to quiet and look expectantly toward the front of the church, a small disturbance occurred at the rear of the hall. It resolved as several gentlemen standing behind the last pews stepped aside, and Mrs. Sherbrook appeared. Looking decidedly harried, she came hurrying down the aisle, scanning the packed pews.

Having deliberately left space between herself and Lady Holbrook, Edwina waved at Mrs. Sherbrook, then shifted closer to the governor's wife, creating just enough space for Mrs. Sherbrook to squeeze in.

"So kind of you, Lady Edwina—thank you." With her gloved hand, Mrs. Sherbrook fanned her face; her color was a trifle high. "My youngest is still fractious over being left with our new nanny—I wasn't sure I would make it in time."

Edwina bestowed a bracing smile. "But you did." She lowered her voice and added, "I had hoped to have a chance to speak with you again. Perhaps at the end of the service, we might find a moment out of the crowd. There's something I would like to ask you."

Mrs. Sherbrook's eyes widened, but she nodded readily. "Yes, of course. I would be happy to assist you in whatever way I can."

The opening of a door to one side of the altar heralded the commencement of the service. Edwina faced forward. As the congregation rose, she counseled herself to patience and, for the moment, gave her mind over to being entertained.

Draped in ceremonial robes similar to those of any Christian priest, a large and imposing African man she presumed was Obo

Undoto led a small procession of altar boys and choristers into the church. The priest proceeded with a firm and stately tread to the pulpit and climbed to the raised platform, while the altar boys, each swinging a censer, took up positions flanking the altar, and the choristers formed up in ranks on the side of the hall opposite the pulpit.

Studying Obo Undoto, Edwina had to admit he looked the part. He was tall—she estimated somewhere over six feet—and was well built, with heavy shoulders and a broad muscled chest. His skin was a deep, dark, burnished brown, reminiscent of polished mahogany. He was either bald or, more likely, deliberately shaved his head; the result made his strong features all the more striking.

Undoto placed his hands on the lectern and looked out over his congregation, then he smiled, raised his hands, and spoke—and Edwina understood why Lady Holbrook had labeled him charismatic.

His voice was exceptional—strong, powerful, yet well-modulated. He spoke with a surprisingly clear diction and had very little accent.

When, after the first prayer, he released them to sit, Edwina settled on the pew and thought: *Someone's taught him.* Of course, she then wondered what had caused her to think that; as with consummate skill Undoto wove his magic over his audience, she continued to watch, to analyze—to look past the smoke and brimstone.

His voice was his principal weapon; a deep baritone, it rose and fell, the cadence a swelling wave that lifted and swept his audience along. Dramatic gestures and finely honed timing played their part; overall, he put on a mesmerizing performance.

When, during the sermon, he thundered, and the pulpit shook beneath his fist, the thought that popped into Edwina's mind was: *Fireworks.* A brilliant flash to temporarily distract.

Indeed, everything Undoto did was as superficial, as insubstantial and illusory, as firework stars.

He had no real passion.

A quick mental comparison with old Reverend Gillings, who had held the living at Ridgware for decades—who spoke softly and whose sermons were models of gently and sincerely expressed thought—confirmed it; even though he spoke quietly, belief—and the passion that nurtured—resonated in Reverend Gillings's every word.

There was no belief behind Obo Undoto's histrionics.

Entertainment, pure and simple, was his creed and what he delivered, albeit wrapped up in the vestments of religion. Glancing curiously at the faces she could see, Edwina had to admit that she doubted any of those attending truly confused this with worship, not in their hearts. This was almost a mockery of true worship; no wonder Reverend Hardwicke was so disapproving of Undoto's ministry.

She couldn't imagine a performance of this ilk being such an attraction anywhere other than in a settlement of this type, where there were so few other sources of entertainment, especially for the wives of the soldiers, administrators, and merchants.

They had to fill their days somehow, and all in all, charlatan though he most certainly was, perhaps in that Undoto could be said to be offering a useful service. Attending pseudo-religious services was unlikely to hurt anyone.

And the hymns were still hymns. Edwina enjoyed singing and saw no reason not to allow the comforting refrains to fill her soul; she could take at least that much genuine enjoyment from the event.

Finally, after the offering plate had done the rounds—in Edwina's view, acting much as a busker's hat—Undoto held out his hands and delivered a blessing. On the heels of that final benediction, he descended from the pulpit and marched up the aisle, both his stride and his expression confident and assured.

Edwina had hoped that, as happened at home, the congregation would file out and then gather in groups outside to chat for a few minutes before dispersing. With Mrs. Sherbrook close behind, she followed Lady Holbrook, Mrs. Quinn, and Mrs. Robey up the aisle.

Undoto stood just outside the doorway, waiting to farewell his parishioners. The other ladies didn't shake hands with him but smiled and inclined their heads. Lady Holbrook complimented the priest on an excellent service, and Undoto smiled, white teeth flashing in his dark face.

Stepping aside, Lady Holbrook gestured to Edwina. "Lady Edwina is visiting from England. She was keen to experience one of your services."

"Indeed?"

Edwina found herself the object of Undoto's dark-eyed gaze. Holding close her cloak of noble superiority, she coolly replied, "My husband and I will be in town for only a few days, so I was pleased I was able to attend today."

Undoto bowed low. "I am honored, my lady."

With her most regal nod, Edwina moved away. Pleased to note that Lady Holbrook had already become engaged with several other ladies in an animated discussion, Edwina halted and waited for Mrs. Sherbrook to join her.

As the other woman came up beside her, Edwina touched her sleeve. "I wonder if we could speak now."

"Yes, of course." Mrs. Sherbrook nodded to one of several benches set to one side of the forecourt. "Let's sit there, out of the noise."

Billings materialized from the crowd; he followed Edwina and Mrs. Sherbrook as they crossed to the unoccupied bench. When Mrs. Sherbrook glanced discouragingly his way, Edwina said, "My footman."

"Oh. I see."

They sat, and Billings halted a few feet away, far enough to give them privacy. Not knowing for how long Lady Holbrook would remain chatting, Edwina plunged in. "Forgive me if my question sounds intrusive, but I, and my husband, too, have grown rather concerned about these odd disappearances."

She glanced at Mrs. Sherbrook in time to see that lady bite her lower lip. Edwina continued, "When the matter came up over tea at Lady Holbrook's, and then again at the Macauleys', I couldn't help notice that you seemed...perturbed."

Her gaze rising to lock on Edwina's face, Mrs. Sherbrook clearly debated, then in a rush said, "We lost our nanny. The one we had before. Or rather, she vanished, just like some of the others we've heard about. She went to fetch a package from the post office and simply never returned. The package was still there—she never reached the post office." Mrs. Sherbrook's face clouded, and there was a touch of belligerence in her tone as she said, "It's all very well for those like Letitia Holbrook to imply that the young women who've vanished are fast and wanton and that they've gone off following men..." Mrs. Sherbrook's gaze steadied on Edwina's face, and her chin firmed. "But Katherine wasn't like that—not at all."

Edwina placed a comforting hand over Mrs. Sherbrook's twisting fingers. "What was Katherine like?"

"She was kind, and the children adored her." Mrs. Sherbrook paused, then went on, "Her name was—is—Katherine Fortescue. She was gentry-bred—more so than I am, truth be told, but her family had fallen on hard times and...well, Katherine was proud and was determined to be independent and no burden on anyone. She answered an advertisement we placed in *The Times* the last time we were in London, and she returned to Freetown with us."

Mrs. Sherbrook seemed to deflate. "She became our children's beloved nanny, and over the last months, she'd also become a dear companion to me." Raising her eyes, she met Edwina's. "There is no possibility at all that Katherine simply went off with some man into the jungle. She was *taken*. By whom or why I have no idea, but she was kidnapped—there's no other viable explanation. My husband has tried to raise the matter with the governor, but over this, Governor Holbrook seems determined to be blind. He just shrugs it off and claims there's nothing to be done."

Edwina sensed the other woman's frustration and distress, but what could she say? "I believe that there are others who are starting to accept that certain people have been taken—kidnapped. But, as you say, by whom or why remains a mystery."

Mrs. Sherbrook's shoulders sagged. "I've kept putting off writing to Katherine's family, hoping against hope... But it's been months now, and we've heard nothing." Staring bleakly ahead, Mrs. Sherbrook drew in a breath, then she straightened her spine. "I'll have to write soon."

Edwina understood Mrs. Sherbrook's sense of helplessness, but helplessness wasn't a feeling she herself ever readily entertained. Perhaps it was something to do with being a duke's daughter, but she was much more inclined to demand answers and resolutions.

"Lady Edwina! Yoo-hoo!" Through the thinning crowd, Mrs. Quinn waved, then pointed at the carriages. "Lady Holbrook is ready to leave, my lady."

Edwina swallowed a sigh and rose. As Mrs. Sherbrook rose, too, Edwina grasped the woman's hand and gently squeezed. "Thank you for telling me about Katherine."

Mrs. Sherbrook nodded. She drew her hand rather nervously from Edwina's and bobbed a curtsy. As she straightened, she said, "If you should learn anything..."

"I'll be sure to let you know." With an inclination of her head, Edwina parted from Mrs. Sherbrook. While the other woman hurried to her own carriage, Edwina went to climb into Lady Holbrook's. She wasn't looking forward to the inquisition that no doubt awaited her as to her opinion on Obo Undoto's performance.

"But at least I learned something for my time." Summoning

a smile, she strengthened her customary armor for dealing with society, stood back to let Billings open the carriage door, then she climbed up to join the other ladies.

She settled beside Lady Holbrook and, bright-eyed, let her gaze pass over the other ladies' faces. "As you all warned me, that was, indeed, diverting." She sat back; with any luck, the resulting exclamations and effusions would last all the way back to Tower Hill.

Declan spent the better half of his afternoon trawling through the likely haunts around Fort Thornton, through the European quarter, and lower on Tower Hill where a single gentleman attached to the governor's office might conceivably have dined.

In a settlement such as Freetown, European gentlemen who were neither army nor navy weren't so thick on the ground that people didn't notice and place each individual. Although he didn't have a physical description of Hillsythe, Declan knew the man's age, where he'd worked, and how long he'd been in Freetown—that should have been enough to pick up his trail.

When his search on Tower Hill proved futile, Declan considered inquiring at the governor's office, located in the fort, but he'd be identified the instant he showed his face, and given the avid interest his story about following a rumor had generated, any questions he asked would be noted and commented on.

And Wolverstone and Melville no longer trusted those in the governor's office.

Declan decided he wasn't yet desperate enough to act against all good sense and continued down the hill. Harboring no real hope regarding Hillsythe and already thinking of what his next move should be, he returned to the tavern where he'd arranged to meet with his men.

One glance at Upshaw's face and his despondent mood evaporated. "What did you learn?"

Higgins and Martin made "get on with it" gestures.

Upshaw all but bounced as he said, "Seems he took a liking to a little place not far from the Customs House. Used to sit in their front window and watch the people walk by as he ate. No name, of course, but the woman who runs the place said as he was a recent arrival and worked up at the fort in the government building. He told her as much."

"Excellent." Declan reflected that he should have known that one of Wolverstone's men wouldn't have let down his guard either near the fort or in dockside taverns. "Did the woman know where he was billeting?"

"He wasn't—billeting, that is. He never told her, but one day she saw him on the street not far from her place, and she saw him pull out a latchkey and let himself in. She pointed out the door to me—she said the shop-owner rents the room above his shop, and that's where our man had been going."

Declan clapped Upshaw on the shoulder. "You'll make bosun yet."

It was a standing joke among his men because no one could imagine replacing Grimsby.

Higgins asked, "So are we going to go around there and take a look-see?"

Declan thought, then said, "We'll go around, but I want you three to hang back. I'll spin a tale about being Hillsythe's replacement and wanting to check if he's left anything in the room. Better you're not seen with me, but you may as well wait outside until we see what I learn."

They did as he asked, waiting in a group on the other side of the street a block away, out of sight of the window of the small tailor's shop above which Hillsythe had apparently slept.

The old tailor who owned the shop swallowed Declan's tale whole and readily unlocked the outside door and showed him up the stairs. Hillsythe had paid the rent for three months, so the tailor had left his things undisturbed. The man also verified that no one else had come to the shop asking after Hillsythe.

The room above the shop was relatively Spartan. It contained a bed, a narrow wardrobe, a small bookcase, a desk set before the single window with a straight-backed chair beside it, and a traveling chest set to one side of the door. With a sweeping glance, Declan took in the brushes and shaving kit on the small shelf above the washstand. *Another one who hadn't expected not to come home.*

He walked to the desk. There were no papers left upon it and no drawer in which anything might have been hidden. Aware of the tailor standing in the doorway and watching him, Declan turned to the wardrobe and opened the door. As he scanned the contents, he felt the hairs at his nape stir.

One evening coat, a hanger with a pair of trousers neatly folded over the bar, an empty hanger, and another with a spare shirt all hung precisely aligned, but on the lower shelf, Hillsythe's dress shoes, a pair of well-worn boots, and a pair of old, comfortable shoes lay haphazardly askew.

Declan forced himself to go through the motions of checking for the papers he'd told the tailor he'd been sent to find. Then he closed the wardrobe and advanced on the chest. A cursory glance inside confirmed that it, too, had been thoroughly searched.

He let the lid fall and, with a resigned sigh, directed a faint smile at the tailor. "Well, it was a long shot, but clearly he didn't leave those papers here."

A minute later, he was back on the street and striding toward his men. He walked straight past them, and they turned and followed. He didn't stop until he was around the corner and back in the busy hubbub of Water Street.

Higgins, Martin, and Upshaw halted before him. Higgins arched his brows. "You found something?"

"Hillsythe's room has been searched. In secret. The tailor knew nothing of it." Declan was still trying to work out what that meant. "They couldn't risk trying to get to Dixon's room at the fort, or Fanshawe's or Hopkins's quarters aboard ship.

But they could easily access Hillsythe's rooms to search, and they did."

Martin blinked. "What were they searching for?"

Declan grimaced. "Presumably for something that might have tipped off someone—someone like me—as to where Hillsythe went, or who he suspected—most likely the same men who took him."

"So..." Upshaw blinked. "Doesn't that mean that there really is someone snatching these men—that they haven't wandered off but that someone's kidnapped them?"

Grimly, Declan nodded. He set his jaw, then glanced around. "I think we've learned all we're likely to about the four men. You three get back to the ship, but there's one more place I need to check."

Higgins, Martin, and Upshaw snapped off salutes, then they turned and headed toward Government Wharf, from where they would row out to *The Cormorant*.

Declan watched them go, then hauled in a deep breath, metaphorically girded his loins, and walked on to the settlement's hospital.

brow, his expression cynical. "The more one hears that excuse, the less believable it seems. However, we did find evidence that all four had expected to return to their quarters as usual. Their belongings were all there—brushes, combs, shaving kits, and clothes all left at the ready. On top of that, Hillsythe's room had been searched, in secret, after he vanished. All of that strongly suggests they've been kidnapped." He paused, then went on, "Following that reasoning further, if they were attacked and captured, then each of them would have fought back—one or more might have been killed. We needed to know, so I went to the morgue."

"Were—had any of them been there?"

"No. Given the weeks that have passed, I didn't expect to find their bodies still in keeping—not in this climate, especially. But I went through the records for the last five months. There were no unidentified European male corpses that might have been them."

He sighed, then swallowed another mouthful of whisky. "Morgues are never pleasant places, but in the tropics…" He still hadn't got the stench out of his nostrils.

"But they weren't there." She frowned. "From that, can we assume they're still alive?" She widened her eyes at him. "Couldn't they have been killed elsewhere and their bodies buried or thrown into the sea?"

He considered, then grimaced. "We can't rule that out, but to my mind, that none of the four have turned up dead anywhere in the settlement significantly increases the likelihood that they're all still alive. Again, because this is the tropics, a dead body is usually found quite quickly. And as the natives have burial rites of their own and are superstitious about such observances, if they find a dead European, they will bring that body to the morgue as soon as possible. Admittedly, our four might have died away from anyone, but… All in all, with no bodies turning up anywhere, the most likely explanation is that they were kidnapped and are still alive, being held somewhere, for some reason."

After a moment, his tone hardening, he added, "There's one more thing. Hillsythe's room being secretly searched after he'd been kidnapped—the reason for that could only be to ensure that he'd left nothing to indicate who had taken him. As one of my men pointed out, that means the kidnappers are no longer hypothetical but demonstrably real—only real people can effect a search, and only real people fear being found out."

"Hmm. That also means they—the kidnappers—were still here, in the settlement, after Hillsythe was taken, and they were willing to act to ensure they weren't detected—which in turn suggests they intended to remain and presumably continue their nefarious activities." She frowned. "If we consider that far more people than just the four men have vanished—and therefore are most likely kidnap victims, too—all without raising any alert, much less a panic, then whoever is behind the kidnappings has been very clever."

"And calm and collected. They've grown confident, apparently with good reason." After a moment, he refocused on her. "So what did you learn? Did you get your chance to speak with Mrs. Sherwood?"

"Indeed." Edwina sat straighter and marshaled her thoughts. "I was right about Mrs. Sherwood being bothered by talk of these 'disappearances.' Some months ago, the nanny they'd brought from England to look after their children vanished." She related all she'd learned from Mrs. Sherbrook. "Of course, she feels responsible for bringing Katherine Fortescue here and so placing her in danger, even though Katherine wanted the position."

Having staff of her own, she could empathize with Mrs. Sherbrook's distress. She could even more definitely empathize with Katherine. If it hadn't been for her brother Julian's sacrifice… In Edwina's head, the words *But for the grace of Julian, I might have been Katherine* tolled. Instead, rather than having to work as a governess to survive, here she was, still received by the ton and all society as the duke's daughter she was, and married to a man she liked, respected, and was learning to adore. A man who could give her, and was giving her, all her heart desired.

In that moment, she made a silent, almost unconscious—certainly instinctive—vow. As a young woman who could have stood in Katherine Fortescue's shoes, if there was anything she could do to rescue Katherine, she would do it.

She raised her gaze to Declan's face and realized he was frowning. "What is it?"

"I just remembered—I don't think I told you that Charles Babington mentioned he knew of a young lady who has also disappeared. I got the impression he was interested in her. He referred to her as a young *lady*, and I doubt he would have even met the Sherbrooks' nanny—I somehow doubt the Sherbrooks' nanny moved in the circles Babington does."

"So we've now got four men—officers and gentlemen—and at least two women—both gentry—known to be missing." Edwina paused, then said, "That suggests that the so-called rumors of children going missing are also very likely to be true."

When Declan accepted her thesis with a grim look and no argument, she spread her hands in mystification. "Why isn't anything being done about this? Why are the authorities behaving with such determined blindness?"

He grimaced. "That's worrying me, too. Especially as even Babington—however reluctantly and against his instincts—appears to have swallowed the prevailing line." A second later, his eyes narrowing, he amended, "Or at least he feels compelled to pretend he has."

Declan took another slow sip of his whisky. After a moment, he said, "As much as I dislike the man, I can imagine an excuse for Decker's inaction on this issue. He's been at sea commanding the squadron for much of this last year. His office here, at least, knows of Dixon's disappearance because they must have passed on Melville's orders sending Hopkins to search for Dixon, and then when Hopkins vanished, they informed Melville, who sent Fanshawe after Hopkins. Decker's office also knows of Fanshawe's disappearance because they notified the Admiralty of it, but given the timing, it's entirely possible that Decker himself has been at sea chasing slave traders since before Dixon disappeared."

"So even if he was here, Decker might not know about Hillsythe being sent in, or Hillsythe disappearing, too."

Declan shook his head. "Neither Decker nor his office would know about Hillsythe. Wolverstone and Melville wouldn't have notified them. They aren't trusting anyone here, and that includes Decker."

"So we can absolve Decker of any negligence, any lack of action on this issue." Edwina paused, then went on, "But Decker isn't here anyway, so we can ignore him for the moment." She looked at Declan. "What about the major who's in charge at the fort? He at least knows Dixon has vanished."

"Major Eldridge." Declan frowned. "Dixon's fellow officers are not happy about the way Dixon's disappearance has been treated, and it seemed they'd been fobbed off with the same story we had from Holbrook…" Declan pulled a face. "I just remembered—Eldridge and Holbrook don't get on. That's not entirely unusual in the circumstances. Eldridge is responsible for the defense of the settlement from attack from outside, but Holbrook sits above him, and it's Holbrook's responsibility to call on Eldridge to act against threats from *within* the settlement."

"So if Holbrook doesn't call on Eldridge to act, he can't?"

"Not without causing a major ruckus. But in this case, Melville might have muddied the waters even further by asking Decker to send men—Hopkins and, subsequently, Fanshawe—to search for Dixon. It's entirely possible Eldridge doesn't know that Hopkins and Fanshawe were dispatched to search for Dixon or that they've disappeared, too." Declan shifted restlessly. "And Eldridge certainly won't have heard about Hillsythe."

"And I suppose there's no reason to imagine that any of the other disappearances—the young women and children—would be brought to the major's attention?"

"No. I can't see why they would." After a moment, Declan said, "Considering the tension I found at the fort, I wouldn't mind wagering that Eldridge, entirely correctly, reported Dixon's disappearance to Holbrook, fully expecting to be given orders to do whatever he needed to find the man. Instead, Holbrook insisted Dixon had gone off on his own account. Holbrook might well have specifically refused Eldridge permission to investigate, and as Eldridge had no evidence that there had been any foul play involved, Eldridge might have been forced to comply—to at least outwardly support Holbrook's line."

Declan paused, then added, "What little I know of Eldridge paints him as a stickler for correctness, so no matter how much he might personally disagree, if Holbrook insisted, Eldridge would toe his line."

"But why would the governor do such a thing? Surely if something nefarious is going on in his town, he'd want it dealt with immediately and as effectively as possible. Why would he deny Eldridge permission to investigate?"

"I think we're missing something. Or rather, we're overlooking something because we don't know enough about it to see how it impacts this situation." Leaning forward and resting his forearms on his thighs, Declan cradled his glass between his hands. "Holbrook's old, but not that old. He's probably got another decade of postings ahead of him. And without a doubt, he'll be hoping his next posting will be to some rather more civilized place than Freetown."

"So you think he views his time here as a stepping-stone to somewhere better?"

Declan nodded. "He might even have been sent here as a trial of sorts—to prove himself under more testing circumstances."

"By sweeping matters of life and death under some carpet?"

Declan's eyes narrowed. He stared unseeing across the room, then he raised his glass and sipped. Lowering the glass, he murmured, "Holbrook might actually believe his nonsense about men going off to seek their fortunes in the jungle. If he feels under pressure to present his tenure here as all smooth sailing, then—and as I said, we don't know enough to be certain—he might have a vested interest in downplaying Dixon's disappearance. We don't know if Holbrook knows about Fanshawe and Hopkins going missing. Decker's office might not have—indeed, most likely wouldn't have—informed Holbrook of that, not without Decker's approval, which couldn't have been forthcoming because he's at sea. But Holbrook will certainly have been informed of Hillsythe vanishing from his own office."

Declan paused, swiftly assessing. "It's possible that Holbrook only knows of Dixon going missing a few months ago, and Hillsythe more recently—and of the Sherbrooks' nanny, assuming he even truly registered the substance of Mr. Sherbrook's complaint. Given Holbrook had fixed it in his head that Dixon had wandered off into the jungle, it might have seemed wise to cling to the same explanation whenever anyone suggested a disappearance. Holbrook might simply be intent on keeping his colony calm, rather than risking what to him might seem unnecessary panic..."

He sipped again, then said, "Actually, I can see that easily enough. Holbrook has to keep Macauley and Babington happy—the company drives all trade in this town. And Macauley especially is of that generation that places a high value on order and calm wherever he does business. Any hint of a panic that might affect his warehouses and Macauley will be writing letters to London."

"When I brought up the subject of people going missing, Mrs. Macauley, at least, knew nothing about it." Edwina grimaced. "But by the end of the conversation, she'd accepted the view that it was nothing to be concerned about."

"That does, however, suggest that Holbrook hasn't mentioned it to Macauley. And although Macauley, businessman that he is, undoubtedly meets with Eldridge and Decker, too, Decker's away and has been for some time, and even if Macauley's recently spoken with Eldridge, the major would have parroted Holbrook's line and wouldn't have mentioned Dixon's disappearance—not something he'd be likely to mention to Macauley anyway."

Edwina frowned. "This is a mess. Foreign office bureaucratic posturing, army, navy, and a lucrative trade monopoly all mixed together."

Declan snorted, then shook his head. "This is one time I'm thoroughly glad that Frobisher and Sons doesn't have much interest in a major trading port." He paused, then went on, "Regardless, Wolverstone and Melville were right. We can trust no one here, and we can't rely on anyone for help. Not even Decker, given he's at sea—Melville's letter to him isn't much use if I can't present it."

Edwina slowly nodded, then refocused on his face. "So what now?"

He dropped his head back and stared at the ceiling. Sifting through all they'd learned took time; deciding whether it was enough took longer still. Eventually, he offered, "We've learned a few things." Enough to make him want to invoke Wolverstone's orders and cut and run, but... He shook his head. "We need something more definite to allow Melville and Wolverstone to build a case for urgent and decisive action. That's what they really sent me down here to get."

And at this point, he had no idea what that something more might be.

Edwina, his wife, who wasn't even supposed to be there with him, set her mind to the problem; squinting across the room, from beneath his lashes, he studied the concentration—the determination—that had invested her features.

Then she looked up and met his gaze, and he knew she'd thought of something.

"What about a list of all those who've gone missing—as many as we can verify? Surely that will underscore the need for action."

He considered it, then sat up. "A list like that...would certainly emphasize Wolverstone's point that something very serious is going on, and that it cannot be allowed to continue to develop, whatever it is." The more he thought of it, the more confident he felt. He refocused on Edwina. "So where can we get such a list? I doubt the governor's office will be any help at all."

He could sense her rising enthusiasm all the way across the room.

"No, indeed." She smiled intently. "But I suspect the Hardwickes will be. Remember I mentioned that Mrs. Hardwicke was the first who told me that the disappearances were widespread? She—and I believe Reverend Hardwicke, too—don't agree with the governor's explanation, but like Eldridge, they've been stymied by Holbrook's insistently dismissive attitude."

She glanced at the clock on the wall. "It's too late to call on the Hardwickes this evening. But I can call on Mrs. Hardwicke first thing in the morning, before she has a chance to go out, and ask her outright if we can assemble a list of all those known to have gone missing—young women and children, as well."

Declan considered that suggestion. Obtaining such a list would go a long way toward accomplishing what they needed, and he couldn't see her being at risk while with the minister's wife. And she would have her guards with her while traveling there and back. He nodded. "Good."

He thought, then drained his glass, lowered it, and said, "While you're doing that, I'm going to investigate one last angle regarding our four missing men." He met her blue eyes, read her inquisitive interest, smiled, and confided, "It's an approach I mentioned when we first came ashore, but one I haven't yet followed up. Did our four men have any contact in common—

someone they knew or some place they all visited?" He envisioned the possibilities. "Did their paths through this colony—all four of them—intersect at some point?"

Edwina sobered. After a moment, she said, "That won't be easy to learn, not without asking a lot of questions—questions that will reveal the true nature of your interest."

He set his glass down with a click. "True. But as I don't see us remaining in Freetown much longer—we need to get back and tell Wolverstone and Melville what they need to know— then I believe it's time we were more open, at least with those who are friends of the missing and who are transparently concerned for their safety."

Edwina nodded. She had to agree. She just hoped he took some of his men with him when he went striding about the settlement.

She let her mind roam over and around all they'd thus far learned. She glanced at Declan, waited until he met her gaze. "What has happened to all these people—the men, women, and children who've been kidnapped? If they haven't been killed, then presumably, whoever took them has some use or need for them. What could that be?"

After a moment of blankness, Declan grimaced. "Slavery instantly leaps to mind, but...that doesn't quite fit."

"Slavery?" She frowned. "I remember you said it was *unlikely* slave traders would operate inside the settlement"—she'd thought his mentioning such villainy had simply been him being over-protective—"but surely, in general, the practice has been outlawed in all British colonies."

"It has been. It is. Sadly, that doesn't mean it's not still going on. That's why the West Africa Squadron is here—or rather, out patrolling the seas off the coast." He paused, then went on, "I would lay odds on there being slave traders still operating in this area. Not through Freetown but out of the inlets up and down the coast. However, from all we've learned, it's only Europeans who've gone missing, and these days, the ramifications of slavers seizing Europeans, especially men, *especially* those in the British armed forces, and then trying to sell them… I can't say that definitely isn't what's happening here, but the odds seem very much against it."

She nodded. "That makes sense. So if not slavery, then…what? What are these people being—for want of a better phrase—collected for?"

He shook his head. "Damned if I know."

Edwina forced herself to wait until ten o'clock the next morning before climbing into the carriage and having Dench drive her the short distance down the hill to the rectory. The Hardwickes lived in a neat little house cheek by jowl with the church. Unlike the bungalows farther up the hill, there were no walls or gates barring entrance. Edwina walked briskly up the garden path, climbed the two steps to the porch, and rapped on the door.

A maid answered the summons and, on being asked for her mistress, conducted Edwina directly into a comfortable parlor where Mrs. Hardwicke sat sewing.

On seeing Edwina, Mrs. Hardwicke's severe features brightened. "Lady Edwina. It's a pleasure to see you." Hurriedly, she set aside her sewing.

But when she made to struggle up from the depths of her armchair, Edwina waved her back. "No—please. This is an entirely informal visit."

"I see." Sinking back, Mrs. Hardwicke eyed her shrewdly and waved to the sofa. "Please, do take a seat."

Once Edwina had complied and settled her skirts, Mrs. Hardwicke continued, "I assume this visit has a purpose, but before we broach it, would you care for some refreshment?"

"Thank you, but no. We—my husband and I—are on something of a deadline. His business here will shortly be concluded, and once it is, we'll be on our way again." Edwina fixed her gaze on Mrs. Hardwicke's face. "I wanted to ask you about these strange disappearances. In particular, it's come to my attention that several young women of good character—two at least, possibly more—have vanished. I believe you also have concerns about children—those from the lower classes who have been deemed to have run away."

Mrs. Hardwicke's face hardened. "I've made no bones about the degree of my concern. You're quite right about the young women. I know of at least four—all perfectly sensible young women—whose acquaintances are at their wits' end. None of those young women would ever have just walked away from their positions."

"Were they all in service?"

"Of one stripe or another, yes. Two governesses, a young woman who worked for the local milliner, and the niece of one of the local merchants who helped in his shop."

"I see." Edwina committed the information to memory. "And the children?"

Mrs. Hardwicke considered her for several moments, then appeared to come to a decision. "You're more nimble than I am—if you would look in the desk drawer"—she pointed to a small writing desk set between the windows—"you will find a leather-bound notebook. If you would bring it to me?"

Edwina rose, crossed to the desk, opened the drawer, and retrieved the notebook. She returned to Mrs. Hardwicke and handed her the book, then resumed her seat on the sofa.

Mrs. Hardwicke flicked through the pages toward the end of the book. "Where...oh. Here it is." She pressed the notebook fully open, then handed it to Edwina. "I grew so concerned, I started to make a list."

Edwina scanned Mrs. Hardwicke's entries. The minister's wife had listed names, ages, family addresses, and dates. "These are the dates the children went missing?" Boys and girls, all under ten years of age.

"Yes."

"Hmm. So..." Edwina counted. "Seventeen in all, starting from three months ago, but none in the last few weeks."

"No. And no—I have no idea what that might mean. Is it a temporary hiatus or a permanent halt?" Mrs. Hardwicke added, "If you turn back a page, you'll find the same details for those four young women."

Edwina flipped back the page and read the information noted. She glanced at Mrs. Hardwicke. "Would you mind if I make a copy of both lists?"

Mrs. Hardwicke's lips compressed. "No need. If you look in the front of the notebook, you'll find a folded sheet. It contains the details of all the women and children missing to date—at least those my husband and I have heard about." She paused, then added, "We have heard of men going missing, too, but in a settlement such as this, with so many single men taking up this job, then that, passing through or simply deciding to move on... Well, with men, it's hard to be sure they actually are missing and haven't simply gone somewhere else. All those we've heard of who seem to have vanished have been the itinerant sort."

Except for the four Declan had been sent to find. Edwina found the sheet, unfolded it, and ran her eye down the listed entries.

Watching her, Mrs. Hardwicke blew out a frustrated breath. "I made that copy for my husband. He took it with him on his most recent visit to the governor, to try to make Holbrook see sense. But, of course, it was a lost cause. Holbrook seems bound and determined not to act. He keeps insisting that there's nothing to be done, that there's nothing to investigate—that the women who've vanished have simply gone off, either following men into the jungle or running off with some sailor. As for the children"—Mrs. Hardwicke's gaze fastened on the list in Edwina's hand—"you will have noticed that all the children are either from slum families or else are ship's brats. This town has its fair share of both, and Holbrook is sadly not the sort of man whose compassion extends to those far beneath him."

Puzzled, Edwina said, "But they are all British?"

"Oh, yes." Mrs. Hardwicke folded her hands. "We've heard nothing about any native children disappearing, and my husband keeps in touch with the local tribesmen and chieftains. If they'd been losing children, we'd have heard about it—a great deal about it—by now."

Edwina was beyond disturbed. She shut the little notebook and handed it back to Mrs. Hardwicke. "Thank you." She folded the list, then held it up. "This is what I came for." She met Mrs. Hardwicke's eyes. "What my husband and I needed."

Mrs. Hardwicke's gaze rested on her, then the minister's wife said, "I really don't think this situation is at all acceptable, but I'm only one woman, and my husband believes he has pushed this particular barrow as far as he can—at least at this point in time. I've been thinking that, given the situation with Holbrook, the only way to get appropriate action on behalf of all those who have vanished is to get that information"—she nodded at the list Edwina was tucking into her reticule—"into the right hands in London. Whoever's hands those might be."

Her gaze intent on Edwina's face, Mrs. Hardwicke arched her brows. "You will be returning to London shortly, will you not, Lady Edwina?"

Tugging the strings of her reticule tight, Edwina wondered how she should reply. In the end, she simply said, "Yes. And I will see to it that this list gets into the hands of those who will be more inclined to act."

Mrs. Hardwicke hesitated, then asked, "Do you know such people?"

Edwina nodded. "Yes. Several, as it happens."

Mrs. Hardwicke softly exhaled. For a long moment, she stared unseeing at Edwina's reticule. Then her chin firmed, and she raised her gaze once more to Edwina's face. "In that case, I believe I should tell you something I have shared with no one else."

Edwina knew better than to speak. She watched while Mrs. Hardwicke gathered her thoughts.

Mrs. Hardwicke's gaze shifted to fix on the door, as if she could see a scene enacted on the panels. "Several weeks ago, a local woman—a vodun priestess—called to see my husband late one night. She said it was critically important—that she had information that affected not just her flock but his."

Mrs. Hardwicke paused, then briefly inclined her head. "To explain, vodun is not...unchristian. It's the local religion and shares many similarities with our beliefs. My husband has always been interested in what he sees as more primitive offshoots of Christianity, so he always reaches out to the priests of the various styles. So he was acquainted with the priestess and she with him. I believe she came to see him because she trusted him. Sadly, I believe she overestimated the power of his position—in vodun, there are few with more power than a priestess.

"She came to enlist my husband's aid in acting against Obo Undoto." Mrs. Hardwicke flushed slightly and cast Edwina a cautious glance. "I am not in the habit of eavesdropping on my husband's meetings with those who consult him, but in the priestess's case, she spoke very loudly. I couldn't help but overhear."

Edwina inclined her head politely. "Of course. But what did she say?"

"She complained that Undoto was a charlatan—something anyone who's attended one of his so-called services would know. However, I believe her primary purpose in coming to see my husband was to warn him. She said"—Mrs. Hardwicke drew in a breath—"and this is verbatim, that if he looked, he would find that all those who had vanished had attended Undoto's services."

Edwina blinked. "Is that so?" Her mind whirled, then she looked at Mrs. Hardwicke. "Do you know?"

Mrs. Hardwicke shook her head. "Sadly, no. I cannot vouch for her claim being true. It might be, but I cannot say from my own experience." She paused, her lips primming, then she confided, "The problem with acting on the priestess's word is that it is patently obvious that she's rabidly jealous of Obo Undoto and his influence, especially among her own kind. My husband considered taking her claim to Holbrook, but in all conscience, felt he could not. He could not convince himself that her version of the truth wasn't colored by a desire to cause trouble for Undoto." Mrs. Hardwicke sighed. "Live and let live is my husband's creed, and with that I cannot argue."

Edwina studied the minister's wife for a moment, sensing the deep concern underlying her resignation. When Mrs. Hardwicke glanced her way, she rose and briskly nodded. "Thank you for your help." She paused as Mrs. Hardwicke got to her feet, then held out her hand. "Rest assured that my husband and I will do whatever we can to cast light on this strange situation."

Mrs. Hardwicke lightly gripped her fingers and bobbed a curtsy.

Edwina put on her smile and took her leave.

But behind her façade, her mind was racing.

Back on the street, she allowed Carruthers, who had accompanied her as her footman, to hand her into the carriage. Before he shut the door, she said, "Tell Dench we have one more stop before returning to the bungalow. I want to visit Mrs. Sherbrook. I don't have her address, but I'm sure if you ask those we pass along the street, someone will be able to direct us."

Edwina was pacing back and forth in the drawing room when she heard the bell for the front gate jangle. She paused in her march, listening as Henry—quietly cursing—strode through the front hall and out to see who it was.

She strained her ears and heard the rumble of male voices

growing nearer. A second later, Declan's firm footstep sounded on the hall tiles. She picked up her skirts and ran for the hall.

On reaching the arched doorway, she ran straight into her husband. She would have bounced off his chest if he hadn't caught her.

Steadying her, his hands, warm and strong, cupping her shoulders, he looked into her eyes and slowly grinned. "Did you miss me that much?"

She arched her brows and made her tone sultry. "As a matter of fact...yes." Then she waved. "But enough of that—I didn't expect you back so soon." It was only midafternoon. "Did you find something?"

He released her and strolled to the tantalus by the wall and poured himself a drink. "By an unexpected stroke of luck, I discovered a place that all four men went to, but in the circumstances, I'm not sure if it's significant or not."

She perched on the arm of the armchair he favored. "What place?"

Glass in hand, he walked to the armchair, sat, sipped, then looked at her. "All four men attended at least one of that priest Obo Undoto's services." He sipped again, then frowned. "Wolverstone's man attended at least three, which, to say the least, seems a trifle odd. Wolverstone's men tend not to be religiously inclined."

She blinked, then blinked again. "Well," she said. Then she smiled intently. "Well, well, well, well, well!"

Puzzled, Declan looked at her.

She shifted to face him. Excitement bubbling in her veins, she told him what Mrs. Hardwicke had revealed about the vodun priestess's claim. "Oh, and I also got a list from Mrs. Hardwicke of all the young women and children who she knows have disappeared." She reached into her cleavage and, with a flourish, produced the folded list.

Declan took it; as he unfolded it and scanned the names, Edwina continued, "I made another copy—you can keep that one and give it to Wolverstone and Melville."

His jaw tightening, he nodded. The list was far longer than he'd expected and included far too many children. The young women were bad enough. He refolded the note and slid it into the inner pocket of his coat.

"And"—a note of triumph rang in Edwina's voice—"there's one thing more. After I left the rectory, I went to visit Mrs. Sherbrook. I asked her if her previous nanny—the one who vanished—had ever attended a service at Undoto's church." She met his eyes; hers were brilliant with purpose. "I thought that a nanny most likely *wouldn't* have gone to such an event—and if she hadn't attended services there but nevertheless had disappeared, then that would disprove the vodun priestess's claim there and then, and we wouldn't be distracted by it."

She drew in a portentous breath; from the light in her face, he guessed the gist of what she was about to reveal before she said, "To my amazement, Mrs. Sherbrook confirmed that Katherine Fortescue, who had also acted as her companion, had accompanied her to several of Undoto's services, the last occasion being on the day before Katherine disappeared."

Declan stared at Edwina's face while he juggled all the pieces of information they'd gathered. When, clearly expecting a more immediate response, she parted her lips, he forestalled her with a raised hand. "I'm thinking. It takes time."

She shut her lips and gave him a look, but consented to allow him a few moments more.

Finally, he grimaced and met her gaze. "First, let me tell you how I learned what I did. I started with Dixon—I was fairly certain Captain Richards at the fort would speak to me and tell me anything he knew. According to him, Dixon was a decent sort, but relatively quiet, which, as Richards pointed out, suits a posting such as Thornton because there's so little to do here. When I asked whether he knew where Dixon visited in the town, Richards mentioned several bars and taverns and that he and Dixon had gone to Undoto's church once, to witness the spectacle, as he put it. He said Dixon had gone a time or two afterward, with others, but just as a way to pass the time."

He shrugged. "There didn't seem to be anything noteworthy about that at the time. I went down to the docks and out to *The Cormorant* to speak with the men I'd had searching for information on Hopkins and Fanshawe. They knew of all the dockside taverns Hopkins and Fanshawe frequented—the usual for officers of the squadron and not the same ones Dixon visited. However, they'd also been told that Hopkins, and later Fanshawe, too, had asked others about Undoto's services. Apparently both attended at least one service, possibly more."

He refocused on Edwina. "That's when unexpected good fortune struck. Billings had come down to the ship to fetch something for Henry. He was waiting to return with me and overheard me say to the others that all I needed now was confirmation that Hillsythe had also attended Undoto's services, but how I was to get that given Hillsythe would not have spoken openly with anyone here… That was when Billings spoke up." Declan paused.

"And?" she prompted.

"Remember when you went to Undoto's church and Billings went with you as your footman-cum-guard?" When she nodded, he mentally girded his loins and continued, "Henry went, too. He was interested in seeing what all the fuss about Undoto was, and I was happy enough for him to be there, keeping a watchful eye over you and Billings from a distance."

Somewhat to his surprise, she merely nodded in understanding and looked at him eagerly, transparently willing him to go on.

He quickly complied. "Henry lurked at the rear of the church and fell in with an old sailor—one-eyed, peg-legged, and very ready to talk to another old tar. The two got on like a house afire. Henry learned that Sampson is a regular at the services—

they're his principal entertainment. He perches on a stool in the back corner and amuses himself by watching all the other Europeans who attend." Declan paused, then went on, "One-eyed he might be, but Sampson has a seaman's sight. He's observant, and most important in this case, he has a very clear, vivid, and detailed memory."

"So you and Billings came back here," Edwina guessed, "then you and Henry went to find Sampson."

Declan nodded. "Henry knew Sampson lived above a tavern not far from the church. He was happy to share all he knew over a meal and a pint of ale." Remembering, Declan shook his head. "He's amazing. He remembers everyone—he described you to a T. It was a part of his game with himself to learn everyone's name—to put names to the faces. Hillsythe stood out in his memory because he hadn't yet managed to track down his name."

"So Hillsythe attended Undoto's services, too."

"On three occasions, according to Sampson."

They fell silent. Declan felt certain they were thinking along the same lines.

After a few minutes, Edwina confirmed that. She met his gaze. "We've nearly got enough evidence to take back to Wolverstone, haven't we?"

"I'm still weighing that up." He settled back in the chair. After a further moment of cogitation, he said, "Undoto's church is the only place we've so far identified that all those people who've vanished who we've also managed to track visited." He raised his gaze to Edwina's face. "Do children attend the services?"

"Not that I saw. Only the altar boys. And I really can't see children—the usual scamps—being interested in Undoto's performance." She paused, then said, "So the children might be a separate group—taken from some other place."

He grimaced. "True. But the principal weakness in our thesis that attendance at Undoto's church is connected in some way with men and young women disappearing is that, given the signal lack of other entertainment in the settlement and the social following Undoto has gained, then attending his church is something virtually everyone here has done at least once."

She looked at him in disbelief. "You're saying attending Undoto's services could simply be coincidence?"

"No." He pulled a face. "I don't believe it's coincidence, but I can see the argument being made—especially by Holbrook if our findings are put before him." He paused, then said, "I'm thinking in terms of our need to give Wolverstone and Melville sufficiently solid evidence to be able to justify immediate and decisive action." He met her gaze. "After all we've uncovered, you and I *know* something distinctly untoward is going on and that it needs to be dealt with."

She nodded decisively. "It needs to be stopped." She studied his eyes. "We need something more."

He nodded and sat up. Reaching out, he set his glass on the side table, then glanced at the clock. "I'll go and see what the vodun priestess can tell us. There has to be more than what she told the good reverend."

Edwina rose from her perch. "I'll come with you."

He got to his feet and drew in a breath, but before he could utter the "No" on his lips, she caught his eye. Her eyes narrowed fractionally as she said, "She's a woman—she will almost certainly talk more readily, more openly, to me."

He hesitated.

"And"—she started toward the door—"we don't have time to waste." She paused in the doorway and watched him walk toward her. There was a challenge in her eyes as, her chin tipping up as she continued to meet his gaze, she stated, "And you'll be with me. We can do this together. It will be perfectly safe."

He halted by her side, read the message in her eyes. The priestess was a woman, after all; she would have defenses, possibly defenders, in place—and she'd wanted to tell someone in authority about Obo Undoto and the missing people. If anything, the woman would welcome them. As a joint venture, visiting the priestess should be safe enough. He grunted. "All right."

Edwina beamed at him, turned, and led the way out.

Eleven

Late afternoon was giving way to evening before Carruthers and Billings, who Declan had dispatched to find Sampson and ask for the vodun priestess's whereabouts, returned with directions.

Eager to be doing, Edwina climbed into the carriage and settled on the seat. When Declan sat beside her and the carriage started off, she could barely contain her smile. While she was keen to learn whether the priestess could give them more details about Undoto and the missing people, the principal source of her inner joy was Declan's acceptance of her position by his side. Of her right to be there, to share in all aspects of this venture—in all aspects of his life.

She'd assumed the priestess would live in one of the more peaceful areas of the settlement, but after traveling down Tower Hill, Dench turned the carriage east. Soon, they'd left the commercial district behind. Rather than turning toward the section of the settlement where Undoto's church lay, Dench continued east at an increasingly slow and difficult pace. The farther they rumbled, the more rutted the road became, and the more dilapidated and crowded the dwellings.

Eventually, the carriage turned, and they headed slightly uphill, away from the coast. Almost immediately, the carriage halted.

"Wait here." Declan swung open the door and stepped outside, shutting the door behind him.

Leaning forward, Edwina peered out, trying to get some idea

of their surroundings. The light was fading fast in that precipitous way night fell in the tropics. "A decent twilight would be helpful," she muttered, but that wasn't going to happen.

About them, deepening shadows cloaked a jumble of tumbledown houses, many little more than shacks. They weren't quite wretched hovels, but they were a far cry from any English cottage.

The road seemed to have ended; she squinted forward, but could see no obvious street or even path ahead.

She could hear Declan speaking in a low voice to Dench and Billings, who had come along as a footman-guard. Although she couldn't make out every word, she gathered that neither Declan nor his men had previously been in this area and hadn't known they were bringing her to such a potentially dangerous place. Their discussion revolved on how best to keep her safe.

Several tense seconds later, Declan opened the door; standing framed in the doorway, he met her gaze. "I don't suppose you would consent to remain here."

She studied what little she could read in his face. "Do you honestly imagine I would be safer here without you than I would be with you?" Besides, she wasn't about to let him go into that jumble of shacks to hunt down a vodun priestess alone.

His jaw firmed until it looked as if it were carved of stone. "The priestess lives among her people." With a tip of his head, he indicated the conglomeration of dwellings behind him. "In there."

Glancing past him, Edwina saw a native woman swathed in colorful shawls slip between two houses and disappear. She looked closer. The narrow gap through which the woman had gone was the opening to a path barely wide enough to be called an alley; as she watched, a man came striding out. He checked and studied the carriage, but then he looked away and continued walking down toward the shore.

Declan had followed her gaze. "She lives in the center of that warren, most of the way up the hill. That path leads to her door."

"Well, then." Edwina shifted forward on the seat and held out her hand. "Apparently, that's the path we have to take."

Declan swung back to look at her; he'd caught the multiple layers of implication in the simple words. After a second's hesitation—a moment of internal debate—his lips set, and he reached out and gripped her hand. "Has anyone ever told you you're an exceedingly stubborn woman?"

"Yes. Quite a lot of people, actually." After he'd assisted her down from the carriage, she slipped her fingers free and shook out her skirts. Straightening, she cast a more comprehensive glance around.

The track of a street Dench had been following ended in a cul-de-sac of beaten earth. Wedged cheek by jowl, dwellings rose ahead and to either side; for the carriage, the only way out was the way they had come. The area was dimly lit by a few smoky torches set in crude supports propped far apart. The flickering light illuminated the façades of the closely packed buildings in a haphazard way; shifting fingers of darkness constantly painted the scene.

There were people in the buildings, some leaning out of windows or sitting on the rough stoops, others gathered in small groups on what passed for front porches. Although no one had reacted to their presence, Edwina was perfectly certain every eye was trained on them.

Raising her gaze to Declan's face, she arched her brows.

His expression one of grim determination, he took her elbow and turned toward the opening through which the shawl-draped woman had gone. Quietly, he said, "Dench will turn the carriage and wait for us here. But in this area, a carriage and horses has significant value, so Billings has to remain with Dench. The fact that we're going to see the priestess should—and that's definitely a *should*—protect us from harm."

Edwina nodded and concentrated on their surroundings. Declan was doing the same. She was glad she'd decided to don her blue carriage dress in place of her day gown; the thicker fabric would afford her more protection in rough surroundings and also through any unexpected danger.

They reached the opening to the path. Declan slid his hand down her arm, grasped her hand, and led the way between the first buildings. She'd wondered whether the path would open up once they were past the entrance, but no; it continued barely wide enough for two people to pass. It wasn't straight, either, but snaked back and forth as it slowly ascended the hill to which the ramshackle houses clung. After the first houses, all subsequent dwellings had what appeared to be front doors that opened directly onto the alley. After they'd passed the first four houses, she glanced back and discovered she could no longer see the entrance to the path, much less the area beyond it.

Facing forward, she continued walking close by Declan's side. He wasn't striding out but keeping his paces short enough so that she could easily keep up. He was also doing his best to look everywhere at once.

The further they went, the more the houses seemed to close around them, until it felt as if they were walking through a maze with solid walls.

They came to an intersection with another, if anything even narrower, path. Declan paused only to confirm the way was clear, then he strode through the intersection and continued on.

She squeezed his hand and whispered, "Do you know where we're going?"

"Her door is on this path and is painted red. Apparently, it's the only red door in the entire warren."

Reassured, she kept her gaze trained ahead, searching for the red door.

They walked steadily for more than fifteen minutes before they spotted it.

Declan paused outside the brilliantly bright red door, then glanced at Edwina. "Ready?"

Her gaze on the door, she nodded.

He wound her arm with his, drawing her closer still, then raised his free hand and rapped on the door.

A wizened old woman of indeterminate age opened the door. She looked out at them without any expression at all.

Edwina spoke before he could. "We don't have an appointment, but we would very much like to speak with the priestess." When the old woman didn't immediately respond, Edwina added, her tone supplicatory, "It's vitally important we speak with her tonight."

The woman studied Edwina, then shifted her gaze to him. Her scrutiny reminded him of the grandes dames of the ton—and even more of his mother.

Finally, the woman stepped back and tipped her head deeper into the house. "Come."

Edwina smiled brightly and stepped forward; he slid his arm from hers, caught her hand, and followed her inside.

The corridor beyond the door was narrow and cramped, and entirely unadorned. The woman closed the door, then squeezed past them. She beckoned them on; she led them to an archway giving onto a small room to the right. Looking over Edwina's head, he saw three women and an older man seated on low sofas draped in the locally crafted brightly hued shawls.

"You wait here with the others." The woman waved them into the room. "I will tell her."

Without even asking their names, the woman walked away down the corridor; he and Edwina watched until shadows swallowed her.

They shared a single glance, then together stepped forward. He had to duck under the lintel; straightening, he took in what was plainly a waiting room of sorts. The other occupants studied them, but did not appear to find anything strange about their presence. Edwina tugged his sleeve, and when he glanced her way, she nodded toward a love seat set beneath the window overlooking the alley.

He escorted her to the love seat, waited until she sat, then sat beside her. From his position, if he turned his head, he could see the section of the alley before the priestess's red door. They'd passed a dozen or more people on their hike up the hill, but the higher they had climbed, the fewer passersby they'd encountered; there was presently no one in sight in the darkened alley.

A door opened and closed somewhere in the house, and then came a quiet exchange. Seconds later, the old woman reappeared in the doorway and beckoned one of the women who'd been waiting. The woman rose and, resettling her shawl about her, followed the old woman deeper into the house.

They had to wait their turn while the priestess tended her flock. Eventually, however, they were the only ones left in the waiting room. Again, they heard the sound of a door opening and shutting. They looked to the doorway, expecting the old woman to appear and beckon them as she had all the others.

Instead, a distinctly brisker, more decisive step sounded on the old floorboards, then a very different woman halted under the lintel of the open door.

She had to be the priestess, Edwina decided. The woman was of average height, with a wealth of curly black hair that sprang from her head in profusion and hung in elbow-length curls over her shoulders and back. Her skin was a rich ebony, her eyes equally dark, her gaze compelling. Full lips completed a face of remarkable strength; the priestess projected an aura of reined feminine power that was impossible to miss.

Edwina didn't remember rising, but she and Declan had both come to their feet.

The priestess's gaze roved over Declan, resting for a second on the sword belted at his hip, then her gaze shifted and traveled even more slowly, more intently, over Edwina.

She parted her lips on a respectful greeting, but the priestess silenced her with an abruptly raised hand.

"You may save your breath." The priestess's voice was low and husky; although clear, her words carried the warmth of an exotic accent. Her gaze, however, was hard and unfriendly. "I do not know who sent you here, but you were misled." The priestess's eyes flashed. "I will not assist you in getting rid of your baby. Life is precious—even more here than in the cities from which you come. Babies are God's gift, and I will have no part in ending such an innocent life—"

"What?" Edwina finally succeeded in finding her tongue. Irritated—frankly insulted—she brusquely shook her head. "No. We're not here for…"

Her words died as she suddenly realized what *hadn't* occurred on their journey south. She refocused on the priestess's eyes; the woman met her gaze, then, brows arching, looked assessingly at her again, her gaze lowering to Edwina's stomach.

Instinctively, she placed a protective hand over the still-flat expanse. Abruptly, she felt cold, then flushed, then decidedly giddy. Definitely shaky. She gripped Declan's arm—the only solid thing within reach—as, at least in her mind, her world reeled.

A child! She was carrying Declan's child!

She looked at him, and he met her gaze. His eyes had widened. His hand closed over hers and gripped.

Seconds passed as they stared at each other, realizing, assimilating—finally knowing. How the priestess had known, Edwina had no clue, but they knew, too; they simply hadn't thought of it, hadn't counted, hadn't realized.

Spontaneously, irrepressibly, she smiled joyously, and so did Declan—a moment of supreme, all-but-incandescent shared delight.

The moment stretched, resonating between them…yet neither had forgotten where they were or why they were there. Gazes locked, they each drew breath, reined in their burgeoning happiness, then, now hand in hand, they faced the priestess again.

Edwina had no idea what their expressions displayed, but the priestess studied them both.

The silence stretched for a moment more, then the priestess frowned, it seemed at herself rather than at them. "I apologize." Her tone had softened. "You did not know." It was a statement, not a question.

"No." Declan sounded as flabbergasted as Edwina still felt. "You'll have to excuse us—it was something of a shock..." His voice trailed away.

Then he shook himself and glanced at Edwina. She saw both joy and faint apology in his eyes, then he turned back to the priestess. "Thank you for telling us—for making us realize. Although we'd like nothing more than to celebrate our new knowledge, that wasn't why we've come to see you, and we have limited time. We're here to seek your help on a serious and potentially grave matter."

"Indeed?" Again, the priestess studied them, this time with more wariness. "And this serious and potentially grave matter is?"

"The people who've gone missing." Edwina stepped forward; she met the priestess's dark gaze. "We understand that you spoke to Reverend Hardwicke about your concerns. My husband and I have an interest in learning as much as we can about what's behind these apparently inexplicable disappearances."

Again, the priestess regarded them measuringly for several long moments.

Edwina held her breath and kept a confident but candid expression on her face.

Finally, the priestess glanced toward the window to the alley. "This is not a discussion we should have in full view of the world. Come to my office."

With that, she turned and led the way out of the room and down the long corridor.

Edwina hurried behind the priestess, Declan at her heels.

The priestess led them to a door at the end of the hall. She opened it and walked into a small, airless chamber that reminded Edwina of a medical man's consulting room. This room had skulls and bones displayed about the walls, too, as well as various animal fetishes, tasseled spears with carved shafts, and other ceremonial items, including several fearsome-looking scimitar-like swords and a collection of daggers. The room was smoky; a curious incense seemed to permeate the space. Edwina glimpsed a polished bowl in a corner, the contents of which were gently smoldering.

Strengthening the similarity between her office and a doctor's rooms, the priestess rounded a heavy wooden desk and sat in the chair behind it. She waved to the pair of rattan-and-cane chairs before the desk. "Sit." To Declan she said, "Please close the door."

He did, then returned to take the chair beside Edwina's.

Sitting rigidly upright, the priestess placed her hands, palms flat, on the desk and regarded Edwina and Declan, looking from one to the other as if seeking some sign. Eventually, she confided, "After speaking with your minister—supposedly a man of God—and having him dismiss all I said as fanciful... Although I admit he did not use that word to my face, I could see that that was what he thought. After that, I did not expect to hear anything more from your people about those going missing. I was given the impression that those missing were consigned to being forgotten, and that in the opinion of your leaders, there was nothing to be done."

Declan said, his voice even yet imbued with the innate authority of a man who commanded, "Those missing have not been forgotten, although I concede that their disappearances have been overlooked by those in authority here. I assure you that that isn't the case with the ultimate authorities farther afield. What I—and my wife—are here to do is to offer you another chance to alter the current situation."

Edwina leaned forward, laying a hand on the desk. "If you will share with us what you know, my husband and I are in a position to ensure your knowledge is communicated to those with the power to effect change here."

Declan kept his gaze trained on the priestess's face and held back the impulse to add further assurances to those Edwina and he had already made. The priestess would either trust them or not, and more fervent assurances from them would only make them look weak—not the sort of people who could deliver what, he suspected, the priestess sought.

After another long minute of studying them—no doubt waiting for them to speak further—the priestess nodded. "Very well." She paused as if gathering her thoughts, then said, "I am called Lashoria—I am a priestess of the vodun gods. As such, I am sworn by those gods to act for my people—for their good in all things, in all ways. I expect the ministers of the other gods— like your Hardwicke—to follow a similar creed, and largely I have found that to be so. However, in this settlement, there is now one who claims to be God-chosen, who follows his own path and seeks riches only for himself, not for his people, not for any god."

Lashoria fixed her dark gaze on Declan. "I am speaking of Obo Undoto." The emotion with which she imbued the man's name went far beyond dislike and solidly into hate. "He came here nearly a year ago. At first, he was merely another priest, another church." She shrugged. "We are tolerant here—there is room for all. So we all thought. But after some time, once Obo Undoto had attracted his congregation, things changed. He became"—she raised her hands up and outward—"bigger. As a man who has found his calling grows big. Confident. Swaggering."

Lashoria paused, then went on, "It was about that time that, one by one, people started disappearing."

Edwina tipped her head. "We've only heard of Europeans vanishing. Have some of your people vanished, too?"

Lashoria shook her head. "None of my people have vanished, but it was my people who brought me word. They do not like that Obo Undoto risks creating bad feelings between the Europeans and us. My people fear what will happen when he and his associates make a mistake, and the English governor and the major at the fort and the admiral of the navy retaliate.

"We do not want war. We do not want recriminations. This is Undoto's doing, not ours." Lashoria paused.

"We accept that is so," Declan quietly said. "The paths of those who vanished all lead to Undoto."

"Precisely!" Lashoria's eyes lit with righteous fire. "If you already know that, then you know that he is at the root of this—that he is orchestrating it." She leaned forward, her eyes wide and compelling. "And I have seen with my own eyes that he is meeting with bad men—men we do not talk about, not under any circumstances, so you must not ask. But I have seen Undoto consorting with these men. I have seen him laugh with them and take their coin." Lashoria drew back and regarded them soberly. "I have seen that with my own eyes, and it is my belief that Undoto is acting with those bad men to spirit people away...because that is what those bad men do."

She was speaking of slave traders; Declan knew the local populace feared saying their names. On that, he doubted Lashoria would bend. He cast about, then asked, "The bad men have so far taken only Europeans and have chosen to take men, young women, and children. Much of that is unusual. Do you have any idea—any suggestion or even vague notion—of what purpose these people have been taken for?"

Pursing her lips, Lashoria shook her head. "That I do not know. But I can tell you this—they are wanted for something they themselves can do, or why the careful picking of this one and not that one? So I believe those taken are still alive and being used to do…something, but as to what that something is, I cannot begin to guess."

Her gaze grew distant. Although she remained in her chair, facing them, her gaze was fixed far away. Then, in a careful, definite voice, the priestess stated, "If you want to learn where your people have gone, ask Obo Undoto."

They got nothing more of substance from Lashoria. Appearing to suddenly deflate and grow weary, she farewelled them and called the old woman to show them to the door.

The door through which the old woman waved them out was not the bright red one through which they'd entered but a nondescript door giving onto a narrow passage. Luckily, Declan's sense of direction was well-nigh infallible. Gripping Edwina's hand, simultaneously trying to calm the pricking of his instincts, he guided her back onto the path they'd walked in upon, joining it several houses down the hill from Lashoria's distinctive door.

It was only early evening, yet night had fallen with black finality. He was conscious of his eyes—his every sense—cutting this way and that, on high alert. It wasn't simply that there were even fewer people about than before but a tickling of presentiment he was far too experienced to ignore.

There could never be true silence in such a warren, with its seething mass of humanity confined in such a small space. But far from being comforting, the undercurrent of normal sounds—of voices, both murmuring and raised, of doors shutting, footsteps near and far, things scraping, pots clanking—made it impossible to hear any of the sounds that might alert them to an imminent attack.

Smells of foreign cooking—of spices, chilies, onions, meat, and fish—and of wood smoke tinged with occasional notes of sulfur and incense wafted around and past, another level of distraction.

His eyes had rapidly adjusted to the gloom; he scrutinized the way ahead, but saw nothing out of place. Despite all they'd learned, both private and mission-wise, neither he nor Edwina made any attempt to talk; from the tension in the fingers he gripped, she was as alert and on guard as he.

He readjusted his clasp about her right hand, shifting her so that she walked a half step behind him to his left—ensuring that his ability to draw his sword was unrestricted. He'd buckled on the scabbard as a matter of course. While many army and naval officers still wore dress swords when going about in society, there was nothing polite about his sword. It was a sharp, well-balanced, double-edged blade with a hilt designed for his hand—perfect for use in cramped surroundings, like on the deck of a ship or, worse, below decks.

Or in narrow, winding alleyways.

His palm started to itch, the need to close his hand about the sword's hilt escalating until he felt it as tiny pinpricks.

To hell with it.

Surrendering to instinct, he reached across and slipped his fingers into the guard, let the hilt settle against his palm, and loosened the blade in the scabbard.

Simultaneously, he squeezed Edwina's hand, whether reassuring her or himself, he wasn't sure. They were most of the way down the hill, approaching the second but last of the cross-alleys. Perhaps he was overreacting, and they would make their way out of the warren unchallenged.

He slowed as they neared the tiny cross-alley, paused at the intersection long enough to check to left and right, but there were no hulking shapes lurking in the shadows. Releasing the breath he'd held, he strode on, keeping his pace definite, confident and sure.

The alley they were following narrowed even more as it

zigged, then zagged between ramshackle houses. They'd gone around the zig and were approaching the zag when he heard what he'd been expecting—the stealthy rush of feet on the beaten earth behind them.

His heart leapt, then pounded. Three racing strides and they were around the zag, and he whirled, placing Edwina behind him as, his sword singing from its scabbard, he turned to confront the cutthroats who had hoped to catch them a few steps earlier—between the zig and zag, where he would have been even more cramped.

Two men rushed past the zag and pulled up, facing him.

Declan almost smiled as he realized there were only two. Two against one, the one being him, was no real challenge in his book—except that he had Edwina with him.

With the fingers of one hand clenched in the back of his coat, she hovered behind him.

The men's gazes traveled over him, then moved on to her—what little they could see of her.

Then the man in the lead smiled, confident and assured.

Declan saw the man's muscles tense for an attack.

Declan struck first.

The man's smile vanished, but his short blade had already been in his hand. He managed to parry Declan's thrust, but Declan didn't retreat, and the man fell back defensively, swearing as he struggled to meet Declan's blade.

At the corner of his vision, Declan saw the second man, who had hung back in the shadows, slide out and to the side.

Whether the man intended to make a grab for Edwina or come at him from the side, Declan didn't wait to find out; in the middle of a flurry of exchanges with the first man, the clang of steel on steel ringing in their ears, he sent a flashing slash at the second man, slicing his forearm and forcing him to leap back.

The second man snarled. Declan ignored him and concentrated on dealing with the first man, who seemed to be the swordsman of the pair.

But then the second man pulled a knife; from the corner of his eye, Declan saw the blade flash. *This is getting serious.* He needed to finish with the first man—

The second man edged around, clearly angling to come at Declan from the side.

This is going to get messy. And his wife—his *pregnant* wife— was too close. The carriage was only a short distance down the winding alley.

The second man, still snarling like a rabid cur, raised his knife.

"Edwina—run!"

"No!"

He had no idea if she was yelling at him or the second man.

Before either he or the man could decide, she darted forward.

The second man—heavy and beefy and at least three of Edwina—saw her fully for the first time. Distracted, he paused and leered as she rushed at him.

Heartened, the first man redoubled his efforts. Declan inwardly swore. He had to keep his attention on the first man's sword. Pushed by desperate fear to end the clash, he delivered a rapid succession of blows, then with a twist of his wrist, disengaged and slashed.

With a cry, the first man dropped his sword and clutched his belly.

Declan didn't wait to see him fall but immediately turned to deal with the second man—

Who was half doubled over, whimpering, with his hands clapped over his face. He'd dropped his knife and was blindly stumbling backward...

Declan glanced at Edwina, saw the battle fury in her face and glimpsed something small, thin, and shiny in her hand. He hadn't seen what she'd done, but now was not the time to discuss it. He grabbed her free hand, pulled her around, and took off down the alley.

They didn't have much farther to go, but the fight hadn't been quiet, and who knew how the local populace would react to what they would no doubt consider violent intruders in their patch?

The prospect of mob justice hovered in his mind as he drew Edwina on as fast as she could manage. She hadn't said a word— had made not a peep after that emphatic "No"; neither had he.

They neared the intersection with the last side-alley they had to cross.

Just before they reached it, two more heavily built cutthroats stepped into their path.

Declan didn't break stride. He released Edwina's hand, hefted his blade, and using the momentum of their downhill rush, went straight through the first man with a thrust to the gut that cut him down where he stood; the man had expected Declan to pull up and hadn't got his blade up in time.

Again, Declan whirled to engage the second man; again, Edwina had struck and more or less disabled the villain. Stumbling back against the nearest wall, the man was clutching his face and howling.

The sound was banshee-like and would certainly bring people out to see.

Declan swung the fist wrapped about his sword's hilt at the man's head and sent him crashing to the ground. Silenced.

With a quick look up the alley, he grabbed Edwina's hand. "Come on!"

They turned and sprinted for the end of the alley.

Five paces on, they cleared the last curve and saw the dusty clearing lying beyond the alley's mouth. All seemed quiet, with no sign of anyone lurking. They couldn't see the carriage, but Declan knew it would be there. He rapidly scanned right and left as they raced on, then he pulled Edwina forward so she ran ahead of him and slipped his fingers from hers. "Go. Straight to the carriage—don't stop. I'll be right behind you."

"You'd better be," she flung over her shoulder. Then she grabbed up her skirts and put on a burst of speed.

He listened for sounds of pursuit, straining his ears as he followed at her heels.

Then she burst into the clearing, and he followed. The carriage stood on the other side of the bare expanse, facing toward the town.

Billings had been lounging against the side. He straightened as he saw them. Eyes going wide as they raced toward him, he swung open the carriage door.

Edwina reached it. Declan caught her about her waist and hoisted her up.

To Billings, he yelled, "Get up!"

Gripping the doorframe, he yelled to Dench, "Get going! Fast as you can back to the house."

Declan hauled himself into the carriage. It lurched as he flung himself on the seat beside Edwina. As the carriage picked up speed, he leaned out, caught the door, and slammed it shut.

He slumped against the seat. His heart was pounding as if it would hammer its way out of his chest. He'd fought in countless battles, fights, and skirmishes—had been in situations where his life had hung on the edge of his blade—yet never had it felt this intense. Never had his every sense seemed heightened to this degree—abraded by a fear far greater than his normal, natural fear of dying.

For long moments, they sat in the dark, the only sounds the dull clump of the horses' hooves, the rattles as the carriage bounced over ruts and through potholes—and their harried breathing.

Like any good commander, he replayed the recent action in his mind, assessing and analyzing. The attack had been well planned; he and Edwina should have been taken.

If she'd obeyed his command to flee, they would have been. She would have run straight into the arms of the two men waiting at the last intersection, and no matter the outcome of his fight with the first pair, that would have been that.

Their attackers hadn't underestimated him. They'd underestimated her.

Hardly surprising. He'd done the same.

The realization...took the wind from the sails of any righteous reaction; upbraiding her for not following his orders but instead acting on her own clearly capable initiative would be gross hypocrisy.

Still...coming to grips with *what* his wife really was—that she was nowhere near as helpless, delicate, and fragile as she appeared, that while he had grounds for the intense protectiveness she evoked, he would be foolish to use his sometimes overblown fears as reason to hold her back—clearly wasn't a change of tack he was going to accomplish in a day.

Or even a week.

That she was now carrying their child wasn't going to help.

The ship of marriage—theirs, at least—was patently going to take time, effort, and shared understanding to find untrammeled winds and an even keel.

They reached better—less potholed—streets, and their breathing evened and slowed.

He felt Edwina's fingers slip into his hand.

He gripped them tightly.

She gripped back.

After a moment, she murmured, "It seems we might have learned something someone doesn't want us knowing."

He considered that, then said, "Did they follow us? Or were they watching the priestess's house?"

Neither of them had an answer.

Eventually, she drew her hand from his. Immediately missing the contact, the anchoring effect, he glanced across to see her hunting in her reticule, which throughout the evening had swung from her wrist. She drew out a handkerchief, easy to see even in the dim light, then lifted something from her lap and with careful strokes, wiped it clean...

He frowned. "What is that?" He reached for it.

She allowed him to take it. "It's a hatpin." While he raised it and, turning it this way and that in the poor light, examined it, she amended, "A modified hatpin."

With a decorative gold head, the tiny weapon—for that was most certainly what it was—possessed a very narrow spike about four inches long. Not a blade—there was no cutting edge—but when he tested its strength, Declan felt the resistance he associated with the very finest tempered steel.

"Julian gave it to me. He gave each of us—Millie, Cassie, and me—a set of six on our sixteenth birthdays." Edwina paused, then added, "He said that as he wasn't able to be there to protect us, then he could at least give us some weapons with which to protect ourselves."

Declan made a mental note to thank his brother-in-law when next he saw him.

Edwina shrugged. "As you saw, they work very well, especially as men never imagine that ladies like us would have such things, much less be inclined to use them."

He had, indeed, seen how open the men had left themselves to her attack.

She reclaimed the pin. After swiping it several more times through the handkerchief, she pulled the wide lapel of her carriage dress forward and slipped the pin into place.

He realized she had a matching pin in the other lapel. "I thought they were hatpins?"

"Hats, hair, scarves, shawls, lapels—they're easy to conceal." Through the shadows, she glanced at him. "When I'm out of the house, I almost always have at least two to hand."

He closed his hand about hers, then slowly, he grinned, raised her hand to his lips, and bussed her knuckles. "Good to know."

The knowledge would never truly ease his mind, but knowing she wasn't helpless—that she possessed real weapons beyond her wits and tongue, and would react to a threat and use them, and not freeze instead—certainly didn't hurt.

As the carriage reached the more civilized areas and the jostling eased, they sat side by side in the shadows and thought of all they'd learned.

Twelve

"We can't leave yet." Edwina paced back and forth, wearing a track in the drawing room rug.

"Wolverstone's orders were unequivocal. The instant I met with any resistance, any reaction whatsoever, I was to leave." Declan sat in one of the armchairs. Experience dictated that he remain outwardly calm for the sake of his crew and Edwina, yet it took effort not to join her. "Having not one but four men attack us constitutes a definite reaction."

She merely humphed and continued pacing.

He studied the set of her chin, the concentration in her features; agitated she might be, but it was an agitation born not of panic but of furious determination. "Wolverstone knows what he's doing." And *he* was still trying to absorb the more personal aspect of the priestess's revelations. In a quieter voice, he said, "They've already lost three men on this hunt."

And he wasn't going to risk losing her.

"Precisely! I'm not going to argue that we need to go any further or probe any deeper. That we were attacked suggests we've already stumbled on a vital clue. More, we've clearly established that whatever's going on is serious, that people are being kidnapped, not just wandering off." She made a scoffing sound. A second later, she halted and met his gaze. "I agree that we need to take what we know back to London. But is what we have to report solid enough to give Wolverstone and Melville what they need to push on and get the situation here—

whatever it is—addressed? Is it enough for them to be able to get those people back?"

Before he could answer, she went on, "Consider what we've learned. We've established that a curious assortment of people have gone missing over recent months. They haven't wandered off. Someone has taken them. However, there's nothing to suggest those missing are dead—most likely they're alive and being held somewhere. We've been told that all the missing adults attended Undoto's church—but that could be deemed coincidence. And if Holbrook is asked for his opinion, that's precisely what he will say. The only evidence we have that Undoto himself is involved, much less slave traders, is the verbal testimony of a vodun priestess. Wolverstone might accept that, but Melville won't, and no one else in the political hierarchy will either."

She paused only to draw breath. "If the priestess's information is discounted—and that's what will happen—then all we've succeeded in establishing as fact is that there are young women and children as well as men gone missing, and there's no sign that any of them are dead. We have no further clue to point to where they might have gone or who might have taken them or even how they were taken—nothing to suggest a direction for any subsequent investigation. We can't even prove they're in danger, and that they don't appear to be dead might very well *reduce* the urgency over finding them!"

Even though the observation supported her direction rather than his preference, he said, "As I understand it, the political pressure to deal with the situation here springs from the fear of the potential ramifications should this prove to be anything like the Black Cobra incident. Wolverstone knows that the only way to meet such a threat is with direct, decisive, and immediate action, however, too often in political circles, fear leads to dithering, and paralysis ensues. And Wolverstone is no longer in a position to simply ignore everyone else and issue orders. He was the one who called me in, but the actual order was Melville's."

"Exactly!" As if she couldn't bear to be still any longer, she started pacing again. Then she halted and swung to face him. "*That's* what I'm worried about—that we'll race home with our news, and Melville and his ilk will just dither over it, finding it murky and difficult and not being able to decide what to do, and ultimately, by default, they won't do anything. They won't believe, they won't understand, and most importantly, they won't *act*."

She captured his gaze; he saw the intensity of agitation in hers and realized there was more to her wish to push on than just a willful, adventurous bent. When she spoke, her tone held no plea; it did, however, hold a wealth of persuasion. "I know you were sent here to find out what happened to the four missing men, but it's the young women and children who've disappeared who most concern me. It's quite literally by the grace of God that I'm not standing in those young women's shoes. If Julian hadn't sacrificed himself for all of us, I might have been reduced to taking a governess or companion position out here. I might have been one of those taken."

Understanding dawned. Loyalty and *noblesse oblige*; she possessed large reserves of both.

He considered her hypothesis and couldn't argue; all she'd said was true.

She drew in a deep breath, then, her gaze steady on his face, said, "They—what might befall them—will haunt me if I don't do the very best, the absolute most I can to have them found and freed and given their futures back." Her eyes didn't leave his as, her voice softer, she stated, "Our good fortune—our continuing to be blessed—only increases the onus on us."

Noblesse oblige, most definitely, but more genuinely and far more deeply felt than the usual superficial nod to convention. She'd been born to the purple; the impulse to aid others and right society's wrongs was inculcated in her bones.

He, too, knew the ties of a higher loyalty, of an unquestioned commitment to an ideal. Why else was he there? Why else did Wolverstone and Melville have the ability to call on his family and be sure they would answer the call?

She seemed to read his understanding in his silence. Her chin firmed, and she gave a little nod. "It's up to us—those who can—to do all we possibly might to help those who cannot help themselves." Her brow furrowing, she recommenced her pacing. "In this case, that means finding some testimony from a more...*respected* source than Lashoria to back up her claims before we flee."

That last word emphasized the dilemma facing them. "Regardless, we do have to flee. Those men who attacked us— the ones who survived—will tell whoever sent them that they failed. I doubt whoever that is will wait to attack us again." He paused, evaluating, then said, "I would expect another attack by dawn. We can't stay here—" He broke off as Henry appeared in the doorway.

"Dinner's served, Captain. Ma'am."

"Thank you, Henry." Declan rose and held out his hand to Edwina. "We almost certainly have until midnight, at least. Let's eat and make plans." When she readily placed her fingers in his, he turned to Henry. "Get the others—all of you bring your plates to the dining room. Dench and Billings will have told you of our rapid departure after seeing the priestess. We need to tell you what happened, and then we need to work out our next moves."

Escorted to the dining room and served a tempting meal, Edwina was content to sit beside Declan and, while she ate, listen to him relate what they'd learned from the priestess. Whether it was a result of the excitement or because she was with child, she was ravenous.

Declan explained that they'd succeeded in getting a list of some of those missing, confirming that the number was much larger and the people more varied than those in London knew, and that courtesy of Sampson, they had enough to suspect that Obo Undoto's services might be a common thread in some of the disappearances. By the time he'd detailed Lashoria's claims that all those who'd vanished had attended Undoto's services, that Undoto himself was involved, and that he was dealing with slave traders, but that such claims would not stand without better proof, Edwina had cleaned her plate and was ready with a suggestion.

"Even though we don't have much time, we should try to find some way to substantiate Lashoria's claims." She pushed her plate away, leaned her elbows on the table, and propped her chin on her clasped hands.

All the men gave her their attention. Staring unseeing across the table, she went on, "Regardless of how much time we have, I doubt we'll find anyone to verify Undoto meeting with the men who no one will name. But if we can find someone with standing to support the *first* part of Lashoria's information—that all the adults who've gone missing attended Undoto's services— that will make the *second* part of her information—that Undoto himself is involved and that he's working with slave traders—difficult to dismiss. At the very least, those latter points would have to be investigated—Melville and his ilk could not let that lie."

She looked at Declan, a question in her eyes.

After a moment of staring at her, clearly turning her words over in his mind, he nodded. "You're right. After the brouhaha over the Black Cobra, if we can verify the link to Undoto via attendance at his services, then the suggestion he has a deeper involvement in what's going on and a possible connection with slave traders becomes impossible—much too dangerous—to ignore."

She nodded. "I've been wracking my brain to think of who we might get to confirm that those who've disappeared all attended Undoto's services. I suspect Sampson could, but like Lashoria, his word is not going to carry sufficient weight—not on its own." She met Declan's gaze. "But others—others in the army and navy who will be believed—have verified that all four of our men attended Undoto's services. What if we can find someone to verify that the four young women who've disappeared—those on Mrs. Hardwicke's list—also all attended? I've confirmed with Mrs. Sherbrook that Katherine did, but have not as yet asked about the other three."

Tapping a finger on the table, Declan frowned. "Eight out of eight is hard to argue away. That might be enough to shore up Lashoria's credibility." He paused, then refocused on Edwina's eyes. "Given time is so short, who are you thinking of asking?"

"I had thought perhaps Mrs. Hitchcock, but like Mrs. Sherbrook, she will probably only know of one, and possibly not one of the four on our list, so that won't necessarily help all that much. However, there is one person whose word would carry significant weight, who I understand has been attending all the services in recent months, and who would most likely know all the British women in the settlement by sight." She held Declan's gaze. "Lady Holbrook."

Lips compressing, Declan shook his head. "We can't trust Holbrook."

"I wasn't intending to. And I gather we'll be away before he might learn of my visit from his wife."

Declan shifted in his chair. Clearly reluctant, he asked, "What do you propose?"

"You want to leave here tonight—I assume you intend us to decamp to *The Cormorant*?"

He nodded. "As soon as we can. When we rise from this table, Billings can run down and alert those on board, hire a dray, and bring some of the others to help." Declan's gaze shifted to Billings, who tipped him a salute. "Meanwhile," Declan went on, "the rest of us will pack everything we brought off the ship and be ready to load up as soon as Billings gets back with the dray."

The others all murmured agreement.

Edwina nodded decisively. "That should fit nicely with what I believe I should do."

She arranged the last details in her mind, then met Declan's eyes. "When we're ready to depart, while you and the others take our baggage to the ship, Dench can drive me to the governor's house." She glanced at the clock. "It'll be late enough by then. I haven't heard of any social gathering being held tonight, and I'm sure I would have heard if there was one. Which means Lady Holbrook should be at home to receive me." She returned her gaze to Declan's face. "I intend telling her that you've received word about some urgent business matter, and so we're leaving in a rush, and as you're overrun with preparations, I've come to make our farewells and to thank her and the governor for their hospitality."

Declan regarded her silently for a full minute, then said, "I thought Lady Holbrook was in full support of her husband's stance regarding the disappearances being nothing worth commenting on. How do you think to convince her ladyship to entertain the notion that the four young women's disappearances are in some way connected with Undoto sufficiently for her to tell you whether they attended his services or not?"

"I don't—meaning I don't intend mentioning the disappearances at all. All I'll ask is whether she knows if those four women attended Undoto's services—that's all I need her to confirm." She paused, then added, "First, I'll lead her to admit that she would know all the British women who've attended. Then she won't be able to say that she simply doesn't know."

A long moment passed.

"I'll come with you." His face set, Declan straightened in his chair.

"You can't." When he frowned at her, she met his gaze. "Holbrook, remember? I can call and ask to see Lady Holbrook and almost certainly she'll receive me alone. Even if Holbrook is there, he and I will exchange greetings and our news, and then he'll leave me to his wife to entertain before I depart. But if you accompany me, Holbrook will attend us and stay with us—and if you're in a rush, we won't be able to dally, so you going off with him to leave me alone with her for long enough for my purpose is going to be difficult to engineer."

Declan transparently did not like her plan. After a moment, he said in his captain's voice, "We'll pack everything up here, and Henry and the others from the ship can take all our baggage down to the docks on the dray and transfer everything across to *The Cormorant*. Meanwhile, you, Dench, Carruthers, Billings, and I will take the hired carriage and go to visit the Holbrooks. I'll remain in the carriage—there's no reason anyone will know I'm there. Billings will see you to the gate. You go in alone, see Lady Holbrook, extract whatever information you can from her, then you return to the carriage, and we'll drive straight down to the docks and board *The Cormorant*."

She envisioned that scenario in her mind. While she had no qualms about entering the governor's house and speaking with such a genial matron as Lady Holbrook, there was no question that she would feel a lot safer on the drive there, and then on to the docks, with Declan sitting beside her. He would no doubt be wearing his sword; when they'd arrived at the house, he'd handed it to Henry to clean, but it was now sitting in its scabbard on the table in the front hall.

Until that evening, she'd never imagined Declan in a real battle. While in the narrow alley she hadn't had much time to study his style, what she'd seen had been more than enough to reassure her that he knew how to wield that sword.

His presence in the carriage, waiting for her while she attempted one last roll of the dice before they quit the settlement, would bolster her confidence.

She smiled, met his gaze, and nodded. "That's an excellent plan."

He humphed, but inclined his head as if sealing a pact. Then he went over his orders with his men.

Content on many levels, when he rose and drew out her chair, she smiled happily up at him, then followed the others from the room and threw herself into their packing.

Two and a half hours later, still garbed in her blue carriage dress, Edwina alighted from their carriage in the street outside the governor's temporary residence. After handing her down, Billings escorted her to the gate, where a bored soldier stood at ease.

In her most regal tones, she stated, "Lady Edwina Frobisher to see Lady Holbrook."

The soldier snapped to attention, saluted, then swung open the gate.

Billings caught her eye, bobbed his head respectfully, then returned to the carriage.

As she walked up the garden path, Edwina heard the carriage rattle on, then halt again. Declan had told Dench to turn the carriage so it faced toward the harbor, ready for a swift departure.

She was smiling fondly as she climbed the steps to the front porch. Declan had been almost humming with a tension that had escalated with every yard they'd drawn closer to the Holbrooks' bungalow. He hadn't—so deeply hadn't—liked letting her come in alone, but even with his instincts plainly riding him, he'd allowed her to step up and do her part.

He'd held back and hadn't tried to prevent her from sharing his life despite the perceived danger—largely illusory though it clearly was.

When the Holbrooks' butler opened the door and, recognizing her, obsequiously bowed her inside, she inwardly shook her head at Declan's irrational fears that any danger could possibly befall her while there—inside the house of the governor of British West Africa.

The butler left her in the front hall for only the bare minute it took him to confer with his mistress, then as Edwina had hoped, he escorted her into the drawing room, where she found Lady Holbrook, sans husband and at her ease.

Lady Holbrook had been reading a novel, which she was in the process of stooping to set aside. She straightened and beamed at Edwina. "My dear Lady Edwina. This is a delightful surprise."

Gliding forward, Edwina extended her hand graciously. "I had to come even though, sadly, it is only to bid you and your husband farewell."

"Farewell?" They touched fingers, her ladyship curtsying appropriately, then Lady Holbrook waved Edwina to the sofa. "I hadn't realized you would be departing so soon."

She sat and waited until Lady Holbrook resumed her seat before saying, "I fear business has caught up with us, and Declan needs must be off—to be perfectly candid, I'm not even sure as to where."

"We will be sorry to see you go. I know there are many here who will have wished to meet with you, but who will not now have that pleasure."

"You are entirely too kind. As I'm sure you will understand, Declan is furiously busy getting the ship ready to sail—we had not thought to depart quite so soon. He has charged me to deliver his good wishes to Governor Holbrook and yourself, and we both wish to convey our thanks for the hospitality you've shown us."

Lady Holbrook accepted the sentiments with a becoming smile and a gracious inclination of her head. "Again, it has been our pleasure to see you both here. If there's anything we can do to assist you before you leave, please do ask."

Edwina could barely believe her luck, to have the perfect opening handed her on a platter. She looked struck, then mused to herself, "Perhaps..." Then she came to herself and refocused on Lady Holbrook. "From our earlier conversations, I gathered that, courtesy of your position, you would most likely recognize all the female population to be found in the settlement—I refer to the British, of course."

Lady Holbrook's expression remained easy and assured. "I take my position at my husband's side quite seriously, so yes, I believe that would be so. Every month, we host a small reception to welcome newcomers to the town, of whatever station. Just a tea, so the lower orders are not overwhelmed. In general, all those invited—which is everyone—attend, so with very few exceptions I have, indeed, met all those here."

"Excellent." Edwina beamed her most ingenuous smile. "In that case, perhaps you might assist me in granting the favors—four, all similar—that certain ladies in London requested of me. Just before we left town, we attended a major ball, and Declan let fall that he was keen to stop in Freetown if time and the weather permitted. The ball was an utter crush, and of course, word got around. Four different ladies approached me and asked if I could make inquiries on their behalf. All had young women who were in some way connected with their families' staffs who had taken positions here. The daughter of the head gardener, the niece of their butler, that sort of thing. Apparently, those in England have been keen for news of their young women, but sadly, the posts haven't obliged, at least not recently." She paused, then lightly frowned. "Now I've put it into words, that sounds a trifle odd, but I'm sure there'll be perfectly normal excuses—too busy to write, rushed off their feet, and so on."

Lady Holbrook shifted, her stays faintly creaking as she sat straighter. "And you may add to that list the occasional bag of mail lost at sea."

Her expression unreadable, Lady Holbrook studied Edwina, and for the first time in their acquaintance, Edwina had no idea what was going on behind her ladyship's gray eyes, behind the pleasant, soft-featured face.

Then Lady Holbrook smiled. "If you will tell me the names of the young women, I'll see if I can dredge news of them from my memory. Sadly, these days, that might take a little time." Lady Holbrook rose. "Allow me to offer you some refreshment—just a cordial I have made up. It's especially refreshing in this heat."

Not wanting to disrupt her ladyship's direction, Edwina inclined her head in acceptance; indeed, it was dreadfully humid, and a refreshing cordial sounded rather nice.

Lady Holbrook glided to the tantalus by the wall. "By all means, tell me the names as I pour."

Edwina relaxed against the sofa. "Katherine Fortescue is one—a governess who I believe took a position with Mrs. Sherbrook. I meant to ask Mrs. Sherbrook when I had the chance, but it completely slipped my mind. Then there's Rose Mallard…" She named the other three women who had been on Mrs. Hardwicke's list.

"Hmm." Lady Holbrook busied herself at the tantalus, then returned with two sherry glasses containing a golden liquid, similar in color to sherry. With a frowning, absentminded look on her face, she handed Edwina a glass, took a sip of her own, then returned to her armchair. "If you will give me a minute…"

Edwina took a small sip of the cordial; it tasted very similar to ginger wine, of which she was fond. She swallowed a larger mouthful, then airily said, "I forgot to ask how long each young woman has been here, but perhaps you might have seen them about town—perhaps at Obo Undoto's services? Such a sighting alone would ease the minds of their families at home."

Lady Holbrook met her eyes.

Her ladyship's gray gaze had sharpened, and her expression had grown strangely watchful. Rather than frown or show any other sign of awareness, Edwina smiled unaffectedly, took another sip of the cordial, then asked, "Do you recall seeing those young women at any of Undoto's services?"

Lady Holbrook's gaze unfocused.

Edwina assumed she was consulting her memory. She sipped

the cordial; as soon as she had her answer, she would take her leave.

Finally, her ladyship refocused. She looked directly at Edwina, then nodded. "Yes. All of them attended at one time or another." A second elapsed, then Lady Holbrook added, "Just as you did."

Edwina blinked. "Are you sure?"

Great heavens! Was she slurring?

Lady Holbrook's lips stretched in a slow smile.

Edwina studied that smile—and felt a chill run down her spine.

"I'm quite sure, my dear." Her ladyship held out her hand. "Now perhaps you had better give me that glass before you drop it—it is one of a set, you see."

In utter stupefaction, only just managing to move her suddenly weighted limbs, Edwina held up the almost-empty glass. She stared at it in mounting horror. Then, moving with increasingly unnatural slowness, she turned her head and looked—really looked—at Lady Holbrook. "You...?"

Her ladyship's smile grew edges. "You're a fool, my dear. You ask too many questions."

Edwina blinked, then blinked again. With one last Herculean effort, she shifted her hand and forced her fingers apart. The glass slid from her grasp and shattered on the tile floor.

A ripe curse—one no lady should even know—fell on her ears.

The sight of Lady Holbrook's face contorting with rage briefly filled her ever-decreasing field of vision.

Then her lids fell and remained down, and she knew no more.

Thirteen

S tuck in the carriage outside the governor's house, Declan couldn't even stand up, much less pace. "What the devil is taking her so long?"

He'd muttered the question several times, with increasing frustration.

He felt helpless, powerless, and he didn't like the feeling. He'd even contemplated going over the wall and skulking through the garden to see if he could catch sight of Edwina in the house… Only the thought of what she would think if she saw him had made him reject the idea.

He'd barely been able to stifle his instincts enough to allow her to walk into the plainly guarded house. Now, as the minutes ticked by and she didn't reappear, he was considering leaving the carriage, striding across the street, and going inside to fetch her. The guard would presumably realize he'd been waiting in the carriage all along, but what did Declan care what the man thought, or that he might later mention Declan's strange behavior to Holbrook…

Damn! He shouldn't—couldn't—call attention to himself in such a manner. He had no idea who Melville and Wolverstone would send to investigate here next, and if it was one of his brothers or cousins…no.

Yet the itch beneath his skin to find Edwina and reassure himself that she was safe and well was growing minute by minute more intense.

His gaze remained locked on the gate of the governor's residence. He filled his lungs and reminded himself that he'd been paranoid enough to set watchers around the house. After the carriage had halted, making use of the shadows, he'd slipped out and, with Billings and Carruthers, had done a quick reconnoiter around the compound; until then, he hadn't realized that the house was the very last house in this neighborhood—it backed onto the slum that straggled down the flank of Tower Hill. He'd left Billings to watch the rear wall and the entrance to the alley that led into the slum, and Carruthers was lounging not far from the gate they'd discovered down one side of the large property. There was no other exit bar the front gate, so she was still in there and presumably—

Billings came pelting out of the narrow walkway that led to the rear gate. The midshipman flung himself at the open carriage window. "Capt'n—you've got to come! They've taken her out and into the stews. Carruthers is following."

Declan had flung open the door, leapt to the street, and was racing for the walkway before he'd even thought. "What happened?"

Reaching the walkway's entrance, he glanced back and saw that Dench had tied off the reins, dropped to the street, and was pounding after them. Declan turned and plunged into the dark passage.

"A local boy slipped out about twenty minutes ago," Billings huffed from behind Declan. "He went into the slum, then returned, bringing along three burly locals. They went in through the side gate, then came out again—one leading the way, one following, and the middle one carrying your missus rolled up in a rug."

Fury, fear, and incipient panic roiled in Declan's gut. "Are you sure it was her?"

"Aye. Not many women around here with such white skin and hair of pale gold. Carruthers saw, and he followed 'em. They passed me by. As soon as they had, I came for you."

"Good man." Declan reached the end of the property; he stepped aside and waved Billings on. "Take point, but keep it quiet."

Billings slipped past, running almost without sound through the shadows along the rear wall of the garden. Declan fell in at his heels, with Dench close behind.

Five paces more, and Billings turned into the alley that plunged and twisted down through the slum. The alley was barely wide enough for two men to move abreast, and its floor was of earth beaten flat by the passage of countless feet. Winding between ramshackle dwellings constructed of timber, daub, rushes, canvas, and woven fabric, this particular alley was merely one of a spider's labyrinth of paths that spread like the veins of a living beast and carried people—the slum's lifeblood—through its heart.

The sensations of close-packed humanity pressing in all around them assaulted Declan's senses; luckily, that very density of life, combined with the composition of the buildings and the dusty path, muted and masked the sounds of their passing.

There was no light save that shed by the moon. Tonight, that was faint, but enough to illuminate their way; eyes accustomed to the blackness of oceans at night had no difficulty piercing what to others would be disorientating gloom.

It was late; most of the slum dwellers rose with the dawn and by now were in whatever passed for their beds.

Declan's paramount fear, the one that had closed claws of iron about his heart—that they wouldn't be able to catch up with Carruthers and the men who had Edwina, that they would lose the trail and he would lose her—escalated as they descended the hill in a series of looping switchbacks.

Then Billings glanced over his shoulder. "I can see Carruthers ahead. They're still moving."

Thank God. Declan's mind had been stalled, absorbing sensory information, but too strangled by imminent panic to make any plans. As the constriction about his heart eased a fraction, his customary faculties kicked to life. After a moment, he asked Billings, "How far?"

"Around the next bend," Billings flung over his shoulder.

His long legs allowing him to easily keep up with his midshipman, Declan seized several moments to plot the action in his mind, then he tapped Billings on the shoulder and leaned nearer to say, "Signal Carruthers—let him know we're here, then I want you and he to stand aside and fall in behind me and Dench."

Billings nodded. He put on a spurt of speed as they rounded the next curve. A few seconds later, he slowed to a cat-quiet stride.

Declan looked past Billings and saw they were coming up on Carruthers. The older man was slouching along, hands in his pockets, his gaze apparently on the ground as he followed seven or so unthreatening yards behind a large armed local thug.

The thug was following another heavyset man who was carrying a rolled rug hefted over one shoulder. A tangle of pale ringlets and one small, very white hand dangled below the edge of the rug.

Fury flared, then turned to icy rage in Declan's veins.

Beyond the two men, Declan caught sight of another armed man in the lead. None of the men seemed in any hurry. They were striding along at an easy pace, heading for the harbor—not for the main wharves but angling toward the cove where local fishing boats were moored.

Carruthers heard them approaching; he glanced swiftly back, and relief etched his face. Billings gave him the sign, and Carruthers stepped to the side, as did Billings, allowing Declan, followed by Dench, to move into the lead.

Declan immediately fell into the same slouching walk as Carruthers had employed. If any of the thugs thought to check behind them, all they would see was four sailors ambling along, no doubt returning to their ship after spending some recreational hours with the female denizens of the slum. That was a common enough sight in that area to raise no alarm.

Swiftly, Declan revised his plan. He leaned closer to Dench. "Change places with Carruthers."

Once that was done, Declan beckoned all three men closer. In case their targets looked back, he kept a smile on his face and occasionally gestured as if he was merely sharing some joke as they rolled home, while in reality he ran down the orders for this battle—one he had to win. They needed surprise on their side, and more than anything else, they needed to get Edwina into their hands unharmed.

When he reached the end of his orders, he drew breath and met Billings's, Carruthers's, and Dench's gazes. "Ready?"

The grim looks in their eyes belying their vacuous unthreatening expressions, the three nodded.

Declan faced forward. He lengthened his stride and, apparently unhurriedly, closed the distance to the last thug in the line of three. As he drew near, he went onto cat-feet, silently placing his boots in the helpfully soft dirt.

The thugs' confidence as they sauntered down the hill hadn't escaped him; this was their territory, and they expected no challenge within it.

Silently, Dench moved into place beside Declan. Carruthers lurked on the far right, while Billings was a step behind.

Declan quietly eased his sword from its scabbard, slowly drawing the blade free with not a whisper of a telltale hiss.

Then he cut his eyes to Dench and nodded.

Dench pounced, going for the nearest man's head, locking his palm over the man's mouth before he could utter a sound.

Declan struck, one single thrust ensuring the man was incapacitated.

As the thug slumped in Dench's embrace, without even a split-second's pause, Declan and Carruthers flowed around Dench and his captive and with rapid strides closed on the man carrying Edwina.

The man's head came up, no doubt sensing the disturbance behind him.

Before he could turn and glance back, a slash of Declan's sword did for the man's hamstrings.

Startled, he yelled. Even before the man's legs folded under him, Carruthers had grabbed the rolled bundle that was Edwina and hauled her free of the man's slackened grasp.

From the corner of his eye, Declan saw her scooped safely into Carruthers's arms. He forced himself to trust her to his men.

Leaving the felled thug for Billings to dispatch—which the midshipman promptly did—Declan stepped into the center of the alley and faced the last thug, the group's point man.

He'd whirled at his mate's cry. In his right hand, the man held a machete, the long wide blade glinting evilly in the weak light.

Declan felt his lips lift in a smile that promised retribution. Sliding his second blade—a long knife—free of his boot, he beckoned the thug on. "Please. I'd like nothing better."

The man's eyes widened. His gaze dropped to his comrades, sprawled silent and unmoving in the dirt, then rose to take in Dench and Billings as they lined up on either side of Declan.

The man sucked in a breath—then he turned and fled as if the hounds of hell were after him.

Declan actually felt disappointed. He listened for an instant, but no sound of imminent attack reached him. He glanced questioningly at Billings.

The midshipman shook his head. "Can't hear anything."

Declan resheathed his blades and stepped back to lift the flap of rug that covered Edwina's face as, rolled up in a fine silk carpet, she lay supported in Carruthers's brawny arms. Her lids were down, her features slack; she appeared to be deeply asleep. Declan slid two fingers beneath her chin, searched, and found her pulse throbbing soundly, the beat strong, the rhythm steady.

"Drugged, I'd say," Carruthers offered.

Declan nodded, then met Carruthers's eyes. "Can you carry her all the way to the wharf?"

"Aye." Carruthers hefted his precious burden, resettling her more securely in his arms. "She's a slip of a thing—she don't weigh more'n a handkerchief."

Declan nodded and turned to the others. They weren't safe yet, and while he would infinitely prefer to have Edwina's warm weight in his arms, soothing and reassuring his abraded emotions, he needed his hands free, needed to be able to defend her. He was the best fighter they had.

He set Billings to scout ahead and put Dench, a blade now in his hand, to guard their rear. Sacrificing stealth for speed, guided by the glint of moonlight on water and the ever-present scent of the sea, they strode swiftly through the rest of the slum, along several narrow lanes bordering the lesser commercial wharves, then stepped onto the solid planking of Government Wharf.

They made it to where *The Cormorant*'s tender was waiting, pulled in close to a set of water stairs, without challenge. They'd discussed the logistics of their departure earlier; the carriage had been hired—it would be found and returned to the stable the next day. Henry, all their baggage, and all his other crewmen had already been ferried to the ship; the tender with its crew of four was waiting to carry them—the last of their party—to where *The Cormorant* bobbed well out in the harbor.

Declan had had Caldwell and the crew move the ship farther out from shore—closer to the open sea—in case anything had gone wrong and they needed to beat a hasty retreat.

As he took Edwina's limp form from Carruthers, then went quickly down the stairs and stepped into the tender, he blessed the instinct that had prompted him to move the ship.

He sat in the bow with Edwina cradled across his lap and tried to think—to imagine what had gone wrong. Clearly something had, but no matter how hard he studied her face, he had to agree with Carruthers. She'd been drugged, but whatever had been used seemed to have merely put her to sleep. Her cheeks were still rosy, her lips soft and full, still their usual luscious pink, and there was no sign of strain or pain about her eyes.

As far as he could see, she was still dressed precisely as she had been when she'd gone through the governor's gate. The strand of South Sea pearls he'd given her as an engagement gift was still about her throat, and the matching earrings still dangled from her lobes. There was no sign she'd been attacked, and she hadn't been robbed. She'd simply been...

Taken.

Frowning, he resettled the rug about her, protecting her face from the droplets flung off the oars. Then he lifted his gaze and stared at the dark but oh-so-comforting bulk of his ship as they steadily drew nearer.

What if he hadn't rescued Edwina? Would she have gone the way of the other young women who had disappeared?

His instincts returned a definite affirmative.

She'd been drugged by someone in the governor's house, then passed on to whoever was spiriting Europeans out of the settlement.

Who in the governor's house?

Edwina almost certainly knew.

She was a duke's daughter; one word from her, and Holbrook would be tossed into shackles and whisked back to London to face his superiors.

But she hadn't intended to see Holbrook.

Regardless...

They reached the ship. Declan settled Edwina over his shoulder and went quickly up the ladder.

He stepped onto the deck, then eased her back into his arms. Instead of heading directly for the companionway, he strode to the stern.

He halted before the ladder to the poop deck and the bridge;

Caldwell was at the wheel, with Johnson standing by—both men's gazes had lowered to Edwina. "Mr. Caldwell—with all due caution and as quietly as possible, up anchor and all hands to the oars."

Caldwell snapped to attention. He knew that tone of voice, understood what the order for caution and silence meant. "Aye, aye, Captain." Immediately, he started issuing quietly spoken orders that Johnson relayed in similar fashion to Grimsby, down on the main deck. The bosun in turn passed the instructions on to the men who, alerted to Declan's return, were streaming up from the bowels of the ship.

The order for silence passed swiftly through the crew; lips were buttoned and footsteps muted. On receiving the order to man the oars, most of the ship's company descended to the lower deck.

Declan shifted his gaze to his navigator, now also alert and awaiting directions. "Mr. Johnson—I want us out of the harbor and the estuary and on the high seas on our fastest course for Southampton as soon as may be."

"Aye, aye, Captain!" Johnson swung down the port ladder and rushed to consult his charts.

Henry popped up at Declan's shoulder, his gaze fixing on Edwina's still face. "Lor' love us. Will she be all right?"

The one question Declan needed an answer to—preferably fifteen minutes ago. He managed to say, "I think she's been given a sleeping draft."

"Well, then." Henry waved him to the companionway to the stern cabin. "Best we get her comfortable so she can sleep it off."

Declan hesitated, then he looked at Henry. "Can you take her down and make her comfortable?" If he took her down, he wouldn't be able to tear himself away, and he needed to be on deck in case those who definitely wouldn't want them to leave attempted to get in their way.

The weight of his captaincy—the responsibility any captain

bore to his ship and his crew—was a burden he'd carried without a thought for more than ten years. He felt that weight now, but he couldn't turn aside from something that was such an intrinsic part of him. And, ultimately, his presence on deck might prove vital to Edwina's continued safety.

"Of course. Give her here." Henry held out his arms, and Declan carefully transferred his precious bundle into his steward's care. Henry settled her in his hold. "Me and the boys will take care of her, never fear."

Declan saw the two cabin boys rushing up to report to Henry. With a nod to them all, he turned to the bridge.

To a man, his crew knew what they were doing; they'd slipped out silently from more than one harbor before. Tonight, with just enough moonlight and starlight to guide them, with the oars repetitively dipping in silent precision, *The Cormorant* slid all but noiselessly through the gentle waves of the harbor and out into the estuary, then it rode the rippling currents as Declan, having taken the wheel, ordered the oars to be shipped and called up the sails.

The wind caught the canvas. The mainsails billowed, then filled and pulled taut.

The resulting surge sent relief flooding through him.

As he brought *The Cormorant*'s bow onto the first tack of the course Johnson had mapped out, heading west-north-west, and the few lights still dotting Freetown dwindled behind them, Declan drew in a huge breath and held it, savoring the salty tang of the sea that was the breath of life to him, then he exhaled and felt the worst of his battle tension leave him.

No one had come after them—no one had stopped them. And now that *The Cormorant* was on the open sea, no one would; he'd back his ship against any other on the waves.

He called up the sails one by one. His crew worked like the well-oiled machine they truly were; soon they'd come around to a northerly tack and were flying over the waves under full sail.

Only then did he hand the wheel to Caldwell and go below.

He'd done all he could to ensure they were out of danger, all he could to ensure her safety as well as his crew's.

Entering their cabin, he found Edwina still sleeping.

Henry had been sitting on the chair before the desk, keeping watch. He came to his feet and saluted. "Not a peep out of her, and her breathing's steady." The steward colored beneath his tan. "Just a suggestion, but you might want to loosen those stays of hers. She'll likely breathe easier."

Declan nodded. "I'll do that."

With a brief salute, Henry went out and quietly closed the door.

Declan crossed to the bed and stood looking down at his wife, at the angelic vision she made with her curls gleaming silver-gilt in the lamplight and the lightest of blushes tingeing her fair cheeks. She looked utterly peaceful, utterly serene.

Distinctly Madonna-like.

His gaze drifted down the body he now knew so well—and stopped just below her waist. Lying as she was, flat on her back, he could almost believe...

He forced in a breath and let it out on a sigh. He wouldn't know more until she awoke. In the meantime, he'd do well not to let his imagination run riot.

Henry, however, had been right. Declan bent over Edwina, gently rolled her to her side, and started undoing the laces of her carriage dress. Once he'd freed her from the folds, he undid the laces of her corset and eased the constricting garment off. He thought for a moment, then removed her shoes and garters and rolled down her fine silk stockings.

Her feet were impossibly delicate and dainty; he curved his hand about one arched sole. The warmth of her foot reassured him, and something deep inside him eased.

They were out on the open sea, where the air was cooler; the temperature in the cabin was steadily falling. Settling her once more on her back, he drew the sheets and coverlet over her chemise-clad shoulders.

That done…he didn't know what else to do. He looked around, but almost immediately, his gaze returned to the bed.

He couldn't seem to shift his attention from it, from her. At the same time, he knew it would be foolish to start imagining, much less try to think anything through, to think back and re-live the last hours. That way lay a morass of useless feelings—feelings he'd felt intensely at the time, but which had little to do with now.

Much less with what came next—not that he knew what that would be.

After several minutes of indecision, he fetched the chair from before his desk, set it beside the bed, and sat. Taking Edwina's hand in his, letting his thumb stroke the fine skin, he waited for her to wake up and tell him—show him—that all the fears he was holding at bay were unfounded.

In the end, he realized there was, in fact, one thing he could do.

He could pray.

Edwina swam slowly up from the depths of a sound and refresh-ing sleep. She wasn't normally a deep sleeper, but this morn-ing she could feel the sheer depth of her relaxation all the way to her bones…

Memory returned in a rush.

On a smothered gasp, she opened her eyes—and saw a fa-miliar ceiling of polished oak dappled with the first glimmer of sunrise reflected off the waves. She'd seen that sight sufficiently often in recent times to instantly be certain of where she was.

Relief washed through her. Whatever had happened after she'd succumbed, Declan had rescued her. And their baby. She spread one hand protectively over her stomach. She and the baby were safe.

But what of him? She was lying in the middle of the bed, not snuggled on the side closest to the wall as usual. Reaching out with her left hand, she confirmed that there was no large hard body sprawled alongside her.

Panic rose and clutched.

Eyes widening, she turned her head—and saw him.

He sat slumped in a chair a mere foot away, apparently as deeply asleep as she'd been. His arm was extended, his hand lying palm upward on the coverlet as if he'd been holding her hand while she slept.

Her gaze raced over him. No bandages; no injury that she could see. Relief flooded her anew.

Then she noticed he'd removed his sword belt and laid the freed sword on the floor next to the scabbard. There was blood on the blade.

What had happened after she'd fallen senseless? Had he had to fight to free her?

For a long moment, she let her senses drink him in, let the sight of his broad chest rising and falling in a regular rhythm reassure and calm her heart. Gradually, something approaching her customary equilibrium returned, yet a sense of emotional vulnerability remained.

Hardly surprising that her emotions were a trifle overset; she—and he—had been through so much in the last day.

Tipping her head back, she looked over her head at the stern windows. It was indeed daybreak; she'd slept through the night.

Looking back at him, she shifted onto her side the better to watch him.

His lids flickered, then rose slightly. Through the screen of his lashes, he stared at her.

Three seconds ticked by, then he sat up, gathered her—sheets, covers, and all—into his arms, hauled her onto his lap, and kissed her.

Kissed her as he'd never kissed her before, a ravenous claiming that stopped her heart.

Then set it beating, pounding, surging anew as she wrestled her arms and hands free, reached for him, speared her fingers through his hair, gripped his head, and kissed him back.

Ferociously.

For uncounted minutes, their emotions clashed, wild as the sea and equally powerful. He nipped at her lips; she tangled her tongue with his. Their lips fused, melded, then parted on a gasp only to come together again in giddy, desperate, greedy need.

He plundered and she rejoiced.

She held him to her, tempted and incited, and he devoured.

Buttons slipped from their moorings; they pushed the covers away. Then she rose up and took him in. With one swift, slick slide, she claimed him—impaled herself on his rigid length—and their world stopped.

Breaths bated, eyes wide, lost in each other's gazes, they froze...

Then sensation gripped them, passion rose and seized them, and their lids fell as they gave themselves up to the wild joy of their togetherness.

Sharing.

Even in this. Even at this extremity of emotion, of unrestrained, unadulterated feeling.

Eyes closed, her lips parted on her panting breaths, she gripped his wrists as his fingers sank into her hips, and he wordlessly urged her on.

Together, they rode—flat out, hearts thundering as they raced for the cliff at the edge of their world.

And, together, soared.

Ecstasy had never shone so brightly, had never shattered them so completely, so blindingly.

Had never scored their hearts so deeply.

Like all storms, this one, too, eventually subsided.

Leaving them, chests heaving, slumped together in the chair. His arms were locked around her. Hers reached as far around him as they could.

Neither wanted to ever let go.

After uncounted minutes of wordless communion, they disengaged. She rose and used the facilities, then returned to his arms, curling her legs and sinking against him, snuggling into his embrace.

Eventually, his hand stroking gently down her spine, soothing him and her both, with his jaw resting against her hair, he murmured, "I don't know if I can do that again." After a moment, he clarified, "If I can survive that again."

She knew he wasn't talking about the past half hour's activities. She still had no idea what had happened through their last hours in the settlement, yet... Without raising her head, she said, "But you did survive it. We both survived it. Not only that, we got all the information we needed to get—and more."

Raising her head, she looked him in the eye. "We triumphed. Together." She held his gaze. "I would never have felt so confident going into the governor's house if I hadn't known you were outside watching over me. I had no idea anything untoward would happen, but if it did, I trusted you would step in and save me. That you would protect me. Me and our child. And you did. I put my faith in you, and you didn't fail me. Or our baby."

She tipped her head, compelling him, convincing him with her eyes as well as with her words. "So we achieved what you'd been sent to achieve—and that will help many others and very likely save innocent lives. That proves this works. That me traveling with you works. We just proved beyond question that together we can achieve far more than if you work alone."

He returned her regard, his gaze equally steady, but a hint of cynical resignation had crept in. After a long moment of gazing at her—during which she held her tongue—he shook his head. "I don't understand how you do it. How you make this"—he gestured between them—"you being with me on a mission, for God's sake, seem entirely reasonable. Indeed, logical. Even desirable."

"Because it is." She made sure her confidence resonated in her tone. "At least for you and me. As far as I can see, we made only one mistake this time, and we'll learn from that."

"We will?"

His skepticism was showing again. She nodded decisively. "The next time I walk into the lion's den, I'll make sure I take you with me."

Declan knew she'd just cast a subtle lure to distract him. He also knew that this was one issue on which he was destined not to win. Not least because, while some small part of him had entertained the vague notion that his marriage to Lady Edwina Delbraith would follow the conventional norm, that small part was massively outgunned by the adventurer that ruled his soul.

He understood her, and heaven help him, she understood him. The questing of the soul that lay at the core of any adventurer was something they shared.

That the duke's daughter he'd chosen to marry would, underneath her golden glamour, prove to be as adventurous as he... Well, Fate was no doubt cackling herself into fits.

Yet even after the excoriating fears he'd endured over the past hours, one fundamental truth, one immutable conclusion—one he'd already, in his heart of hearts, reached—remained.

If he couldn't take her with him, he wouldn't go adventuring again. The thought of leaving her behind...he knew he'd never do it. That was the one thing he truly wouldn't be able to bear. Not seeing her sweet face on his pillow every morning. Not hearing her musical voice, not having her smile light up his day.

Those were now his treasures. His most precious pleasures.

The bright jewels of his soul he could no longer live without.

And yet, because she was who she was—the adventurous

woman behind the glamour—he would never have to make that choice.

She'd sworn to cleave to him through sickness and health, through life and death—through danger and mayhem.

He knew that was how she saw it and how she intended to honor their marriage.

He could do no less.

She challenged him even in this—and even in this, he could not, and would not, fail her.

She was watching him still, waiting, guessing, no doubt, what track his mind had taken. She was waiting to see how he would respond—whether he would reach for her olive branch and step over the tiny rift in their road and continue hand in hand with her, or whether he would argue further.

His eyes locked with the bright blue of hers, he arched his brows. "So who was the lion?"

She didn't hesitate. "Lady Holbrook."

He blinked. "*She* drugged you?"

She nodded.

"Did the governor know?"

"I don't believe so. In fact, he might not even know I called. The only people who saw me were the soldier on the gate, the butler, and her ladyship."

"What did she drug you with? Do you know?" He forced his second worst fear into words. "Might it harm the baby?"

"No. It was laudanum, and lots of ladies take that, even when they're expecting. I'm sure it was that because I've had it before—when I broke my arm years ago. The effects were exactly the same. And she had to have had it there on the tantalus—as she very likely would if she used it herself—because she only decided to drug me after I asked about the four young women. She didn't have time to fetch anything else, but offered me a special cordial to drink while she dredged her memories for the answer to my question."

"What exactly did you ask her? And did she answer?"

Edwina thought back. "First, I led her to confirm that she would recognize all the British women in the settlement. Then I asked her..." She closed her eyes, bringing the moment to mind. "Whether she recalled seeing those four women at Undoto's services." She opened her eyes and fastened them on his. "And *yes*—once she saw that I'd drunk enough for the drug to take effect, *before* I succumbed, she told me plainly that all four women had attended Undoto's services—just as I had." She looked away, remembering. "She put a certain emphasis on those last four words, as if that—attendance at the services—was a prerequisite for people being taken."

"Just as Lashoria said."

She met his eyes. "Was I taken—kidnapped—too?" When his lips tightened and he nodded, she settled deeper into his arms. "Tell me what happened."

He did; she felt certain he skated over the bloodier aspects, but his story filled in the time until she'd been laid out on the bed.

She glanced at the window; as the ship's bow rose on a wave, she caught a glimpse of nothing but blue-gray sea stretching all the way to a very distant horizon. "So we're on our way back to London."

"Yes." The ship dipped, and he continued, "We're running under full sail again, so you can expect a bit of pitching."

She shrugged; she'd grown accustomed to the rise and fall of the decks on their way down to the settlement. "So how long before we reach Southampton?"

"At least twelve days." Declan paused, then met her eyes. "I suggest we spend some of that time putting together every piece of the puzzle that we found. Whatever's happening down there—wherever those missing people have been taken—they deserve to be rescued. Something has to be done."

She nodded in her customary decisive fashion. "Indeed.

Wolverstone and Melville have to act immediately, and it's up to us to ensure they do."

He tried to suppress his grin, but failed.

She saw and, distinctly imperiously, arched her brows. "What?"

"I was thinking about our upcoming interview with Wolverstone and Melville."

"And?"

"How much I'm going to enjoy watching their expressions while you lecture them on what they must do."

She gave him a chiding look. "I certainly won't be lecturing them—that's not how it's done."

His father's words rang in his head: *They know how to manage things.* He widened his eyes at her. "Oh? So how *is* it done?"

She gave a confident toss of her head. "It's easy. All one has to do is lead them to make the conclusion you wish them to make and ensure they believe that it was all their idea."

"Ah." He sensed that knowledge might well prove pertinent to his own future. His future dealing with her—being managed by her.

"So..." She leaned into him again, sinking against him. "I agree we'll need to spend some of our time working on our presentation of the facts." She looked up at him through her lashes, the blue of her eyes aglow with the warmth of England's summer skies. "Do you have any suggestions about how we might pass the rest of the next twelve days?"

The artful minx slid another of the buttons on his shirt free.

He licked his lips. "I believe I might have one or two...exercises you might like to try."

"Indeed?" Her smile turned gloriously eager. "You'll have to show me."

He looked into her eyes, returned her smile, and happily resigned himself to untold hours being artfully managed by his wife.

Fourteen

They sailed up the Solent and into Southampton harbor twelve mornings later. The sun was just rising, painting the scene in shades of pewter and rose. Against the dawn sky, the forest of masts stood like so many sleeping sentries, the first sunbeams glinting off countless brass fittings. It was early, the day as yet more anticipation than fact; the scene was drenched in silent splendor, with only the occasional caw of a swooping seabird and the soft lap of the waves against myriad hulls to say it was real.

Edwina stood at the starboard railing and drank in the sight. Nearer at hand, all was bustle and life—the now-familiar calls, the crack of flapping sails, the rattles and the clangs as the crew brought *The Cormorant* around and in—while beyond the wharf, neat ranks of slate roofs filled the still-sleeping town and straggled up the cliff, above which rolled the green fields of England.

She breathed in and felt her heart swell, buoyed by a sense of coming home to…not a new start but their next start, the beginning of the next phase of her and Declan's shared life. She glanced back to where he stood on the bridge, legs braced, hands clasped behind his back as, with his gaze on his sails, he directed his men to furl this one, trim that one, and *The Cormorant* slid gracefully through the crowded lanes, making directly for the company's wharf.

She studied her husband for several minutes more, seeing the concentration in his handsome face as he captained his ship. She also caught the swift glance he threw her; he knew she was there, just as he always seemed to know where she was at any given time.

That, she'd accepted, was important to him. It was something she was prepared to live with.

Looking back at the wharf, she leaned against the rail and watched as Southampton and the next stage of their lives drew nearer.

As they'd discussed, they'd spent the days of the voyage polishing their presentation to Wolverstone and Melville with an eye to ensuring that further immediate action was taken to locate and rescue the missing people. They'd also spent long, dreamy hours in the billows of the big bed in the stern cabin reassuring each other that they were hale and whole—and that on that level at least, nothing about their marriage had changed.

They'd also spent long hours talking. Walking the decks arm in arm, over the table while sharing their meals, and in the quiet of the evenings when Declan had taken the helm and she had stood, wrapped in her shawl, beside him.

In the instant in the Holbrooks' drawing room when she'd realized she'd unwittingly played the fly to her ladyship's spider, she'd understood—with a stunning clarity that had blazed across her mind—just how much, how very much, she'd risked.

But Declan had been there to save her.

She'd owned to her reaction, admitted it, spoken of her shock, of her leaping fear, and yet, against that, stood her resolution. As he termed it, her inherited *noblesse oblige*. Wherever it sprang from, she could no more turn aside from her need to right wrongs and act for those who could not protect themselves than she could turn back the sun. She wouldn't be who she was without that deep-seated compulsion.

They'd spoken of it—considered that its intensity might in part stem from having had her brother act in the self-sacrificing way he had to save their family, leading to a consequent need in her to balance the universe's scales.

Declan, in turn, had reached deep, searched, and found words to convey the hollow terror he'd felt when he hadn't known what was happening—and the icy fear he'd experienced once he'd known she was in the hands of the enemy, the nearly paralyzing self-questioning as he'd plotted to seize her back.

They'd shared what they'd learned, not just about each other but also about themselves.

For hours, they'd walked, and talked, and shared all they were, down to their last, most closely guarded emotion.

They'd come to understand each other so much more deeply than they had before.

Looking out at the wharf as it neared, hearing her husband's crisp orders and Grimsby's yells as crewmen battled to furl the last sails while others leapt to the rails with ropes and still others manned the anchor, she remembered how she'd viewed their married life as she'd been carried aboard in her trunk—such a simple, naive view.

She thought of how she now saw that same thing—their shared life, their marriage, their future—and marveled at how dramatically her view had expanded, had taken on depth and detail.

She would never regret stowing away for her first voyage on her husband's ship.

They had gained so much. Had learned so much. About each other, but even more about themselves.

About the reality of their weaknesses and how they could counteract or work around them, about leaning on each other, and having confidence in the other, of knowing how each other would react.

About their marriage—the reality of what that living entity was and how best to make it work.

Beneath all lay an acceptance, recognized and voiced by them both, that together they had achieved, could achieve, and likely always would achieve more than either might alone. Together, they were more—more powerful, more effective, stronger.

Better able to be the people each of them wanted to be.

Better able to create the life they wanted for them and their children.

They'd spoken of that, too, and decided on some of the details. Neither wished to raise their children in London; they'd settled on finding a small manor somewhere not far from Southampton, that being the principal port from which *The Cormorant* sailed. Perhaps on the outskirts of the New Forest. They'd also discussed his father's hopes that Declan would be the one to take responsibility for the London office and oversee contact with the government. Out of that, they'd accepted the need for a London base and had elected to exercise the option to purchase the Stanhope Street house, which, all in all, had suited them.

Future voyages was one arena they'd agreed would need to be negotiated step by step—voyage by voyage. But Edwina had learned that Declan's youngest brother, Caleb, had been born at sea, so she felt confident she would have Declan's mother's support should she need it. Regardless, Declan had agreed that, in the main, there was no good reason she couldn't accompany him on his voyages—and, indeed, as they'd proved in Freetown, there were sound reasons why, if at all possible, she should.

Yet if that practical aspect of their marriage was still a work-in-progress, so much more had now locked into place. Their appreciation of each other's strengths, their understanding of how best each could support the other, the comprehension of just how completely their paths—their desires, their hopes, their dreams—were aligned. All those aspects were now settled, recognized, and acknowledged between them.

Sensing Declan's approach, she glanced to her right as he strolled up to stand alongside her.

He looked out at the town, then he raised his gaze and looked further. After a moment, he glanced down and met her eyes.

The light in his—challenging, amused, understanding, and loving—made her heart leap. His lips gently curved. He arched a brow. "Ready?"

"Yes." She knew he wasn't referring to them leaving the ship.

His gaze locked with hers, he closed his hand about one of hers and raised it to his lips. Brushed a kiss across her knuckles. "Prior to this voyage, I would never have imagined I would ever say these words, but thank you for caring enough—about me, about us—to stow away."

Her smile bloomed; she had to blink to clear her eyes, but she didn't take her gaze from his face as they clung to the connection for a moment more.

Then, as one, they drew breath and looked across the wharf to the town.

"Where first?" she asked, as the ship bumped against the wharf.

"I have to call at the company's office to register the ship's return and arrange for the crew's wages to be paid. Once I've done that"—he shifted his hold on her hand, lowering it and engulfing it in his—"we'll take a fast carriage to London."

He glanced at her. "Do you want to go to a hotel to wait?"

She looked up and smiled into his eyes. "No. I'll go with you."

He grinned, grasped her hand more firmly, and turned her to where the gangplank waited.

They reached Stanhope Street shortly after midday. A note sent to Wolverstone at his London residence, mentioning Edwina's integral role, resulted in a summons to attend a meeting with Melville and the duke at Wolverstone House in Grosvenor Square later in the day.

Rather curious as to the chosen venue, Declan and Edwina duly presented themselves at Wolverstone House at four o'clock. The butler, as imperturbable as any of his kind, bowed them inside and escorted them into a well-appointed and distinctly sumptuous library.

The duke rose from one of the armchairs angled before the Adam fireplace. He came forward to greet them. "Frobisher. Lady Edwina." Sharp dark brown eyes studied her, then as if content with what he saw, he bowed over her hand. "I am very glad to see you both. I had no idea you had planned to accompany Frobisher south."

Edwina had met Wolverstone socially on several occasions; she was aware of his somewhat exalted position and had learned from Declan that during the wars, under another name, Wolverstone had commanded many men on dangerous missions, and so many still viewed him as having some undefined authority. But she knew nothing of that for fact, and as someone who knew a great deal about façades, she decided to ignore his. She smiled sunnily at him. "It was our honeymoon, after all, and I couldn't see why Declan should have all the excitement of an adventure while I stayed at home."

Wolverstone blinked.

A light laugh drew Edwina's attention to the lady who had risen from the sofa; she recognized Wolverstone's duchess, Minerva.

"I believe you've rendered my husband momentarily speechless, my dear." Minerva's eyes danced. "Quite a feat." As they were already acquainted, she touched fingers and cheeks with Edwina, then, with a wave, invited her to join her on the sofa. "I confess I am dying to hear of your adventure, but we should wait on Melville—he shouldn't be long. In the meantime, perhaps we can have tea."

The duchess looked at Wolverstone, who obligingly crossed to the bellpull and tugged it. Then he glanced at Declan. "I believe Frobisher and I, and most likely Melville as well, will require something stronger."

Minerva acquiesced with a regal nod. While she gave her

orders to the butler, Wolverstone and Declan repaired to the sideboard and returned with cut-crystal glasses in their hands.

Wolverstone waved Declan to one of the pair of armchairs facing the sofa before resuming his seat in the armchair a little way from his wife.

Declan sipped the amber liquid in his glass, then asked, "Why here?"

Wolverstone calmly replied, "Given that we cannot, at this juncture, be certain of our trust in Governor Holbrook, Major Eldridge, or Vice-Admiral Decker, Melville agreed that all future meetings on this matter will be better conducted outside Admiralty House."

Declan's brows rose, but before he could comment, the door opened, and the butler announced Melville.

The First Lord joined them. He was plainly disconcerted by Edwina's presence, and if he harbored any wariness toward Wolverstone, it was as nothing to what he felt over Wolverstone's wife.

After Melville had bowed to the ladies and shaken hands with the men, and Wolverstone had supplied Melville with a much-appreciated glass of brandy, Minerva directed Melville to the second of the armchairs facing the sofa. As the others resumed their seats, she said, "Perhaps we might start at the beginning, Mr. Frobisher, when you and Lady Edwina arrived in Freetown."

Declan was happy to oblige; together, he and Edwina delivered their carefully constructed report, detailing their findings day by day. They submitted the list Mrs. Hardwicke had compiled and otherwise restricted themselves to stating facts, and studiously avoided drawing any conclusions.

Melville grew increasingly agitated with every fact they advanced. The instant they fell silent, he exclaimed, "Holbrook's *wife*? Great heavens!"

His dark gaze acute, Wolverstone asked, "What is your assessment of Holbrook himself?"

Declan shook his head. "Based on what we know, it's impossible to say whether or not he's involved."

After a second, Wolverstone shifted his gaze to Edwina. "Lady Edwina?"

"I did not spend sufficient time with the governor to get any real feel for his character. However, although he is the one most people cite as being dismissive of all attempts to focus official scrutiny on the missing people, I do wonder if, in that, he might not have been greatly swayed by his wife."

Melville frowned. "How so?"

"Well, I can readily imagine Lady Holbrook emphasizing the social and commercial ramifications of officially acknowledging an epidemic of missing people occurring in the settlement." Edwina raised her hands, palms out. "Panic would ensue, and all those who could leave would flee, which would create a political furor. In addition, those missing came largely from the lower classes, and I understand the governor has a blindness in that regard."

She paused, then added, "If, as my husband and I believe, Lady Holbrook was instrumental in selecting those who would subsequently vanish, then knowing of her husband's prejudice, she would, of course, favor those whose disappearance was least likely to provoke him to action."

"And given the tension between Holbrook and Eldridge," Declan put in, "if Holbrook wishes to ignore the disappearances, then as the majority of those missing are civilians, there's little Eldridge can do." He paused, then added, "I can't comment on Decker—he wasn't there while we were."

A short silence ensued, then Wolverstone steepled his fingers before his chin, his expression harsh and unyielding. "I believe you've brought us enough solid facts to reach several conclusions. First and foremost, there is, indeed, something very serious going on in Freetown. Some villainous scheme the authorities cannot ignore or, as happened with the Black Cobra cult, it will blow up into something much worse." He slanted a sharp glance at Melville. "In other words, Melville, you have no choice but to act quickly and decisively."

Melville grimaced; he shifted in his chair, but didn't disagree.

Minerva humphed. "If this has reached the point where the governor's wife has been suborned, then that is unarguable proof that whatever is going on, there's a great deal of money, or power, or both involved."

Wolverstone inclined his head in agreement. "Just so."

Melville looked as if he was sucking a lemon, but he, too, nodded. "Indeed."

"Secondly," Wolverstone continued, "as to the details of the plot, such as we know them, an unknown number of men of working age, including Dixon, Hopkins, Fanshawe, and Hillsythe, plus at least four young women and seventeen children— all thus far identified being British—have vanished from the settlement over the last four months. These disappearances are not random, but rather as if those taken have, for some reason or reasons we haven't yet determined, caught the eye of the villains—there is certainly a suggestion that those taken were selected rather than being arbitrarily or opportunistically captured.

"In that respect, Captain Dixon being one of those taken early, perhaps even being the first to vanish, might be pertinent. As an expert sapper, managing tunneling and explosives is his acknowledged strength. For someone starting a mine, his talents would be attractive. But why young women and children might be required for such an enterprise is more difficult to discern. Without further information, our villains' purpose remains undefined."

Wolverstone paused, then went on, "Given your questions to Lady Holbrook and her responses and actions, we can accept as fact that she is involved in some capacity, possibly through selecting the victims, and is in contact with those orchestrating the disappearances. And, further, that attendance at Obo Undoto's services is in some way necessary. How, exactly, we do not know. However, the vodun priestess Lashoria—whose evidence has proved accurate in at least one respect, namely that all the missing adults had attended Undoto's services—has specifically implicated Undoto himself. At this point, we should regard Undoto as one of our villains, possibly the one with whom Lady Holbrook interacted. He is also thought to be working with slave traders, although whether slave traders are directly involved with the disappearance of our missing people remains to be established."

Lowering his hands, Wolverstone looked around at them all, but while they'd followed his careful summation, no one had anything to add. "Very well. In light of the foregoing, let's turn to our next step." He looked at Declan. "In your opinion, who in the settlement can we trust?" Wolverstone's lips twisted wryly. "Alternatively, who might we consider allies?"

Declan acknowledged the qualification with a tip of his head. "Lashoria, for a start. Captain Richards at the fort, and possibly others there, too, might be willing to help."

"Mrs. Hardwicke," Edwina put in. "And also most likely her husband—at least in terms of information. There's also Mrs. Sherbrook, although I doubt she knows more than she's already told me."

Declan nodded his agreement, then looked at Wolverstone. "There's one other I wish I'd had time to question more closely. Charles Babington. He's concerned about one of the missing young women—I don't know which one. Charles would know a great deal about what goes on in the settlement, and he has the ability to find out more if he so chooses. He might well be willing to help."

"That's better than I'd hoped for," Wolverstone said. "Whoever we send down next will have a decent foundation from which to start."

Melville frowned. "We should get the Foreign Office to re-call Holbrook at once."

"No." Wolverstone's negation was as cold as iron and equally inflexible.

Melville's frown turned perplexed. "But if they get him back here, his wife will come, too, and even if Holbrook himself is oblivious to what's been going on under his nose, we'll be able to question his lady and learn a lot more." Melville stared at Wolverstone. "Why wouldn't we have him recalled?"

"Because as things stand," Wolverstone replied, "that won't advance our cause and, instead, may cause irreparable harm. Consider—it's been thirteen days since Lady Holbrook tried to have Lady Edwina abducted and Frobisher seized her back. By the time any packet reaches Freetown, do you honestly believe Lady Holbrook will still be there?"

Melville blinked. "You think she'll have vanished, too?"

"No. I think that, when our next operative arrives in Free-town, he'll find one of two situations at the governor's house. If Holbrook is as guilty as his wife, they will both have departed, most likely taking ship for the New World, leaving some ex-cuse like a family emergency or similar to cover their tracks, at least long enough for them to leave. Alternatively, if Holbrook has been, as you say, oblivious, then he will still be there, alone, having waved his wife off on a similarly justified jaunt." Wolver-stone met Melville's gaze. "Of one thing I am quite certain. By the time any communication reaches Freetown, Lady Holbrook won't be there."

Wolverstone paused, then continued, "Now consider what our villains' current view will be. Regardless of whether Holbrook and his wife manufactured some story and decamped together or her ladyship fled on her own, I guarantee the villains will have no inkling that anything is amiss. Whatever the story spread to cover Lady Holbrook's departure, with or without her husband, there will be nothing in it to alert or alarm anyone. If the villains asked about Lady Edwina, to save her own skin, Lady Holbrook will have downplayed and dismissed Lady Edwina's importance and the potential ramifications—and if she's dealing with the likes of Undoto, who is there to gainsay her? Thus, at present, the villains know only that their people were called on to take a lady from the governor's house, but after an armed clash, she was rescued by sailors, and they and she left Freetown. Regrettable, but nothing to cause any major alarm. Subsequently, but entirely unconnectedly, the governor's wife, with or without the governor, was called away on a family emergency."

Wolverstone regarded Melville evenly. "Neither the Holbrooks, nor the villains, nor anyone else in Freetown knows Frobisher as anything other than a trading ship's captain and sometime explorer. They know even less of Lady Edwina—she was a tonnish noble lady passing through, nothing more. As far as I can see, the villains have no reason to think that an official investigation is being focused on them. Which is exactly what we need."

He paused, then, his voice growing colder, went on, "Against that backdrop, whether Holbrook is in Freetown or not, if he's recalled, the order will cause an instant scandal that will spread like wildfire throughout the settlement and immediately alert the villains that official attention has been engaged. What will the villains then do?"

Into the ensuing silence, Edwina said, "They may very well kill the people they've taken—men, women, and children."

"Precisely." Wolverstone inclined his head to her, then refocused his steely gaze on Melville. "*That*, regardless of all other considerations, is the outcome we must strive to avoid. Thus far, as Frobisher's commendably thorough reconnaissance has shown, there is no evidence that any of the missing people have been killed. We must do nothing to jeopardize their safety."

After a moment of studying the obviously frustrated Melville, Wolverstone stated, "As a member of His Majesty's government, you are, with others, responsible for managing the situation in Freetown. However, any solution to the problem cannot involve sacrificing innocent lives. After all, innocents are the ones we— all of us—are, in one way or another, committed to protect." After an instant's pause, Wolverstone continued, "And I hardly need remind you that in the wake of the Black Cobra, any further slaughter of innocents—and in this case, they are British— will not go down well with the public."

Along with Wolverstone, Minerva, Edwina, and Declan all looked at Melville and waited.

The First Lord all but squirmed; the temptation to seize the moment and be seen to act decisively—and publicly—clearly called to his politician's soul, but eventually, he grimaced and rather petulantly said, "Very well. So if we can't recall Holbrook, what do you suggest?"

Declan switched his gaze to Wolverstone.

His ex-commander did not let him down. "I propose that we send a second operative to Freetown immediately, with orders similar to those we gave Frobisher, but our new man will be starting his investigation at a point further along the villains' enterprise. While our ultimate aim must be to rescue those missing and shut down this scheme, whatever it is, the next step is, while maintaining all possible secrecy, to determine how those missing were taken or, alternatively, who took them. I suspect that learning where or why they've been taken will come after we answer the previous questions." Wolverstone glanced at Declan and arched a brow.

Declan nodded. "That would be the direction I would advise."

"Excellent." Several seconds ticked past, then Wolverstone rose.

Everyone else came to their feet.

Wolverstone offered Declan his hand. "Thank you." As Declan gripped and they shook hands, Wolverstone continued, "Your mission is complete. Your contribution in this matter is, as always, greatly appreciated." Wolverstone released Declan, turned to Edwina, and smiled. "As is the very real contribution made by Lady Edwina."

Edwina returned Wolverstone's smile, curtsied, then made her farewells to Minerva and Melville, and accepted Declan's arm. Wolverstone accompanied them as they walked to the door.

As Wolverstone reached for the doorknob, Edwina asked, "So you *will* be sending someone down to pick up where we left off?"

Wolverstone met her gaze and smiled a smile that was as intent as she could have wished. "Indeed. Just as soon as I can lay my hands on a suitably qualified and able soul."

"When you find him," Declan said, "we would be happy to give him a more detailed description of the settlement and its dangers." He met Wolverstone's gaze. "Anything to make his road easier and hopefully successful."

Wolverstone's smiled deepened. "I'm sure he'll appreciate that." With a nod, he opened the door. "Rest assured he and I will be in touch."

They returned to the house in Stanhope Street—shortly to be theirs—to a household delighted to have them home again.

Humphrey beamed in a most unbutlerlike way, and on being informed that they would be dining in, Mrs. King and Cook threw themselves into preparing a banquet fit for returning heroes.

Not that either Edwina or Declan gave any details over where they had been, much less what they had done, yet their satisfaction with their accomplishments and with each other was, apparently, obvious enough to infect their staff. Everyone went around with a smile on their face and a bounce in their step. Even Wilmot, who had been so relieved to see Edwina walk in the door that she'd promptly burst into tears, had recovered and was actually humming while she sorted and brushed Edwina's clothes.

With her household happy and contentedly busy, Edwina seized an hour to indulge in a long soak in a bath scented with her favorite perfumed oil. Head back against the tub's rim, she closed her eyes and let her memories of all they'd seen, all they'd been through—all they'd learned—rise and wash through her.

It was unarguably true that neither Declan nor she were the same people they had been when they'd left London.

They'd grown and, like twining trees, they'd grown together.

Satisfaction, contentment, and quiet joy rose and wrapped around her like steam. She lay back, eyes closed, and let the emotions sink into her heart, into her bones, into her very soul.

Downstairs in the small library, Declan sorted through his correspondence; for once, he felt happy to be home. To have time to savor the best of tonnish life with Edwina by his side, before they again set sail. He no longer doubted, let alone questioned, that "they." She had proved herself a true adventurer's wife, a perfect soulmate for him; she was intent on holding his hand as well as his heart, and somewhere during their voyage home he'd made peace with that.

They'd been absent for only four weeks; he found no startling news in the pile of letters—just the usual bills, two chatty letters from friends, and a note from his brother Robert. Dispatched from New York, the note stated that, as Robert would be sailing into the Pool of London to put the ambassador he'd been sent to ferry home ashore, he would call on Declan and Edwina in Stanhope Street.

Declan smiled in anticipation and made a mental note to warn Edwina. Judging by the date of the note, Robert would be arriving any day now.

He flicked through the letters again, then set them aside. As usual, his senses had yet to adjust to the fact that the floor did not pitch and tilt.

The door opened, and Edwina swept in, her pocket-Venus

figure draped in cornflower-blue silk, her curls up and tumbling in artful disarray about her delicate face—and his senses stilled, then expanded like his heart.

He realized he was smiling in a witless fashion as he rose and, setting aside the letter knife, went to take her hand.

She smiled brilliantly up at him. "Good evening, dear husband. Are you busy?"

He opened his mouth to deny it, and the doorbell jangled.

Both he and she glanced at the door.

Then he cast her a questioning glance. "I thought we were dining alone."

"So did...I." Consciousness infused her expression. "Oh, dear. I sent word to Mama, and my brother and sisters."

Declan inwardly sighed, stole a quick kiss from her rosy lips, then wound her arm in his and led her out to the front hall to meet the invading horde.

There was no hope of repelling them. Not only Lucasta and her companion, Anthea, but Millicent and Catervale, and Cassie and Elsbury were shrugging out of coats and handing over hats and canes in the hall. And in an appearance that underscored the fact that, despite Edwina's recommendations not to worry, her family assuredly had, Lord Julian Delbraith and his wife, Miranda, had just arrived to join the fray.

It was chaos from the first—a joyous babel of questions and answers all offered at once. Hugs and kisses, handclasps, and claps on shoulders ensued, and exclamations and exhortations abounded; eventually, between them, he and Edwina succeeded in herding everyone into the drawing room.

Theirs wasn't a large house, but no one minded the coziness, the closeness. It was the middle of the Season, and their visitors were dressed for the evening; they doubtless had events to attend later, but when Edwina slipped out—presumably to consult with Cook—then returned and issued an invitation for dinner, everyone accepted with alacrity.

After the first wave of questions—Were they well? Where had they been?—had been answered, everyone settled comfortably, and after swearing their visitors to secrecy, he and Edwina commenced their story.

Unlike their earlier report delivered at Wolverstone House, they started at the true beginning. Naturally, all the ladies approved of Edwina's insistence on accompanying him on his mission and applauded her resourcefulness in devising how to successfully stow away, but his brothers-in-law were as horrified and as supportive as he might wish—and equally resigned to the inevitable outcome.

"So," Edwina said, "we eventually sailed into Freetown harbor."

She broke off as Humphrey entered to announce dinner.

They all rose and removed to the dining room, and at their visitors' urging, he and Edwina immediately took up their tale. By mutual consent, carried in several glances shared down the length of the table, they skated over some of the more personal details, including her expectant state. Nevertheless, in the main, they described the situation as they'd found it, and their subsequent actions and discoveries, their conclusions, and the questions arising that remained to be answered.

Their recitation, unhurried and frequently interrupted by requests for descriptions or further elucidation, carried them through the five-course meal and back into the drawing room. No one even suggested that the ladies and gentlemen separate for the men to enjoy port and brandy—not in that company. The men had no intention of missing out on any revelations.

"So these poor people have been kidnapped, and as yet no search has been ordered?" Lucasta's tone held censure of the sort only a dowager duchess could command.

"That's correct." Declan glanced at the others. "That's essentially the wrong we've started to put right. We've done the groundwork, establishing the need for a full-scale, albeit secret, investigation. Whoever is sent in next will commence the search proper, but they'll have to tread warily. The last thing we want is for the kidnappers to kill their captives in order to cover their tracks."

Sober looks and nods of grim understanding were exchanged.

Melville would most likely have an apoplexy over such openness, but Declan had no qualms about revealing such details; this was a company who knew how to keep secrets.

This was family.

Finally satisfied that their tale was fully told, the company moved on, and the talk turned to the social highlights they'd missed while out of town. Declan glanced around again, taking in the expressions—relaxed, animated, openly reflecting interest and concern, connection, and affection—and realized that this was one of the very best aspects of tonnish life. Family. A home. And a wife to call his own.

More, a wife who was delighted and determined to go adventuring with him.

And their first child was on the way.

He couldn't ask for more; there wasn't anything more he wanted.

Eventually, their visitors recalled their evening's engagements; with hugs and kisses, they took their leave. The ladies arranged to meet for morning tea at Catervale House. The gentlemen shook hands and agreed to meet in Dolphin Square the following afternoon, the better to discuss several investment prospects Julian had stumbled upon in more conducive surrounds.

At last, when they'd waved everyone away and Humphrey had shut the door, Edwina heaved a huge but transparently happy sigh. She met Declan's gaze and smiled a touch wearily. "I love them all, yet I'm glad they've gone."

He held out his hand, palm up. "It's been a very long day. You were up before dawn."

"I was, wasn't I?" She slipped her fingers into his hand. "That said, I'm glad I didn't forgo the chance to see dawn break over the Solent."

He turned her to the stairs.

Side by side, they started to climb.

Then she shot a sidelong look his way. "Even though I'll doubtless see it many times more in my life—"

He had to grin.

Her chin lifted challengingly. "—the first time deserves a special place in my memories."

He reached for the knob of their bedroom door, sent it swinging wide, and met her gaze. "Indubitably."

Her smile was glorious, lighting her eyes, illuminating her expression.

Lighting up and brightening—gilding—his life.

She was his lodestone, the fire on the cliffs that would always lead him to safe harbor. But she was also a star burning brightly in the firmament of his heaven, her light striking to his soul; with her commitment to travel with him, she would always be there to guide him over the seas, through the shoals of the ton, safely home to the house they would find in the country, to the children they would have, to the hearth they would call their own.

With her by his side, he would never lose his way.

In her, he'd found his ultimate adventure.

With a smile in her eyes and curving her rosy lips, she walked backward into the room, her hand still in his, drawing him with her. He pushed the door shut and let her lead him on.

Into her arms. Into their bed.

Into their own special heaven.

Clothes were shed and fell, landing where they would.

Discarded as they stripped themselves bare.

As they came together with no barriers between—neither on the physical plane nor on that plane where their hearts dwelled.

Their lovemaking had changed over the past days. The intensity was still there, still acute, yet was no longer so shocking. The urgency had eased, allowing them time to savor, to appreciate every last gasp, every kiss. Every trembling touch, every arching moan, every driven, demanding caress.

That she was carrying his child—that in fact they were three and no longer just two—fascinated him. The barely detectable rounding of her stomach was a consuming delight.

As for her…he couldn't comprehend how just four weeks could have so matured her, yet her confidence—in him, in herself, in them together—now infused every action. Every touch, every look, every bold word. And here, in their bed, her newfound assurance combined with his self-confidence and expertise to elevate their play, to extend it and the connection it carried into realms he'd never previously breached.

Into realms that touched, then forged their souls.

Into one. As one.

Desire surged. Passion whipped.

Pleasure rose at their command. They let it roll on, over and through them, until it rose in a towering wave and broke over them.

Ecstasy followed, sharp and bright, then waned into fathomless satiation.

Bliss.

A marriage built on solid rock and tended with devotion.

He disengaged from her, rolled to his side, and gathered her to him. She came, snuggling her head into the hollow of his shoulder as she always did.

When he'd married her, he'd had no real idea of what marriage to her might demand. What it might take—what it might ask of him. Although he'd had a vague view, that had dissipated rather quickly as he'd learned the truth of her, of the woman she truly was.

Now…while he knew very well that many of his peers would feel uncomfortable within the marriage he and she had wrought, for him, she and this marriage were perfect. She and it met his every need, including those needs he hadn't previously known he had.

He wanted this marriage—their marriage—every bit as much as she did.

If anything occurred to threaten its fabric, she would fight for it—and he would fight beside her.

Together. Side by side. That was how they—he and she—were meant to be.

Settling her within one arm, in her usual sprawl across his chest, he raised his other arm and, elbow bent, slid his palm beneath his head. He stared upward, not at all certain where his thoughts would lead him, yet they seemed curiously insistent. Relaxing completely, he let them stream through his mind as they would.

He and she had all this—everything any sane couple could want.

Their future glowed, stretching before them, just waiting for them to claim it.

All well and good, yet still he was prey to a nagging sense of…a job left undone.

Of a goal as yet unattained.

Gradually, the source of his unsettledness solidified in his mind.

He hesitated, then, with his senses, he reached for her—and realized she, like he, was still awake.

He wasn't sure how to broach the subject; she might not feel as he did. After casting about for several moments, he murmured, "We'll need to go house hunting in the country."

"Not until this is done."

Thank God. "Indeed." Now he knew she felt the same, he let his mind range ahead. "I still can't imagine what on earth could be behind this…"

"This strange snatching of souls." She paused, then whispered,

"Regardless, neither of us will be able to turn aside until we see it brought to an end."

Confidence in herself. Confidence in him.

"True." He thought, then went on, "Wolverstone will bring his next operative to meet us—I think we can count on that. We'll see who it is and try to gauge what comes next. Assuming Wolverstone makes the same stipulation—that as soon as this agent learns something, he returns immediately with the news rather than following any trail…" Eyes narrowing, he stared unseeing at the ceiling as he followed that train of thought to its logical end. "Then I suspect that whoever it is will focus on Undoto and through him try to pick up our missing people's trail."

Her hair slid like silk over his skin as she nodded. "We'll need to inveigle this new agent to share his news with us when he returns."

"Depending on whom they send, that might be tricky, but between us, we'll manage."

After a moment, she rose on one elbow to look into his face. "You weren't expecting to sail until July. Whoever goes down to Freetown to investigate will be back long before that." She tipped her head. "Can *The Cormorant* remain at Southampton in case we need her again?"

His grin was all teeth. "Now I've got her out of Royd's clutches, I'm not inclined to let him have her back. I'll go to the office tomorrow and give orders for her to remain moored in Southampton Roads." He met her gaze. "And I'll send word to Caldwell and Henry to have her ready to sail to West Africa again on half a day's notice."

She looked into his eyes, then she stretched up and touched her lips to his. "Thank you. It might just be my *noblesse oblige* prodding, but I feel as if we have unfinished business in Freetown. That while we accomplished what you were sent to do, that's not the end of what we can—and should—do." Her ex-

pression sober, she whispered, "To help those who, in these circumstances, are powerless to help themselves."

Meeting her gaze, he nodded. "We'll stand by, ready to answer whatever call comes and to do all we can to bring those
lost souls home."

After several seconds contemplating his expression, she narrowed her eyes at him. "You're not going to argue that, now
that I'm expecting, I have to remain in London?"

He looked into her face, thought of all he'd learned over the
past weeks—ever since he'd found her in her trunk, a stowaway
in his cabin. "No." He hesitated, then gave his tongue free rein
to express the hope, the joy, the love that filled his heart. "You
belong by my side. We'll find a way."

He was an adventurer to his soul, and so was she.

And their marriage was the biggest adventure of all—one that
would last them a lifetime.

★ ★ ★ ★ ★

If you enjoyed Declan and Edwina's adventure,
don't miss the next installment in
Stephanie Laurens'
The Adventurers Quartet,
a set of sultry, sweeping adventure-romances
featuring four buccaneering brothers
and four adventurous ladies.

Read on for a sneak peek from Volume Two,
A BUCCANEER AT HEART,
to find out who picks up the baton
and takes on the challenge in the next stage
of the on-going mission.

Available from MIRA Books on April 26th

One

Captain Robert Frobisher strolled at his ease along Park Lane, his gaze on the rippling green canopies of the massive trees in Hyde Park.

He'd steered his ship, *The Trident*, up the Thames on the previous evening's tide. They'd moored at Frobisher and Sons' berth in St. Katherine's Dock, and after he'd dealt with all the associated palaver, it had been too late to call on anyone. This morning, he'd dutifully gone into the company office in Burr Street; as soon as the customary formalities had been completed and the bulk of his crew released for the day, he'd jumped into a hackney and headed for Mayfair. But rather than driving directly to his brother Declan's house, he'd had the jarvey let him down at the end of Piccadilly so that he could take a few minutes to drink in the green. He spent so much of his life looking at the sea, being reminded of the beauties of land was no bad thing.

A self-deprecating smile curving his lips, he turned the corner into Stanhope Street. Barely ten o'clock was an unfashionably early hour at which to call at a gentleman's residence, but he felt sure his brother and his brother's new wife, the lovely Edwina, would welcome him with open arms.

The morning was fine, if a touch crisp, with the sun intermittently screened by gray clouds scudding across the pale sky.

Declan and Edwina resided at Number 26. Looking down

the street, Robert saw a black carriage pulled up by the curb farther along.

Premonition swept cool fingers across his nape. Early as it was, there was no other conveyance waiting in the short residential street.

As he continued strolling, idly swinging his cane, a footman perched on the rear of the carriage saw him; instantly, the footman leapt down to the pavement and moved to open the carriage door.

Increasingly intrigued, Robert watched, wondering who would descend. Apparently, he wouldn't need to check the house numbers to discover which house was his goal.

The gentleman who, with languid grace, stepped out of the carriage and straightened was as tall as Robert, as broad-shouldered and lean. Sable hair framed a face the features of which screamed his station.

Wolverstone. More precisely, His Grace, the Duke of Wolverstone, known in the past as Dalziel.

Given Wolverstone was plainly waiting to waylay and speak with him, Robert surmised that Wolverstone's status as commander of British agents outside of the isles had, at least temporarily, been restored.

Robert's cynical, world-weary side wasn't all that surprised to see the man.

But the gentleman who, much less elegantly, followed Wolverstone from the carriage was unexpected. Portly and very precisely attired, with a fussy, somewhat prim air, the man tugged his waistcoat into place and fiddled with his fob chain; from long experience of the breed, Robert pegged him as a politician. Along with Wolverstone, the man turned to face Robert.

As Robert neared, Wolverstone nodded. "Frobisher." He held out his hand.

Robert transferred his cane to his other hand; returning the nod, he grasped Wolverstone's hand, then shifted his gaze to Wolverstone's companion.

Releasing Robert, Wolverstone waved gracefully. "Allow me to present Viscount Melville, First Lord of the Admiralty."

Robert managed not to raise his brows. He inclined his head. "Melville." What the devil was afoot?

Melville curtly nodded back, then drew in a portentous breath. "Captain Frobisher—"

"Perhaps," Wolverstone smoothly interjected, "we should adjourn inside." His dark eyes met Robert's gaze. "Your brother won't be surprised to see us, but in deference to Lady Edwina, we thought it best to await your arrival in the carriage."

The notion that consideration of Edwina's possible reaction held the power to influence Wolverstone even that much... Robert fought not to grin. His sister-in-law was a duke's daughter and thus of the same social stratum as Wolverstone, yet Robert would have wagered there were precious few who Wolverstone would even think to tip-toe gently around.

Curiosity burgeoning in leaps and bounds, at Wolverstone's wave, Robert led the way up the steps to the narrow front porch.

He hadn't previously called at this house, but the butler who opened the door to his knock recognized him instantly. The man's face lit. "Captain Frobisher." Then the butler noticed the other two men, and his expression turned inscrutable.

Realizing the man didn't know either Wolverstone or Melville, Robert smiled easily. "I gather these gentlemen are acquainted with my brother."

He didn't need to say more—Declan must have heard the butler's greeting; he appeared through a doorway down the hall.

Smiling, Declan strode forward. "Robert—well-met!"

They grinned and clapped each other on the shoulders, then Declan noticed Wolverstone and Melville. Declan's expression shuttered, but then he looked at Robert, a faintly question evident in his blue eyes.

Robert arched a brow back. "They were waiting outside."

"Ah. I see."

From Declan's tone, Robert gathered that his brother was uncertain whether Wolverstone and Melville's appearance was good news or bad.

Yet with assured courtesy, Declan welcomed Wolverstone and Melville, shaking their hands. "Gentlemen." As the butler shut the door, Declan caught Wolverstone's eye. "The drawing room might be best."

Wolverstone inclined his head, and the butler moved to throw open the door to their left.

Declan waved Wolverstone, Melville, and Robert through; as Declan started to follow, Robert heard the butler ask, "Should I inform her ladyship, sir?"

Without hesitation, Declan replied, "Please."

Sinking into one of the numerous armchairs spread around the cozy room, Robert was surprised that Declan hadn't even paused before summoning his wife to attend what was clearly destined to be a business meeting—although of what business, Robert couldn't guess.

Declan had barely had a chance to offer his guests refreshments—which they all declined—before the door opened and Edwina swept in, bringing all four men to their feet.

Fetchingly gowned in cornflower-blue-and-white-striped silk, she looked happy and delighted—glowing with an uncomplicated enthusiasm for life. Although her first smile was for Declan, in the next breath, she turned her radiance on Robert and opened her arms. "Robert!"

He couldn't help but smile widely in return and allow her the liberty of an embrace. "Edwina." He'd met her several times, both at his parents' home as well as at her family's, and he thoroughly approved of her; from the first, he'd seen her as precisely the right lady for Declan. He returned her hug and dutifully bussed the smooth cheek she tipped up to him.

Drawing back, she met his eyes. "I'm utterly delighted to see you! Did Declan tell you we planned to make this our London base?"

She barely paused for his answer—and his quick look at Declan—before she inquired about *The Trident* and his immediate plans for the day. After he told her of his ship's position and his lack of any plans, she informed him that he would be staying for luncheon and also to dine.

Then she turned to greet Wolverstone and Melville. The ease she displayed toward them made it clear she was already acquainted with them both.

At Edwina's gracious wave, they resettled in the armchairs and sofa, and the next minutes went in general converse led, of course, by Edwina.

Noting the quick smiling looks she shared with Declan, noting his brother's response, Robert felt a distinct pang of envy. Not that he coveted Edwina; he liked her, but she was too forceful a personality for his taste. Declan needed a lady like her to balance his own character, but Robert's character was quite different.

He was the diplomat of the family, careful and cautious, while his three brothers were reckless hellions.

"Well, then." Apparently satisfied with what Wolverstone had deigned to share about his family's health, Edwina clasped her hands in her lap. "Given you gentlemen are here, I expect Declan and I had better tell Robert about how we've spent the last five weeks—about the mission and what we discovered in Freetown."

Mission? Freetown? Robert had thought that, while he'd been on the other side of the Atlantic, Declan and Edwina had remained in London. Apparently not.

Edwina arched a brow at Wolverstone.

His expression impassive, he inclined his head. "I daresay that will be fastest."

Robert didn't miss the resignation in Wolverstone's tone.

He felt sure Edwina didn't either, but she merely smiled approvingly at Wolverstone, then transferred her bright gaze to Declan. "Perhaps you had better start."

Entirely sober, Declan looked at Robert and did.

Between them, Declan and Edwina related a tale that kept Robert transfixed.

That Edwina had stowed away and joined Declan on his run south wasn't really that much of a surprise. But the puzzling situation in Freetown—and the consequent danger that had stalked them and, beyond anyone's ability to predict, had reached out and touched Edwina—was a tale guaranteed to capture and hold his attention.

By the time Edwina concluded with a reassurance that she'd taken no lasting harm from the events of their last night in Freetown, Robert no longer had any doubt as to why Wolverstone and Melville had been waiting on the doorstep to waylay him.

Melville huffed and promptly confirmed Robert's assumption. "As you can see, Captain Frobisher, we are in desperate need of someone with similar capabilities as your brother to travel to Freetown as fast as may be and continue our investigation."

Robert glanced at Declan. "I take it this falls under our… customary association with the government?"

Wolverstone stirred. "Indeed." He met Robert's eyes. "There are precious few others who could do the job, and no one else with a fast ship in harbor."

After a second of holding Wolverstone's dark gaze, Robert nodded. "Very well." This was a far cry from his usual voyages ferrying diplomats—or diplomatic secrets of whatever sort—back and forth, but he could see the need, could appreciate the urgency. And he'd sailed into Freetown before.

He looked at Declan. "Is this why there were no orders waiting for me at the office?" He'd been surprised to learn that; the demand for his services was usually so great that *The Trident* was rarely free for more than a few days, and Royd and his Corsair often had to take on the overload.

Declan nodded. "Wolverstone informed Royd the government would most likely need to call on another of us once *The Cormorant* got back, and fortuitously, you were due in. I received a missive from Royd, and there's one waiting for you in the library—we're free of our usual business and are to devote our services to the Crown."

Robert dipped his head in acknowledgment. He tapped his fingers on the chair's arm as he sifted through all Declan and Edwina had revealed, adding in Wolverstone's dry comments and Melville's few utterances. He narrowed his eyes, in his mind studying the jigsaw-like picture he'd assembled from the facts. "All right. Let's see if I have this straight. Four serving officers have gone missing, one after another, along with at least four young women and an unknown number of other men. These disappearances occurred over a period of four months or more, and the few instances known to have been discussed with Governor Holbrook, he dismissed as due to those involved having gone off to seek their fortune in the jungle or elsewhere. Some such excuse. In addition, seventeen children from the slums are also missing, apparently disappearing over much the same period, with Holbrook brushing their vanishing aside as children running off—nothing more nefarious.

"Currently, there is nothing to say if Holbrook is trying to suppress all interest in this spate of missing people because he's involved, or whether his attitude springs from some other, entirely noncriminal belief. Regardless, Lady Holbrook has proved to be definitely involved, and it's doubtful she'll still be in the settlement, but you would like me to verify whether Holbrook himself is still at his post. If he is, then we presume him innocent—or at least unaware of whatever is driving these kidnappings." Robert arched a brow at Wolverstone. "Correct?"

Wolverstone nodded. "I haven't met Holbrook, but from what

I've been able to learn, he doesn't seem the type to be involved. However, he might well be the type of official who will refuse to react until the unpalatable truth is staring him in the face— until circumstances force him to it."

Robert added that shading to his mental jigsaw. "To continue, in the case of the missing adults, there are reasonable grounds on which to believe that they're being selected in some way and that attendance at the local priest Obo Undoto's services in some way facilitates that. We know nothing about how the children are taken, other than that it's not through any connection with Undoto's services."

Declan shifted. "We can't even be sure the missing children are being taken by the same people or for the same reason as the missing adults."

"But given that young women have been taken as well as men," Edwina put in, "there has to be a possibility that all the missing, children as well as adults, are being…used in the same way." Her chin firmed. "By the same villains."

Robert paused, then said, "Regardless of whether the children are going to the same place, given the priestess's claims—none of which have yet proven unfounded, so let's assume she spoke true—Undoto and his services are clearly the obvious place to look for the beginnings of a trail."

No one argued. After a second of considering the picture taking shape in his mind, Robert went on, "If I've understood correctly, the vodun priestess Lashoria, Reverend Hardwicke, and even more his wife, an old sailor named Sampson, and Charles Babington are people you"—he glanced at Declan and Edwina— "consider safe sources."

Both nodded. Declan stated, "They're potential allies and might well be willing to play an active hand in helping you learn more." He met Robert's eyes. "Babington especially. I believe he has a personal interest in one of the young women who has gone missing, but I didn't get a chance to pursue that or him further. But he can command resources within the settlement that might prove useful."

Melville cleared his throat. "There's also Vice-Admiral Decker. We have no reason to imagine he has any involvement in whatever heinous crime is under way in the settlement." He all but glowered at Declan. "I gave your brother a letter enabling him to call on Decker's support. I believe I worded it generally, so it will apply to you as it would have to him."

Declan dipped his head. "Decker wasn't in port while I was there. I still have the letter—I'll give it to you."

Robert wasn't fooled by Declan's noncommittal tone; he wouldn't be tripping over his toes to ask any favors of Decker, either. Indeed, he hoped the vice-admiral remained at sea throughout his visit to the settlement.

"Regardless," Wolverstone said, "I cannot stress enough how critical it is that whatever occurs while you're on this mission, you must not at any point do anything to alert the perpetrators to any level of official interest. We must protect the lives of those taken—sending in a rescue team who find only dead bodies isn't something any of us wish to even contemplate. Given that we cannot be certain who of those in authority in the settlement is involved, and conversely who is safe to trust, every action you take must remain covert."

Robert nodded curtly. The more he heard—the more he dwelled on all he'd learned—remaining covert first to last seemed his wisest choice.

"So, Captain," Melville said bracingly, "we need you to go into Freetown, follow the trail your brother has identified, and learn all the details of this nefarious scheme."

Melville's expression was a blend of belligerence and something much closer to pleading. Robert recognized the signs of a politician facing a threat beyond his control.

Before he could respond, Wolverstone softly said, "Actually, no." Wolverstone caught Robert's gaze. "We cannot ask you to learn all the details."

From the corner of his eye, Robert saw Melville's face fall as he stared at Wolverstone, who, in this matter, was effectively his mentor.

As if unaware of the angst he was causing, Wolverstone smoothly went on, "From what your brother has said, and from all I've learned from others over recent days, given that those effecting the kidnappings are slave traders, then I gather that in Freetown, as generally in that region, the slave traders will be operating out of a camp. They will hold their captives at that camp until they have a sufficient number to take to whoever they're supplying. Further, the camp will almost certainly be outside the settlement's borders, somewhere in the jungle, possibly some distance away."

Wolverstone glanced at Declan, who, his expression impassive, nodded.

Imperturbably, Wolverstone continued, his gaze returning to Robert's face, "Consequently, this mission is highly unlikely to be accomplished in only two stages. There will be however many stages we require to learn what we need to know, all without alerting the villains involved. Your brother"—he paused, then inclined his head to Edwina—"and Lady Edwina got us the first vital clues. They identified Undoto's services as being a part of the scheme and gave us the connection to the slave traders. They also confirmed that those in high places in the settlement are involved, something we must strive never to forget. If Lady Holbrook was suborned, almost certainly others will have been as well."

Wolverstone's gaze cut to Melville, but although he looked dejected and, indeed, disgruntled, the First Lord made no attempt to interrupt.

"Therefore," Wolverstone continued, "your mission must be to confirm the slave traders' connection to Undoto and, by following the slavers, to identify the location of their camp. Your orders are specifically that. Locate the slavers' camp, then return and report. You must not follow the trail further, no matter the temptation."

Wolverstone paused, then added, "I appreciate that, very likely, that will not be an easy directive to follow—it's not one I take joy in giving. But in order to mount a rescue of all those taken, it's imperative we learn of the location of that camp. If you go further and are captured yourself... Put simply, all those missing can't afford that. If you are taken, we won't know until your crew return to tell us. And once they do, we'll be no further forward than we are now—no nearer the point of knowing enough to effectively rescue those taken."

Wolverstone glanced at Melville; when he looked back at Robert, his features had hardened. "Running a mission in successive stages may seem like a slow way forward, but it is a sure way forward, and those taken deserve our best attempts to successfully free them."

Robert met Wolverstone's gaze; two seconds ticked past, then he nodded. "I'll locate the slavers' camp and bring the information back."

Simple. Straightforward. He saw no reason to argue. If he had to sail to Freetown and do this mission, he was glad enough that it should have such a definite and definable endpoint.

Wolverstone inclined his head. "Thank you." He looked at Melville. "We'll leave you to prepare."

Melville rose, as did everyone; he offered Robert his hand. "How long before you and your ship will be ready to depart?"

Robert gripped Melville's hand. "A few days." As hands were shaken all around and they moved toward the door, Robert thought through the logistics. He halted at the doorway and spoke to all. "I'll send *The Trident* to Southampton to provision from the stores there. I imagine I'll be able to set sail in three days."

Melville humphed, but said no more. From his expression, Robert surmised that the First Lord was even more deeply troubled by the situation in Freetown than Wolverstone.

Then again, Wolverstone had no real responsibility to shoulder in this instance, while Melville… As Robert understood it, as First Lord, Melville had his neck metaphorically on the block, at least politically, and possibly even socially.

Robert returned to the armchair opposite the sofa. While Declan and Edwina farewelled their unexpected guests, he swiftly reviewed all he'd been told.

When Declan and Edwina reentered the drawing room and resumed their seats, he looked from one to the other. "All right. Now tell me all."

As he'd assumed, the pair had a great deal more to impart to him of society in Freetown, of all the characters who had played even small parts in their own drama, of the sights, sounds, and dangers of the slums, and so much more that, he knew, could well prove helpful, and perhaps even critical, once he was on the ground in the settlement.

The hours slid by unnoticed by any of them.

When the clocks struck one, they repaired to the dining parlor and continued their discussions over a substantial meal. Robert grinned when he saw the platters being brought in. "Thank you," he said to Edwina. "Shipboard food is good enough, but it's nice to eat well when one can."

Eventually, they returned to the comfort of the drawing room. Having exhausted all the facts and most of the speculation applicable, they finally turned to the ultimate question of what purpose lay behind the strange kidnappings.

Slumped in the armchair he'd claimed, his long legs stretched out before him, his booted ankles crossed, Robert tapped the tips of his steepled fingers to his chin. "You said that Dixon was the first to vanish. Given he's an engineer of some repute, assuming he was chosen for his known skills, I agree that that suggests the enterprise our villains are engaged in is most likely a mine."

Lounging on the sofa beside Edwina, Declan nodded. "At least in those parts."

"So what are they mining?" Robert met his brother's blue eyes. "You know that area better than I. What's most likely?"

Declan twined his fingers with Edwina's. "Gold and diamonds."

"I assume not together, so what's your best guess?"

"If I had to wager, I'd go for diamonds."

Robert had a great deal of respect for Declan's insights into all matters of exploration. "Why?"

Declan's lips twisted. He glanced at Edwina. "I've been thinking about why those behind this have chosen to take young women and children—what uses they might have for them. Children are often used in gold mines to pick over the shattered ore—they'd be just as useful in mining for diamonds, at least in that area. But young women? They have no real role I can think of in gold mining. But in mining for diamonds in that area?"

Gripping Edwina's hand, Declan looked at Robert. "The diamonds there are found in concretions, lumped together with other ore. Separating the ore from the stones is fine work—not so much precision as simply being able to work on small things. Young women with good eyesight could clean the rough stones enough to reduce their size and weight so that the final product, while keeping its value, would fit into a relatively small space— easy to smuggle out, even by mail."

Declan held Robert's gaze. "If I had to guess, I would say our villains have stumbled on a pipe of diamonds and are busy retrieving as many stones as they can before anyone else learns of the strike."

Later that same day, in a tavern in Freetown located on a narrow side street off the western end of Water Street—an area

frequented by clerks and shopkeepers and others more down-
at-heel—a man rather better dressed than the other denizens sat
nursing a glass of ale at a table in the rear corner of the dimly
lit taproom.

The tavern door opened, and another man walked in. The
first man looked up. He watched as the second man, also better
dressed than the general run of the tavern's clientele, bought a
glass of ale from the man behind the counter, then crossed the
room to the table in the corner.

The men exchanged nods, but no words. The second man
drew up a stool and sat, then took a deep draft of his ale.

The sound of the door opening reached the second man. His
back was to the door. He looked at the first man. "That him?"

The first man nodded.

Both waited in silence until the newcomer had bought an ale
for himself and approached the table.

The third man set his glass down on the scarred surface, then
glanced around at the others in the taproom before pulling up
a stool and sitting.

"Stop looking so damned guilty." The second man raised his
glass and took another sip.

"All very well for you." The third man, younger than the
other two, reached for his glass. "You don't have an uncle as
your immediate superior."

"Well, he's not going to see us here, is he?" the second man
said. "He'll be up at the fort, no doubt busily sorting through
his inventory."

"God—I hope not." The younger man shuddered. "The last
thing we need is for him to realize how much is missing."

The first man, who had silently watched the exchange, arched
a brow. "No chance of that, is there?"

The younger man sighed. "No—I suppose not." He stared
into his ale. "I've been careful to keep everything we've taken

off the books. There's no way to see something's missing if according to the books it was never there."

The first man's lips curved without humor. "Good to know."

"Never mind that." The second man focused on the first. "What's this about Lady H? I heard through the office that she's decamped on us."

The first man flushed under his tan. His hands tightened about his glass. "I was told Lady H had gone to visit family, and for all I know, that might still be the case. So yes, she's gone, but as she knows nothing about my connection to our operation, she didn't see fit to explain her reasons to me. I asked around—indirectly, of course—but apparently Holbrook doesn't know when she'll be back."

"So we might have lost our ability to vet our kidnapees?" The second man frowned.

"Yes," the first man replied, "but that isn't what most concerns me." He paused to take a sip of his ale, then lowered the glass and went on, "Yesterday, I heard from Dubois that Kale claims he lost two of the three men he sent to the governor's house to fetch some lady Lady H had sent word to them to come and get."

The third man looked puzzled. "When was that?"

"As near as I can make out, it was fifteen nights ago. Three days before Lady H sailed. I spent the evening in question dealing with dispatches, so I knew nothing about it at the time." The first man paused, then more diffidently went on, "From what I could gather, it was Frobisher's wife, Lady Edwina, who came to see Lady H that evening, but I can't be certain Lady Edwina was the lady Lady H called Kale to come and get, and I see no point in asking too many questions of the governor's staff.

"According to Dubois, Kale said that the lady his men picked up was drugged and asleep. All his man—the one who survived—could tell him was that the lady had golden hair. In their usual team of three, Kale's men wrapped her in a rug and carried her out through the slum behind the house, but then they were attacked by four men—sailors, according to the survivor. The sailors killed two of Kale's men and took the lady back. Kale's third man ran, but then doubled back and trailed the sailors to the docks. He saw them get into a tender and be rowed off, but in the dark, he couldn't tell which ship they boarded."

The second man continued to frown into his glass. "If I'm remembering aright, Frobisher's ship was in the harbor that night. It wasn't there the next day—they must have left on the morning tide."

The first man humphed. "Word is that they—Frobisher and Lady Edwina—were on their honeymoon and were headed to Cape Town to visit family there. If that's so, then even if it was Lady Edwina who Lady H drugged—God alone knows why the silly bitch would do such a thing, but if she did—I can't imagine we'll hear any more about it."

The third man stared at the first. "But…surely Frobisher will lodge some sort of official complaint with Holbrook?"

The first man grinned. "I doubt it. Lady Edwina's the daughter of a duke—very highly placed within society in London. I really can't see Frobisher wanting to draw attention to his wife being in the hands of the likes of Kale's men, in the night, in the slum, no one else about. Not the sort of thing he'd want known about his wife."

"I agree." The second man nodded. "He's got her back, and by the sounds of it, no harm done. He'll leave it at that." He paused, then added, "If Frobisher had wanted to make anything of it, he wouldn't have sailed without pounding on Holbrook's desk. He didn't, so I agree—that's that." He cut a glance at the third man. "No need to borrow trouble on that account."

The first man leaned his chin on one hand. "And I don't think we need to fear Lady H giving us up to anyone, either. She has far more to lose than we do. The only reason she agreed to Undoto's suggestion was for the money—that's really all she cared about. And if it was Lady Edwina she tried to drug and send off to Kale, then once she learned that Lady Edwina had been rescued, I can quite understand Lady H wanting to make herself scarce. I would, too. But if that's the case, it's better for us that she's taken herself off—we wouldn't want her to be waiting here to be asked any awkward questions if any are ever directed this way."

The second man grunted. "She doesn't know enough to point the finger at us, anyway."

The first man dipped his head. "True. But she might have pointed at Undoto, or given up her contact with Kale, and that might have started things unraveling... No. Overall, we should be glad she's gone. But if she has done a flit for good and all, then the one thing we do need to work on is how to cover for her expertise." The first man looked at the other two and raised his brows. "Any notion how we're to vet those we take to make sure their disappearance doesn't set off any alarms?"

Silence ensued.

Finally, the second man raked his hand through his thick black hair. "Let's leave that for now, but keep alert for any possible other way. As of this moment, Dubois has enough men for his needs."

"But he says he'll need more," the first man countered. "He said Dixon's not far from opening up the second tunnel, and once he does, if we want to increase production like we've promised our backers, then Dubois will need more men."

"So he'll need them soon, but not immediately." The second man nodded. "No need to panic. We'll find a way."

"What about women and children?" the third man asked.

"Dubois said he has enough of both for now." The first man turned his glass between his hands. "He won't need more until they start hauling rock from the second tunnel."

The three fell silent, then the second man humphed. "I hope Dixon can be trusted to do what's needed."

The first man's lips quirked. "Dubois was very confident that in order to keep Miss Frazier safe and unmolested, Dixon will perform exactly as we wish."

The second man grinned. "I have to say that Dubois's notion of using the women's safety to control the men has proved nothing short of inspired."

The first man grunted and pushed away his empty glass. "Just as long as the men don't think ahead and realize that, when we have all we need from them, it's all going to come to the same thing in the end."

A gray dawn was breaking far to the east as Robert steered *The Trident* down the last stretch of the Solent. The day was overcast and blustery, the waves a choppy gray-green, but the wind gusted from the northeast, which made it damned near perfect sailing, at least to him.

He'd risen in the small hours and had jockeyed *The Trident* into position to be one of the first ships to heel out on the surging tide. With the way clear before the prow, he'd called up the sails in rapid succession. Ships like *The Trident* were best sailed hard, with as much canvas flying as possible; they were designed to race over the waves.

The buoys at the Solent's mouth came into view, rising and falling on the swell. Robert corrected course, then, as the first of the Channel's rolling waves hit, swung the wheel. He called rapid sail changes as the ship heeled; the crew scurried and shouts flew as the sails were adjusted, then *The Trident* was shooting into the darker waters of the Channel, prow unerringly on the correct heading to take them out into the Atlantic on the most southerly tack.

Once the ship steadied, he checked the sails, then, satisfied, handed the wheel to his lieutenant, Jordan Latimer. "Keep her running as hard as you can. I'll be back for the next change." That would come when they swung even further to the south to commence the long haul to Freetown.

Latimer grinned and snapped off a salute. "Aye, aye. I take it we're in a hurry?"

Robert nodded. "Believe it or not, *The Cormorant* made the trip back in twelve days."

"Twelve?" Latimer let his disbelief show.

"Royd put a new finish on the hull and fiddled with the rudder. Apparently, if running under full sail, it shaves off nearly a sixth in time—Declan's master reported *The Cormorant* was noticeably faster even on the run from Aberdeen to Southampton."

Latimer shook his head wonderingly. "Pity we didn't have time for Royd and his boys to doctor *The Trident* before we set out. We'll never make it in twelve days."

"True." Robert turned to descend to the main deck. "But there's no reason we can't make it in fifteen, as long as we keep the sails up."

If the winds held steady, they would. He went down the ladder to the main deck, then paced along the starboard side, checking knots, pulleys, and the set of the spars, listening to the creak of the sails—the little things that reassured him that all was right with his ship.

Halting near the bow, he glanced back and checked the wake, all but unconsciously noting the way the purling wave broke and the angle of the hull's canting. Seeing nothing of concern, he turned and looked ahead to where, in the far distance, the clouds gave way to blue skies.

With luck, when they reached the Atlantic, the weather would clear, and he would be able to cram on yet more sail.

The ship lurched, and he gripped the rail; as the deck righted, he leaned against the side, his gaze idly sweeping the seas ahead.

As he'd predicted, it had taken three days for *The Trident* to sail from London to Southampton and to be adequately provisioned from the company's stores there. Add fourteen more days for the journey south, and it would be eighteen days since he'd agreed to this mission before he sighted Freetown. Fourteen full days before he could start.

To his surprise, impatience rode him. He wanted this mission done and squared away.

The why of that had been difficult to define, but last night, as he'd lain in his bed in the large stern cabin—his cold, lonely, and uninspiring bed—he'd finally got a glimpse of what was driving his uncharacteristically unsettling emotions.

After three full days spent with Declan and Edwina, he wanted what Declan had. What his brother had found with Edwina—the happiness, and the home.

Until he'd seen it for himself, until he'd experienced Declan's new life, he hadn't appreciated just how deeply the need and want of a hearth of his own was entrenched in his psyche.

Put simply, he envied what Declan had found and wanted the same for himself.

All well and good—he knew what that required. A wife. The right sort of wife for a gentleman like him—and that was definitely not a sparkling, effervescent, diamond-of-the-first-water like Edwina.

He wasn't entirely sure what his wife would be like—he had yet to spend sufficient time dwelling on the prospect—but he viewed himself as a diplomat, a man of quieter appetites than Royd or Declan, and his style of wife should reflect that, or so he imagined.

Regardless, all plans in that regard had been put on hold. This mission came first.

Which, of course, was why he was so keen to have it over and done.

He pushed away from the side and headed for the companionway. He dropped down to the lower deck and made his way to his cabin. Spacious and neatly fitted with everything he needed for a comfortable life on board, the cabin extended all the way across the stern.

Settling into the chair behind the big desk, he opened the lowest drawer on the right and drew out his latest journal.

Keeping a journal was a habit he'd acquired from his mother. In the days in which she'd sailed the seas with his father, she'd kept a record of each day's happenings. There was always something worthy of note. He'd found her journals as a boy and had spent months working his way through them. The insight those journals had afforded him of all the little details of life on board influenced him to this day; the impact they'd had on his view of sailing as a way of life was quite simply incalculable.

And so he'd taken up the practice himself. Perhaps when he had sons, they would read his journals and see the joys of this life, too.

Today, he wrote of how dark it had been when they'd slipped their moorings and pulled away from the wharf, and of the huge black-backed gull he'd seen perched on one of the buoys just outside the harbor mouth. He paused, then let his pen continue to scratch over the paper, documenting his impatience to get started on this mission and detailing his understanding of what completing it would require of him. To him, the latter was simple, clear, and succinct: Go into the settlement of Freetown, pick up the trail of the slavers, follow them to their camp—and then return to London with the camp's location.

With a flourish, he set a final period to the entry. "Cut and dried."

He set down his pen and read over what he'd written. By then, the ink had dried. Idly, he flicked back through the closely written pages, stopping to read entries here and there.

Eventually, he stopped reading and stared unseeing as what lay before him fully registered. Unbidden, his gaze rose to the glass-fronted cabinet built into the stern wall; it contained the rest of his journals, all neatly lined up on one shelf.

The record of his life.

It didn't amount to much.

Not in the greater scheme of things—on the wider plane of life.

Yes, he'd assisted in any number of missions, ones that had actively supported his country. Most had been diplomatic forays of one sort or another. Since his earliest years captaining his own ship, he'd claimed the diplomatic missions as his own—his way of differentiating himself from Royd and Declan. Royd was older than him by two years, while Declan was a year younger, but they were both adventurers to the core, buccaneers at heart. Neither would deny that description; if anything, they reveled in being widely recognized as such.

But as the second brother, he'd decided to tread a different path—one just as fraught with danger, but of a different sort.

He would be more likely to be clapped into a foreign jail because of a misunderstood insult exchanged over a dinner table, while his brothers would be more likely to be caught brawling in some alley.

He was quick with his tongue, while they were quick with their swords and fists.

Not that he couldn't match them with either blades or fists; growing up as they had, being able to hold his own against them had been essential—a matter of sibling survival.

Thoughts of the past had him smiling, then he drew his mind forward, through the past to the present—then he looked ahead.

After a moment, he shut the journal and stowed it back in the drawer. Then he rose and headed for the deck.

Given how boring his recent life had been—more like existing than actively living—perhaps it was a good thing that this mission was not his usual diplomatic task. Something a little different to jar him out of his rut, before he turned his mind to defining and deciding the details of the rest of his life.

A fresh and different challenge, before he faced a larger one.

Climbing back onto the deck, he felt the wind rush at him and lifted his face to the bracing breeze.

He breathed in and looked around at the waves—at the sea stretching forever on, as always, his path to the future.

And this time, his way was crystal clear.

He'd go to Freetown, learn what was needed, return to London and report—and then he would set about finding a wife.

Two

Good morning." Miss Aileen Hopkins fixed a polite but determined gaze on the face of the bored-looking clerk who had come forward to attend her across the wooden counter separating the public from the inner workings of the Office of the Naval Attaché. Located off Government Wharf in the harbor of Freetown, the office was the principal on-land contact for the men aboard the ships of the West Africa Squadron. The squadron sailed the seas west of Freetown, tasked with enforcing the British government's ban on slavery.

"Yes, miss?" Despite the question, not a single spark of interest lit the man's eyes, much less his expression, which remained impersonal and just a bit dour.

Aileen was too experienced in dealing with bureaucratic flunkies to allow his attitude to deter her. "I would like to inquire as to my brother, Lieutenant William Hopkins." She set her black traveling reticule on the counter, folded her hands over the gathered top, and did her best to project the image of someone who was not about to be fobbed off.

The clerk stared at her, a frown slowly overtaking his face. "Hopkins?" He glanced at the other two clerks, both of whom had remained seated at desks facing the wall and were making a grand show of deafness, although in the small office, they had to have heard her query. The clerk at the counter wasn't deterred, either. "Here—Joe!" When one of the seated clerks reluctantly raised his head and glanced their way, the clerk assisting her prompted, "Hopkins. Isn't he the young one that went off God knows where?"

The seated clerk shot Aileen a quick glance, then nodded. "Aye. It'd be about three months ago now."

"I am aware that my brother has disappeared." She failed to keep her accents from growing more clipped as her tone grew more severely interrogatory. "What I wish to know is why he was ashore, rather than aboard H.M.S. *Winchester.*"

"As to that, miss"—the first clerk's tone grew decidedly prim—"we're not at liberty to say."

She paused, parsing the comment, then countered, "Am I to take it from that that you do, in fact, know of some reason William—Lieutenant Hopkins—was ashore? Ashore when he was supposed to be at sea?"

The clerk straightened, stiffened. "I'm afraid, miss, that this office is not permitted to divulge details of the whereabouts of officers of the service."

She let her incredulity show. "Even when they've disappeared?"

Without looking around, one of the clerks seated at the desks declared, "All inquiries into operational matters should be addressed to the Admiralty."

Her eyes narrowing, she stared at the back of the head of the clerk who had spoken. When he refused to look around, she stated in stringently uninflected tones, "The last time I visited, the Admiralty was in London."

"Indeed, miss." When she transferred her gaze to him, the clerk at the counter met her eyes with a wooden expression. "You'll need to ask there."

She refused to be defeated. "I would like to speak with your superior."

The man answered without a blink. "Sorry, miss. He's not here."

"When will he return?"

"I'm afraid I can't say, miss."

"Not at liberty to divulge his movements, either?"

"No, miss. We just don't know." After a second of regarding her—possibly noting her increasing choler—the clerk suggested, "He's around the settlement somewhere, miss. If you keep your eyes open, perhaps you might run into him."

For several seconds, her tongue burned with the words with which she would like to flay him—him and his friends, and the naval attaché, too. Ask at the Admiralty? It was half a world away!

Thanking them for their help, even if sarcastically, occurred only to be dismissed. She couldn't force the words past her lips.

Feeling anger—the worst sort, laced with real fear—geysering inside her, she cast the clerk still facing her a stony glare, then she picked up her reticule, spun on her heel, and marched out of the office.

Her half boots rang on the thick, weathered planks of the wharf. Her intemperate strides carried her off the wharf and up the steps to the dusty street. Skirts swishing, she paced rapidly on, climbing the rise to the bustle of Water Street.

Just before she reached it, she halted and forced herself to lift her head and draw in a decent breath.

The heat closed around her, muffling in its cloying sultriness.

The beginnings of a headache pulsed in her temples.

Now what?

She'd come all the way from London determined to learn where Will had gone. Clearly, she'd get no help from the navy itself...but there'd been something about the way the clerk had reacted when she'd suggested that there was a specific reason Will had been ashore.

Her older brothers were in the navy, too. And both, she knew, had served ashore at various times—dispatched by their superiors on what amounted to secret missions.

Not that she or their parents—or even their other siblings in the navy—had known that at the time.

Had Will been dispatched on some secret mission, too? Was that the reason he'd been ashore?

"Ashore long enough to have been captured and taken by the enemy?" Aileen frowned. After a moment, she gathered her skirts and resumed her trek up to and around the corner into Water Street, the settlement's main thoroughfare. She needed to make several purchases in the shops lining the street before hiring a carriage to take her back up Tower Hill to her lodgings.

While she shopped, the obvious questions revolved in her brain.

Who on earth was the enemy here?

And how could she find out?